# MADLY YOURS

OTHER BOOKS AND AUDIOBOOKS
BY ELLE M. ADAMS

*Engaging Emma*

The anticipated sequel to *Engaging Emma*

# MADLY YOURS

a novel

# ELLE M. ADAMS

Cover image: *Woman Sitting on Wooden Dock* © phpetrunina14, stock.adobe.com

Cover design copyright © 2025 by Covenant Communications, Inc.

Published by Covenant Communications, Inc.
American Fork, Utah

Copyright © 2025 by Elle M. Adams
All rights reserved. No part of this book may be reproduced in any format or in any medium without the written permission of the publisher, Covenant Communications, Inc., PO Box 416, American Fork, UT 84003. The views expressed within this work are the sole responsibility of the author and do not necessarily reflect the position of Covenant Communications, Inc., or any other entity.

This is a work of fiction. The characters, names, incidents, places, and dialogue are either products of the author's imagination, and are not to be construed as real, or are used fictitiously.

Library of Congress Cataloging-in-Publication Data

Name: Elle M. Adams
Title: Madly yours / Elle M. Adams
Description: American Fork, UT : Covenant Communications, Inc. [2025]
Identifiers: Library of Congress Control Number 2024938333 | ISBN 9781524427764
LC record available at https://lccn.loc.gov/2024938333

Printed in the United States of America
First Printing: January 2025

31 30 29 28 27 26 25    10 9 8 7 6 5 4 3 2 1

*For single mothers everywhere,
with a prayer that
He will make your burdens light*

# ACKNOWLEDGMENTS

Many thanks to Rebecca Tuft and Kami Hancock for helping me find my way to the best version of this story. Thanks to Ashlyn LaOrange and Shara Meredith for their patience and for getting me out there at the very edge of my comfort zone. Everyone at Covenant is a dream to work with. I am fortunate indeed.

I owe a debt of gratitude to Dean Hughes for being my first reader. It takes a man's man to be able to lay hold of a piece of women's fiction and offer spot-on advice on how to make it better.

A special thanks to Officer Brian Markland for sharing his expertise and knowledge about the obligations and duties of a police officer. He was generous with his time and patient in answering all my questions. Any mistakes are my own.

Like the protagonist in this story, I am a single mother. It's tricky, but when God closes a door, he opens a window. I am blessed to have a rock-solid tribe of women who have encouraged, lifted, loved, and supported me. Heading them is my mother—a tenacious woman who protects her own and steps in when I need her (and sometimes when I don't). Thanks to my cheerleaders: Eden Carter, Laura Turner, Laura Hales, and Laura Laycock. I would have vaporized long ago without you.

Thank you, Julianne Donaldson. For good or ill, you get it more than anyone else. So happy that you broke our pattern. Maybe someday I'll follow in your footsteps.

Michelle, thank you for offering honest feedback. Thanks also for sticking with me and being perpetual shelter during the storm.

I was fortunate to grow up in a small Missouri town surrounded by a community of people who embody the word "home." They are also the reason a part of my heart still lies in that small midwestern town. So, thank you to the Stephens family, the Marrs, the Cochrans, and the Rutts. I'm grateful y'all give me an excuse to come home.

And thanks to my children. I love you. As you travel along your own paths, know that my love and support follow you no matter where you roam.

# PROLOGUE

THE STORM CAST WICKED SHADOWS against the wall as lightning slashed through the branches outside. Whippet's bed was right under one of the dormered windows in the room she shared with her older brother every time they visited their grandmother. She looked across to where Tucker was fast asleep. The night-light by her bed showed him lying there, legs akimbo, mouth slack, and snoring. No use to her at all.

Three sharp blasts of thunder, one after the other, made the room shiver. Seven-year-old Whippet Madsen shot up in bed and screamed, "Mama!" Her parents' room was at the other end of the hall, next to Grandma Lily's. Pulling the covers over her head, Whippet counted to see how many seconds it would take for her mother to make the trek down the hall.

One. Two. Three. Four. The hall light went on and there was the telltale sound of her mother's feet softly hitting the wood floor. Whippet slowly unfurled and poked her head out from her pink princess blanket. The door creaked open, and Whippet felt the mattress dip under her mother's weight.

"Storm got you scared, little friend?" her mother whispered as she smoothed back the covers and righted Whippet's pillow.

"A little," she responded, not wanting to sound like she was too afraid.

Her mother pushed the wispy blonde hair from Whippet's face and started to hum. That's what Mama did; she hummed the storms away. She never sang. Daddy always said Mama couldn't carry a tune in a bucket. Whippet closed her eyes for a second and imagined her mother in her long white nightgown, trying to balance an old wooden bucket full of black musical notes. In her mind, her mother walked along the spindly branches of the oak tree outside the window, balancing that bucket while she hummed. The thunder and lightning liked the humming too. They got quieter and quieter so they could listen.

"Hey! Why wasn't I invited to this party?" a voice came from the door.

"Daddy!" Whippet exclaimed. He put a finger to his lips, pointing to her sleeping brother. "Daddy," she whispered.

Her mother smiled and made room for her dad. Daddy slipped an arm around Mama's shoulders and kissed her forehead. "You go on back to bed. I've got this." Her mother blew her a kiss on her way out the door.

"Now why all the fuss, missy?" he asked, his voice quiet so as not to wake Tucker.

"There are monsters in the tree out there," Whippet insisted, pointing to the window behind her bed.

"Well, let's see about that." Her father got up to investigate, opening the shutters to the gloomy night.

"No monsters," he said, glancing out. "But Whippet, look at this."

Whippet twisted in her bed to peek over the low headboard. Her father pointed to a branch just below the window.

"I don't see anything," Whippet whispered. A flash of lightning revealed a little nest resting in the branches of the tree. Whippet counted three pretty blue eggs inside and became instantly concerned.

"Where's the mama bird?" she asked.

"Oh, I bet she's nearby," her father answered.

"Will they be all right?"

Her father nodded. "Look, the wind is rocking them to sleep." Whippet watched as the wind lifted the branch, rocking it gently up and down, up and down. Soon, her own eyes got heavy and, satisfied that the little eggs were safe, she settled back into bed. The thunder had moved on. "Whippet, remember to give your ring a twist when you feel the worry coming on, okay?" He pointed to the ring on her thumb, silver with a coral bead set in it. Her dad had given it to her on her last birthday.

"All set?" her father asked.

Whippet nodded and snuggled in deep, waiting for the words she knew were coming. Wonderful, light words that would carry her into sleep. Her father said them almost every night.

"Who can do anything she sets her mind to?"

"Me," she whispered.

"Who do I love to Pluto and back?" Pluto because it was even farther away than the moon.

"Me."

"Who is my best girl?"

"Me!"

"You'll remember that, won't you Whippet? No matter what?"

"Yep." She yawned and closed her eyes. "But if I forget, you'll just tell me again."

But she did forget.

Time had a way of changing things. Time took away the storm. But time also took away her daddy and stole her mama's easy smile. And time eventually made her forget that she was her father's best girl and that she could do anything.

# CHAPTER ONE

*Twenty-one years later, present day*

At the sound of a siren coming up fast behind them, Whippet uttered a very unladylike word and slowed down. Her nine-year-old daughter gave a whoop of delight and rattled the glass jar in her hands before pushing it between the front seats.

"Deposit please," Everly said in a sing-song voice. "Look at all the money I have! I might have enough to buy a puppy all by myself!"

It looked like the police car was serious. Whippet gripped the steering wheel tighter and pulled over. She took a couple deep breaths then reached over to pull a dollar bill from her wallet. She replaced the wallet in her purse then bent to push her purse underneath the passenger seat. "You and your darn swear jar," she muttered as she deposited the money.

"A whole dollar!" Everly exclaimed.

"Yes," Whippet replied blithely. "That's to buy your silence while I'm dealing with the cop. Read your book and don't listen to what I say."

Everly sighed. "That means you're going to lie."

"I'm not going to lie. I'm just going to bend the truth a little," Whippet reasoned.

"Same difference. Gramma Fancy says liars go to—"

"Say it and you have to give me the dollar back."

Everly closed her mouth.

Whippet checked her reflection in the mirror, ran her fingers through her hair, and bit her lips. If she thought it would help, she would have prayed. She rolled down the window and pasted on a smile, thinking of the handful of unpaid tickets now residing in her glove box. She fervently hoped that the great state of Texas would not be able to share that particular bit of information with Normal, Missouri's police department.

Within moments a tall, broad-shouldered officer was at the side of the car. Sunglasses hid his eyes, but he didn't seem much older than her twenty-eight years. He had dirty-blond hair cut short. He was cute too. Maybe she could flirt her way out of a ticket.

"Welcome to Normal," the man said flatly. "License and registration please."

Whippet shaded her eyes with her hand. "Was I speeding?" she asked coyly.

"Fifty-seven in a thirty-mile-per-hour zone."

"Thirty? I haven't made it to town yet."

"You hit city limits two miles ago," he said.

Whippet looked around. Google maps said they were about a mile from her grandmother's farmhouse. They were surrounded by trees and pastures. A cow stood chewing grass not twenty feet from her car. "Are you sure about that? There's nothing here."

The officer's jaw tightened. "Yes, ma'am."

"Mom! He 'ma'amed' you!" Everly popped her head between the seats. "She hates it when people call her 'ma'am.'"

"Hush," Whippet said through gritted teeth. Her mind wandered once again to those radioactive tickets in her glove box. If the cop ran her plates . . .

Desperation might be the mother of invention, but she also gave birth to a few lies here and there. Whippet unbuckled her seat belt and got out of the car.

"Ma'am, please stay in your vehicle," he said.

Ignoring him, Whippet said, "Officer"—she looked at the placard on his shirt—"Beaufort. My name is Daphne Carmichael." She extended her hand, which he did not take. "My family lives over on Christopher Street, and I was speeding because I'm trying to make it home. Family emergency." She finished with a stage whisper.

Okay. She was lying. But flirting wasn't working and lying was better than spending the night in jail. Besides, she did know Daphne Carmichael. Sort of. As children they used to play together when she visited here in the summer. She hoped to heaven Daphne was long gone from Normal.

"Daphne Carmichael?" the cop said slowly.

"Y-yes." Whippet swallowed hard.

"The same Daphne Carmichael I helped pack up before she moved to Iowa three months ago? Red hair, brown eyes. Sound familiar?"

Well, darn. "Maybe?" she said, twisting the ring on her pinkie finger.

The good officer's jaw clenched. "License and registration . . . please."

"Um, the thing is," Whippet started, "I seem to have left my purse at home, so if you want to give me a warning, I promise—"

"You mean that purse?" Officer Beaufort nodded toward the car window. Whippet turned. The traitorous bag was only half hidden under the seat. Whippet silently uttered a curse word that would have cost her five bucks, easy.

"Fine," she said, getting back in the car. She grabbed the purse and jerked her license from her wallet. She retrieved the registration from the glove box and handed both to him through the window.

"Thank you, Daphne," the cop said, not smiling. She watched through the mirror as he got back into his squad car.

"Please don't run the plates," she whispered. At this point, she would take a ticket and be grateful.

"Is everything okay, Mom?" Everly asked, a note of worry in her voice.

"Just fine," she lied.

She shouldn't have come. This proved it. Her family could have read Gran's will and phoned her with any news. Her presence was not necessary and getting here had been a trial of Odyssean proportions.

She'd been fired from yet another job. Two days ago, when she'd asked for the time off, her boss, Anthony Bannon, had backed her into a corner and told her to ask him "real nice." That hadn't ended well. She shuddered at the memory. Unfortunately, her boss had also been her landlord. So, as of yesterday, she was homeless as well as jobless. Last night she and Everly had emptied their small, furnished apartment and stuffed everything they owned into the back of her Chevy Cobalt. Not so long ago, she would have handled a week like this by having a drink or two.

Whippet shook off the thought and closed her eyes. She was fine. It was going to be fine. She'd be at her grandmother's house soon and her mother would . . .

*Oh,* her mother would have something to say about this. Whippet tapped her fingers against the steering wheel. She could almost see Mom standing there, making a tsking noise and saying, "Oh, Whippet."

She turned to look at Everly. Her daughter seemed oblivious to the catastrophe unfolding around them, focusing instead on the copy of *The Witch of Blackbird Pond* Whippet had given her for the drive.

She leaned against the headrest and closed her eyes. Suddenly, she wanted her grandmother with a longing so deep and sharp, it nearly took her breath away. Gran would have smoothed things over. She would have told Whippet to stop taking herself so seriously, to relax. Gran would have made it seem like losing her job had been the plan all along. She would have turned it into a good thing.

Whippet looked at the police car through the side mirror and chewed on her thumb. She hoped a ticket wasn't a sign of disastrous days ahead. Frankly, she needed a break. For the last few years, it seemed her only luck had been bad.

She saw the cop walking toward her again. When he was next to the car, he motioned for her to get out.

He handed her the drivers' license. "Well, Orla—"

Whippet cringed at the sound of her given name. "Daphne is fine!" she said.

Her mother had named her Orla, thinking it an honor to bestow the name of a long-ago ancestor. And it might have been if she'd been born in 1882. As it was, she'd been nicknamed "Orca" in grade school.

He raised an eyebrow at her. "Right. Well, the DLC is telling me your license has been suspended."

"Um, what's the DLC?" she asked, twisting her hands together.

"The Driver's License Compact. Your driving record follows you wherever you go."

"Great." Whippet gave him an uneasy smile. "So, I guess what happens in Texas doesn't necessarily stay in Texas?"

"You are correct."

"That's not good." Whippet gave her pinkie ring a twist as she looked at her daughter in the back seat.

Officer Beaufort scrubbed a hand down his face then motioned for Whippet to follow him to the squad car. "Listen, driving with a suspended license is a class one misdemeanor. It means jail time and fines."

"What?!" There was no keeping the panic from her voice.

The cop held up a hand. "I'm going to have to impound your car. I'll give you a ride to the station." He paused. "Do you have someone you can call?"

Whippet took a slow breath and exhaled. "Yes, I do."

# CHAPTER TWO

The ride back to the station was tense and mostly silent.

Sam looked in his rear-view mirror as he switched lanes. He caught a glimpse of his passengers huddled together in the back seat. Whippet Moran had her arm around her daughter. He could just make out the sound of her whispering soothing words into the child's ear. She seemed like a good mom. That was something, at least.

He felt bad. He tried to give people a break, especially the tourists who buzzed through town on their way to grander destinations. The mayor liked to lecture Sam on how the town depended on visitors passing through. But twenty-seven miles an hour over the limit wasn't going to be tolerated. Especially on a nice spring day when kids were out riding their bikes and folks were speed-walking in the warm sun. Attending to a fatal crash was not the way he wanted to start the day.

He had managed to get some information out of Whippet on the way. He wondered briefly how being nicknamed after a dog breed was better than the name Orla, but after serving several years in law enforcement, he'd heard stranger things.

The other pertinent information he'd been able to drag out of her was that she was Tucker Madsen's little sister. Tucker was the town doctor, and his family was respected around Normal. This member of the Madsen clan seemed to have a talent for bending the truth. But then, who was he to judge? He didn't know her.

They walked through the glass doors of the station, and Sam showed Whippet's daughter—Everly was her name—to a small reception area with a couple of vinyl couches and a coffee table covered with magazines.

"You wait here, okay, sweetheart?" Whippet said, smoothing a hand down her daughter's hair. "It's going to be okay."

Sam held the door to his office for Whippet, then took a seat behind his desk.

A yellow sticky note on his computer screen read, *Sharon O'Neil called*. Sam frowned, plucked the note off, and tossed it into the garbage. He looked up at Whippet Moran. "Have a seat."

She remained standing stick-straight in front of him. She kept biting her lip and twisting the ring she wore on her pinky finger. Sam felt a twinge of guilt. He didn't enjoy this part of the job. "This might take a minute, so would you like to take a seat?" he repeated and gestured at the metal folding chair next to his desk. She sat down.

Sam bent over to switch on his computer. He hadn't been in the office yet today. He'd spent the morning out on patrol. He'd parked his cruiser on the side of the highway in plain sight, but Whippet had blown past the speed check without so much as a sideways glance.

She was pretty, with her long blonde hair and stormy eyes. But he was practiced at ignoring such things. He had a taste for difficult women and had learned the hard way that it was best to avoid them.

"So are you here long?" he asked as he worked on his computer, finding the website she'd need to visit to get her license reinstated.

She turned sharp eyes on him. "Why? Are you going to make me wear one of those orange vests and pick up trash along the side of the road?"

Sam suppressed a smile. "Uh, no." He picked up the handset and handed it to her. "You should call your brother," he said.

"I've got it, thanks," she said, holding up her cell phone.

A little while later, Tucker Madsen walked through the door, stethoscope still around his neck. His shoulders seemed to relax when he saw his sister.

"Is she under arrest?"

"Nice to see you too, brother dear," Whippet said, arms folded across her chest.

"No," Sam answered, standing to shake Tucker's hand. "But she was driving with a suspended license, so I had to impound the car." He looked at Whippet and she glared back at him. "She has several outstanding tickets. Might want to get that cleared up before a warrant is issued for her arrest."

"I'll make sure of it," Tucker said.

Tucker glanced down at her. "Whippet, why don't you wait out front while I talk to Sam?"

"Are you sure?" Sam said, leaning back in his chair. "She seems like a flight risk to me." One eyebrow rose as he looked at her.

Whippet stood and swung her purse over her shoulder. "Very funny. I'll go find Ev."

Tucker nodded, and Whippet went out into the lobby.

"She *should* be under arrest, am I right?" Tucker asked and Sam shrugged. Tucker rubbed a hand down his neck. "Is there a fine for today?"

"Nah. Just makes sure she takes care of those tickets."

"Thanks, Sam. I'll make sure she does."

They went back into his office, and Sam wrote down the websites Whippet would have to visit to take care of her outstanding tickets and her driver's license. Tucker thanked him again and went back out into the lobby.

He watched as Tucker pulled Whippet out of her chair and into his arms for a hug. "Welcome to Normal!" he said.

A minute later the front doors closed behind them and Sam found himself muttering, "Good luck, Doc. You've got your hands full with that one."

\* \* \*

They piled into Tucker's Explorer and drove down the street a couple of blocks. Whippet looked up at the old brick building as they got out of the car. "It looks good, Tucker."

The old mercantile building had been in the Madsen family forever. A century ago, it had been a thriving dry-goods store. But it had languished in disrepair for years until Tucker took it over, remodeled it, and transformed it into his medical office.

"Thanks," he said, pushing through the front door.

"Guys, this is my nurse, Barb," Tucker said, introducing Whippet and Everly to the middle-aged woman sitting behind the reception desk. With Barb's short, curly gray hair, pink cheeks, and sharp eyes, Whippet got the impression the nurse was both capable and kind. "This is my sister, Whippet, and my niece, Everly," Tucker addressed Barb, and Everly gave a little wave. "My sister and I are going upstairs to my office. Can Ev hang out with you for a while?"

"You bet!" the woman said. "You hungry, sweet pea?"

"A little," Everly confessed.

"Your Uncle Tucker keeps the breakroom stocked," Barb said, and Everly followed her down the hall.

Thirty-five minutes later, Whippet's frustration had come to a head. "Twenty-one days!" she exclaimed looking at Tucker, who shrugged.

"Sorry, Whippet. That really stinks."

She looked at the computer screen. The great state of Texas kindly informed her that it would take twenty-one days for her compliance documentation and fees to be processed. After that, her license would be reinstated, and she could rescue her car from the impound yard. "What am I supposed to do without a car for the next three weeks?" She sighed and glanced at her big brother. "Thank you, Tucker," she said, because, yep, he'd paid. For everything. The warrant fees, the processing fees, reinstatement fees, and the four unpaid tickets that had gotten her into this mess in the first place. It had been a serious chunk of change.

"Merry Christmas," he said, arching an eyebrow at her.

"Yeah," she replied weakly, getting out of his chair.

"So, this is your office?" she asked, looking around. "It's nice." She ran her finger along the wainscoting. "You have an office. You're, like, a real grown up."

Tucker sat down. "Come on in, the water's fine." He grinned at her.

"Ha, ha," she said and stuck out her tongue.

"So," Tucker started, "want to tell me why you showed up unannounced? Mom said you weren't coming until next week."

Whippet twisted her ring. "Uh, would you believe spring break started early?"

Tucker stared at her. His silence did the trick and seemed to pull the truth right out of her.

She flopped into the chair next to his desk. "It's not spring break, but if you tell Mom—"

"Don't worry about Mom right now. Tell me the truth."

"My, uh, employment has been terminated," Whippet explained.

"You got fired again?!" Tucker threw his hands in the air.

"Don't say it like that!"

"How would you like me to say it? Isn't this the second job you've lost this year? Whip, It's only April."

"I know what month it is!"

"Tell me what happened," he said, more calmly.

She exhaled long and loud. "A couple of days ago, I went into my boss's office to ask for some time off, you know, so I could come out here for the reading of Gran's will, and he . . . well, he fired me."

Tucker leaned forward. "There's got to be more to the story than that."

"When I approached him, he, uh, told me to ask him nicely."

Tucker's brows came together. "What does that mean?"

Whippet looked down. This was so uncomfortable. "He backed me into a corner and told me to ask him *nicely*." She did not want to talk about this.

"He backed you into a corner?" Tucker's voice had turned to ice.

"Yes. And then he put his hands on me, so I put my knee—"

"Okay! I think I've got the idea. Tell me this guy is in jail now."

She paused. "There's more."

Tucker's expression turned thunderous.

"You know Everly and I have been living with Cal's mother since he took off?" Tucker nodded, and she kept going. "Well, a couple of months ago, she kicked us out. Cal accused her of being disloyal to him by letting me live there."

"Great guy, your ex."

She twisted her ring. "Yeah. Well, we moved to a little apartment next to the Maxi Mart where I worked. But it was owned by one Anthony Bannon, my boss. So when he—"

"When he fired you, he kicked you out too."

"Yes." She took a deep breath. "We packed everything up and headed to Normal."

"You don't seem bothered by this," he said.

"Well, I'm not thrilled I lost my job," she replied.

"Are you kidding me?!" Her brother looked angry. "What this guy did was not only inappropriate; it was illegal. You need to do something about it."

"I did do something. I kneed—"

"That's not what I mean!" Tucker exclaimed, turning back to his computer and typing again.

"What are you doing?" she asked.

He turned the screen toward her, and she recoiled. He'd pulled up the web page for the Texas Workforce Commission. Her mouth opened. "You want me to file a complaint?"

"Absolutely." Tucker nodded. "And if you don't, I will."

Whippet glanced at Tucker's fisted hands. There was a sick feeling in the pit of her stomach. "I-I don't . . . Tucker, it wasn't that big of a deal," she whispered.

"It's a very big deal. Think for a second. If he did this to you, then he's probably doing it to other employees too."

That gave her pause. Whippet thought about Meggie Desoto, her coworker for the past two months. Meggie relied on the money she made at the Maxi Mart to help pay for college. Anthony made inappropriate comments to both of them, but what if he set his sights on Meggie next?

"Here," Tucker said, handing her a piece of paper. "That's the web address. Use it."

Whippet grimaced but took it anyway.

"I can't force you to file a complaint, but, Whippet, think about it. This guy used his position to make unwanted advances and then fired you when he didn't get what he wanted. And I bet this wasn't the first time. Am I right?"

Whippet shrugged and looked away.

"You don't deserve to be treated like that by anyone." Tucker shook his head. "If you change your mind, that website will tell you what steps you need to take, okay?"

She gave a jerky nod.

Tucker sat back in his chair. "So, you're homeless."

Whippet tucked a strand of hair behind her ear. "If you're going to change the subject, could you pick a subject that's a little less depressing?"

"What about your driver's license? How come you didn't know it was suspended?"

Whippet crossed her arms over her chest. "How was I supposed to know that if I got four tickets in a year they'd suspend my license?"

"Four tickets? Whippet, it's only April!"

"Stop telling me what month it is! I only got those tickets because I was trying to get Ev to school on time. I didn't realize my license had been suspended. Maybe I got a letter or something, but honestly, Tucker, I'm too busy to pay attention to stuff like that."

"Well, that's just great. Now all your worldly goods are locked inside the impound yard."

Whippet sagged in her chair. "Yeah."

Tucker took a deep breath. "Sorry I yelled at you," he said. He reached over and gave her an awkward pat on the shoulder. "It'll work out. C'mon," he said, standing up. "Let's go get Everly."

Whippet followed her brother out of his office. The second he walked ahead of her, she tucked the little piece of paper he'd given her into her wallet.

Just in case.

# CHAPTER THREE

Whippet plucked anxiously at the hem of her T-shirt and took a deep breath to calm the feeling of dread that was slowly creeping up on her as they drove south toward Miss Lily's House, where Whippet's brother lived with his wife, Emma. Everly peppered Tucker with questions about Normal from the back seat, blissfully unaware of Whippet's distress.

"Mom will be at our house for dinner," Tucker informed her. Their mother, Sophie, lived just down the road in the house Emma had turned into a bed-and-breakfast. Mom was the manager.

Whippet shook her head. "Don't tell Mom about . . ." she looked back at Everly, ". . . you know," she whispered. There would be no rest if her mother found out what had happened with her old boss.

Tucker looked annoyed. "I won't, but you should." He turned left, and they wound their way closer to the house. "Mom will be happy to see you."

Whippet doubted that. She wasn't looking forward to this reunion. Her mother had an innate sense for deception. It was eerie, really, the way she could sniff out duplicity even amid the most practiced of liars. And Whippet had told some lulus in her day. Like the time she'd told her mother she was spending the weekend with her best friend, Winnie Petersen, and had actually gone to Lake Jacomo with her boyfriend, Cal Moran, a lie that had resulted in Everly. Would her mother be suspicious when they showed up a week early for the reading of Gran's will? Definitely. Especially since Whippet had asked her mother to arrange the appointment with the lawyer around Everly's school break.

Whippet felt every muscle tense as they pulled to a stop. She undid her seat belt and looked up at the beautiful old house, a grand Queen Anne Victorian with a wide, welcoming front porch. This used to be her grandmother, Miss Lily's, home, a place of wonderful childhood memories. The towering oak trees swayed their welcome as she slid out of the car. Her feet had barely hit the ground when she heard the screen door swing open. Whippet's attention went to the front door where her mother emerged, wringing her hands in her apron. She wasn't smiling.

It seemed like Whippet hadn't seen a smile on her mother's face in years. Not since the afternoon a police officer had come to the door and informed them that Daddy had been killed in a car accident on the way home from his job at a preparatory academy in Kansas City.

That day had marked the end of Whippet's childhood and the beginning of trouble with her mother. It hadn't started in earnest until high school, when Whippet had exchanged reasonable, responsible behavior for partying with Cal. She still found it amazing how quickly she'd become addicted to alcohol. Truthfully, she'd found it marvelous the way a couple of drinks had made everything slip away. The fights with her mother, the stress of school, the pain of losing her dad—all obliterated in an alcoholic haze.

"Whippet?"

Tucker's voice brought her back to the gravel driveway. Whippet looked at her mother and waved, pretending at a casualness she didn't feel. Mom walked to the edge of the porch, and Whippet watched for the worry to appear on her mother's face. A look only Whippet seemed to inspire.

"This is unexpected," her mother said, walking down the front steps. "What's this about?" she asked, a furrow showing between her eyes. "Did I get the dates wrong?" she asked, and Whippet gave her an uneasy smile. "You didn't get fired again, did you?" her mother asked, and Whippet's smile fell.

"Mom, no!" Whippet exclaimed. She saw Tucker shake his head as he passed them on his way inside. "We just wanted to surprise you, that's all," Whippet said, dodging the issue entirely. "Surprise," she said faintly.

"Mm-hmm," Sophie muttered, pulling Whippet in for an awkward pat on the back. Mercifully, her mother was distracted by the sound of the car door opening.

"Grammy!" Everly flew out of Tucker's Explorer and ran toward Sophie.

"There's my sweet girl!" Mom exclaimed. Whatever her faults, Sophie Madsen was excellent with Everly. She had nothing for *her* except unabashed grandparental love. Her mother wrapped Everly into a hug and turned to Whippet. "Honey," she said, "where's your car?"

Whippet placated her mother with yet another lie about car trouble, and Mom walked them into the house, her arm around Everly's shoulders.

"How was the drive?" she asked.

"Fine," Everly said. "You should see all the money I have in my swear jar!"

"Swear jar?" her mother asked, cutting Whippet a look.

"Yep!" Everly was all enthusiasm. "Whenever Mom says a bad word, she gives me a quarter. I got tons of money on the drive here."

Sophie's eyebrow's rose. "Is that right?"

"Whippet!" Emma squealed from behind them. She charged down the hall and threw her arms around Whippet.

Tucker had hit the jackpot when he'd married Emma. With her long auburn hair and green eyes, Emma was not only beautiful, but warm and kind. One of the most real people Whippet had ever met.

"Sorry to show up unannounced," Whippet apologized.

"Oh, please! I'm so excited you guys are here." Emma reached down to include Everly in her embrace. "You must be exhausted. I'm sure it's been a long day." Emma gave her a meaningful look, and Whippet got the distinct impression that her sister-in-law knew exactly how taxing the day had been. "You guys want to wash up? Dinner will be ready soon."

\* \* \*

Twenty minutes later, Whippet came downstairs, halting on the landing when she saw her suitcases stacked neatly in the entryway. Tucker walked through the front door carrying Everly's blanket and pillow. He spied her and said, "Sam brought these over on his way home."

Whippet tilted her head. "Sam?"

"Sam Beaufort. The guy who pulled you over."

Whippet crossed her arms over her chest. Cute or not, Sam had ruined her day. "You mean the self-righteous jerk who impounded my car?"

"No. I mean the generous guy who kept you out of jail by letting you off with a warning."

Whippet scowled. "Twenty-one days without a car, Tucker."

"I know, Whip. Soon we'll all be feeling the sting of your bad choices. Sam said you could go by the impound yard sometime and—"

"Get my car?" She clasped her hands in hope.

"No. Get the rest of your stuff."

"Fine," she said, raising her nose in the air and breezing past him. Whippet stopped before going into the kitchen and took a deep breath. *It's going to be okay. Everything will be okay.* She would keep telling herself that until it was true. She pushed through the door.

"Want some dinner?" Emma asked, sliding a basket of rolls onto the table. Whippet smiled. This was her favorite room in the house. This was where Grandma Lily had taught her how to make bread, telling her that kneading built character. *Punch that dough, Whippet!* Gran would say. *It's better than punching your brother.* Debatable. It was also where Gran showed her the finer points of baking as she pulled flour, sugar, and baking powder from the cupboards with the glee of a mad scientist.

Whippet took the seat next to her daughter just as Tucker walked in and sat next to Emma. Their mother said grace, and everyone quickly dug in to the delicious fried chicken dinner.

"So, sweetheart, how long are you staying?" her mother asked as she passed the peas.

Whippet froze.

"Yeah, Whip," Tucker said, shooting her a look. "How long?"

Big brothers. So overrated. Whippet wasn't ready for this conversation, so she deflected. "Oh, probably just the week." She avoided looking toward the judgmental end of the table.

Everly's head shot up, her mouth stuffed full. "But, Mom, I thought you said—"

"I know. You're anxious to get back to school," she said with a stiff smile, "but it's okay. I, uh, talked to your teachers before we left." Everly knew her well enough to just roll her eyes and finish her meal.

Whippet turned toward her mother. "Mom, did you make this chicken? It's so good!" Her tactic worked, sort of. Everyone complimented her mother on dinner, and soon the conversation turned to the drive from Texas and Everly's swear jar.

Surprisingly, Whippet enjoyed the meal and the company. Everly answered her uncle's questions about their life in Texas quickly and intelligently. Whippet's smile grew as she listened to her daughter. How she'd ended up with a child so much smarter than her was a mystery. Tucker and Emma seemed charmed by her beautiful girl. Halfway through dinner, Whippet glanced over and saw her mother watching her. Mother quickly looked away, but not before Whippet spied the ever-present worry in her eyes.

After dinner, before going down to her own place, her mother showed Whippet and Everly where they would be sleeping.

"I thought you could stay in here, Everly," her mom said, pushing open the door.

Everly looked between Whippet and her grandmother Sophie, and Whippet rubbed her daughter's back. "Look at that nice, big bed, Ev. I bet it's comfy. Did you know that when I was a little girl, this was the room I would sleep in when we came to visit my grandma?"

A faint smile crossed her mother's face. "Remember the time you and Tucker left the window open all night, hoping fireflies would make their way up to your room?"

Whippet nodded. "A bat flew in instead, and you chased it around with a broom. Poor thing flew back out the window in self-defense." Whippet grinned and, surprisingly, her mother smiled too.

They showed Everly the bathroom. After she changed and brushed her teeth, Everly jumped into bed.

"It's comfy!" she exclaimed, and Whippet sat down next to her. "Mom," Everly said as she reached for her book, "you don't have to tuck me in. I'm not a baby."

"Don't I know it," Whippet said mournfully. "You're growing up too fast."

"I think I'm just right," Everly said, snuggling into the feather pillow.

Whippet smiled. "I think you are too. Okay, don't stay up too late reading. I love you."

"Love you too," Everly mumbled, already engrossed in her book.

Whippet closed the door and followed her mother down the hall. "Let's get you set for the night. I thought you might like this room again." Her mom pushed the door open. This had been the room Whippet's parents always claimed when they'd visited. It had wide-framed windows with views that stretched all the way down to the lake. Whippet had stayed in this room a couple of months ago when she'd come out for Gran's funeral. It was a fairy-tale room with a four-poster bed and lush white bedding. The small chandelier made her feel a bit like a princess. Whippet put her purse on the bed and sat down. "Thanks, Mom. I love the way this room catches the morning light."

"It is a nice room." Her mother put her hand on the door to leave but turned at the last second. "Have you heard from *That Man* lately?"

Whippet bit down on a smile. Her mother categorically refused to utter Whippet's ex-husband's name. It was as if her mom believed that in speaking Cal's name, she might accidentally conjure him. Whippet's answer was the same as every other time her mother asked about him lately. "Not since he signed away his parental rights eleven months ago."

Her mother nodded, mouth tight. "Well, you're here now," she said, as if that solved the world's problems.

Whippet heard her mother walk down the hall muttering something about "That Man."

That Man indeed.

# CHAPTER FOUR

"Yes, Mrs. Moretti. I sent Officer Coleman over." Sam hit the blinker and turned up the drive to his house.

"But the Coleman kid, he hasn't been out of the academy that long, has he? You sure he knows what he's doing?" Marian Moretti had called the station just as Sam was leaving for the day, swearing she'd seen someone in the woods behind her house. She called at least once a week with the same complaint. There was never anyone in the woods. Sam thought maybe she was just lonely. Tonight, he'd dispatched Whit Coleman to tromp around outside and reassure her.

"Yes, ma'am. And he'll give me a call if it turns out to be anything." It wouldn't.

"Well, if you're sure—"

Sam suspected Marian's hesitancy stemmed more from the color of Whit's skin rather than his ability to handle the job. Social mores died slowly around here.

"Well, I suppose I can trust you," Mrs. Moretti said, still sounding doubtful. "After what you did for—"

"Oh, hey, Mrs. Moretti. I have another call coming in," he lied before she could mention the fire. "You take care now."

Sam pulled into his driveway. He'd taken this job almost two years ago, thinking it would be a restful change from the work he did with the Chicago PD. It was different, all right. But restful was not the word he would use.

Sam let himself into the house.

"Honey, I'm home!" he called. Two seconds later, he heard the scrambling of nails scratching on the newly refinished floors. The sound always made him wince. He moved into the dining room and prepared for impact. He bent down as a furry rocket launched itself into his arms.

Sam had never pictured himself owning a dog. Didn't want the responsibility. A few months ago, this straggly beast had set up camp on his back porch, a little worse for wear. Sam had tried to find the owner. He'd posted fliers in every window in town, but had heard nothing.

Dale Richards, the town vet, told Sam he thought the dog was a lab mix, no more than a year old, which explained the pup's cheerful exuberance. Sam was still trying to resign himself to dog ownership and hadn't quite gotten around to giving the thing a name yet. "What about Scout?" he asked the mutt. The dog quirked his head to the side. "Okay, maybe not. Don't worry, pal, I'll figure it out." He scratched the dog behind the ears and said, "Okay, buddy. Scram. I've got things to do." The dog trotted off, and Sam walked into the entryway again, throwing his keys onto the table next to the mahogany pier mirror.

He'd made it home in record time today. He'd only stopped once, pulling over to help Mike Treemonton move his car off the road where it stalled at the only stoplight in town. He'd stopped by the Madsen place to drop off a couple of suitcases, but that hardly counted. Tucker Madsen was his nearest neighbor. Tucker had purchased the house from his grandmother, Miss Lily, about a year and a half ago. From what Sam heard, Tucker had given up a lucrative medical practice in California to come back to Normal and take over as town physician for the semi-retired Doc Braithwaite. Tucker was good people. His sister, on the other hand, with that tangle of long blonde hair and wide blue eyes, seemed a bit sideways. Prettier than a field of cornflowers, but bent. He'd be better off to steer clear of that mess. Sam was glad Tucker had answered the door when he stopped by.

Tucker had thanked him and turned to go back into the house. At the last second, he'd paused and turned around again. "You okay?" Tucker had asked.

Sam had shrugged and said, "Any reason why I shouldn't be?"

Tucker gave a nod. "Heck of a thing you did for the O'Neils. The kind of thing that might leave you a little on edge afterward."

"I'm good," Sam said. "It's the O'Neils you should be talking to."

"I have. Sharon O'Neil has a textbook case of PTSD," said Tucker.

"Glad she's getting help," Sam said and got back in his car, heading for home.

He was fine. It was the O'Neils that everyone should be worried about. Not him.

Sam wished everyone would stop talking about the fire. He shook off the conversation and ran upstairs to his room, hanging his gun belt in the closet before changing into a T-shirt, jeans, and work boots.

Sam had just started for the stairs when his phone vibrated with a text from a number he didn't recognize.
*We need to talk.*
He knew exactly who it was. Emory. It had to be. The ex-wife who'd left him after deciding she'd "outgrown" their relationship. Sam wished she'd outgrow the habit of trying to reel him back in. Sam took a deep breath. It was time to get busy. He pocketed his phone and headed downstairs.

Sam had moved to Normal just after his divorce was final. His original intention had been to care for his ailing great-uncle. That was his story anyway. Unfortunately, not everyone bought it.

"You're running away," his mother had said, seeing right through him.

"Maybe so," came his reply. "But I don't see anyone else lining up to help Uncle Harlan."

"That's because he's an ornery old goat!"

Sam had heard tales of Uncle Harlan, of course. A bitter, lonely man who wanted nothing to do with the rest of the family.

Harlan had been all that and more. Contrary, ungrateful, and cheap, Harlan had greeted Sam on that first day with a snarled, "I'm not as rich as they all say, you know!" Things devolved from there.

Harlan's health had started to decline, and the old grump had stopped going into town altogether. Instead, Harlan had ruled his kingdom from behind his antique walnut desk, scribbling notes and letters that he'd insisted Sam post for him. No email for Harlan, who was convinced the internet was a pre-apocalyptic tool of the government.

Sam walked into the dining room and stared at his current project: removing the disgusting flocked wallpaper that covered every wall. The stuff was as stubborn as Harlan had been. Sam moved the ladder closer to the wall, climbed up, and started scraping.

This had once been Harlan's room. When the stairs had become too difficult for Harlan to navigate, Sam had set up a bed for him in here. Depending on someone else had bothered Harlan, so instead of expressing gratitude, his hostility had increased. Sam hadn't minded. Harlan and the endless household repairs had been excellent distractions from the things Sam had left behind in Chicago: the pressures of his job and the end of his marriage. It had worked for a while, but Sam eventually got wrapped up in the mystery of Harlan himself. Sam's grandfather, Joe, was Harlan's younger brother, and no better man than Joe had ever walked the earth. It gave Sam pause. How could two men from the same family be so different?

A year and seven months after Sam arrived, Harlan had died in his sleep. It had been a peaceful way to go for such a rancorous old man. Sam made sure his uncle got a proper burial, a memorial service only a handful of good people showed up for, and got ready to move out of the big old house on the hill.

Then something surprising had happened. His uncle's attorney informed him that Harlan, who reused Ziploc bags and turned soda cans in for the recycling money, was in fact quite wealthy. At his passing, the old miser had left a stock portfolio valued at over two million dollars to be divided among his survivors. In addition, he'd left Sam the house and more than enough cash to fix it. It was an unexpected move, and Sam was oddly touched. Harlan had left no explanation, just a note saying the will was iron clad.

So Sam inherited a five-thousand-square-foot home-improvement project. From the outside of the house, it looked like he'd won the lottery. From the inside, not so much. It was like the 1970s had exploded, splashing itself against the floors and walls in a cacophony of color. Burnt orange, avocado green, puce. The first time Sam had seen it, it had kind of made his eyes want to bleed. It wasn't all bad though. The nasty shag carpet had protected wide-planked oak floors, leaving them in near perfect condition. Since he'd moved in, Sam had spent evenings and weekends ripping up carpet, painting walls, and restoring woodwork.

The dog barked, ready for his dinner, and Sam walked into the kitchen. It was a disaster; he'd demoed everything in here. The only thing left was an old trestle table he used as a work bench and a few cans of paint waiting to be opened. Sam sighed. There was still a lot to be done tonight. At least work took his mind off the fact that he rattled around this big old house on his own, just like his uncle before him.

Sam felt a nudge at his knee and looked down at the dog, waiting patiently beside him. He fed the mutt and patted his head before grabbing a screwdriver and prying the lid off a can of paint. "Back to work," he said aloud, but there was no one there to hear him.

# CHAPTER FIVE

"When are you going to tell Mom the truth?" Tucker asked, eyeing her. They were at the courthouse for the reading of Gran's will.

Whippet froze. "Tucker, I told you—"

Her brother shook his head. "I meant about losing your job, not *how* you lost your job. Although, you do need to file that complaint." Tucker paused. "You know it's going to be pretty obvious that something is up when you don't head back to Texas, right?"

"Oh, yeah. Uh . . . soon. I'll tell her soon," she said, looking up at her brother and rotating her pinkie ring. "I should probably come clean with Emma too."

"Emma already knows. I told her the night you got here."

"Oh. Right." Tucker probably had one of those marriages where there was honesty and communication, all the things she'd missed out on during her foray into matrimony.

"You need to tell Mom so we can help you figure things out," Tucker insisted.

Whippet's head jerked back, eyes widening. "What do you mean, 'we'? I don't need help figuring things out."

"Really?" he said. "You have a plan?"

Whippet's brows came together. "Yes, I have plan. We're going back to Texas as soon as I can get some money together."

Tucker shook his head. "Texas? Why would you go back to Texas?"

"Well, I—" Whippet stopped. It was a good question. Her mother-in-law had kicked her out, Cal was long gone, and—oh yeah, she had no job. "I guess I don't know."

"Exactly," Tucker said. He walked over to her and put his hands on her shoulders. "You should stay." He nodded like it was already decided. "Your family is here."

He walked past her as Emma came through the courthouse doors. Mom walked in right behind, holding Everly's hand. Mom had taken Everly to lunch today. "Just the two of us," she'd said when she asked Whippet. It was the kind of thing she used to do with Whippet before her father died.

Maybe staying for a while wouldn't be such a bad idea. Just until she could save a little money and decide what to do next. Then she'd leave before her family made her too crazy.

They'd been in Normal for five days, and Whippet had enjoyed showing Everly all her favorite spots on Gran's farm. The weeping willow out back—a great place to disappear when avoiding chores—and the dock that stretched out over the lake where her dad had taught her to swim. They made cookies together in the kitchen using the same melamine bowls Gran had used when she taught Whippet how to bake. Last night, the two of them had snuck up into the cupola, Whippet's favorite childhood hideout. The door was stuck, warped by the ever-present humidity, but Whippet managed to get it open using a flathead screwdriver she'd found in the junk drawer in the kitchen. They'd cleared away cobwebs as they went up the narrow stairs into a room that smelled like wet cardboard. An array of dusty stuffed animals surrounded a small table, assembled for a tea party that had never happened.

Her dad had been the only one who had known to look for Whippet up here. He'd kept her secret too, sticking his head around the corner and calling, "Come down for dinner before your mother comes looking, missy."

"Mom." Everly pulled on her arm, and Whippet's thoughts snapped back to the courthouse. "This town is really small," she whispered, probably so Sophie wouldn't hear. "Really, really small."

"I know, hon. It's not that bad, is it?" Whippet whispered back.

Everly shrugged. "How long are we staying?"

That was turning out to be the question du jour.

Their little party walked upstairs to the attorney's office. Tucker sat next to Emma on a small sofa in the back. Her mother gestured to a wingback chair in front of the lawyer's desk, and Whippet sat down. Everly sat on a folding chair next to her and held Whippet's hand.

The door opened again. "Sorry to keep you waiting," a man said, stopping to shake her mother's hand before he nodded to Tucker and Emma. He turned to Whippet and held out his hand, his nice midwestern manners on display.

"I'm Hopper Spickett, attorney for your grandmother. I'm sorry for your loss. Miss Lily was—well, she was extraordinary."

"She was. Thank you." Hopper seemed like a nice guy. Very cute too. Emma told her last night that she'd been engaged to Hopper a few years ago. Whippet turned to look at her sister-in-law, and Emma gave her a wink.

"Shall we get started?" Mr. Spickett said, going to sit behind his desk.

There weren't any surprises. Gran forgave the debt on Miss Lily's House for Tucker and Emma and left them the surrounding land. Miss Lily made provisions for Mom as well, and as the attorney went on, Whippet found her mind wandering to what Tucker had said before.

Last night, Whippet had pulled out the piece of paper Tucker had given her in his office and looked up the website. She scanned it quickly and found, to her disappointment, that she would have to file a complaint with the corporation that owned the Maxi Mart first. She knew the name of the company; it had been on every paycheck. Still, she hesitated. The corporation that owned the chain of convenience stores was run by her boss's family. Would it do any good to file a complaint? Would they do anything more than just give her boss a slap on the wrist? She didn't like thinking about it, so she pushed it to the back of her mind.

Maybe she should stick to her plan to make a little money or ask for a loan so she could get back to Texas. College Station was a lot bigger than Normal. That meant more opportunity.

Whippet took a deep breath. Her mother had her arm on Whippet's chair. There was something reassuring about being surrounded by her family. Maybe she should stay. Like her brother said, there wasn't anything for her in Texas. Not anymore.

"Did you hear that, Whippet?" her mother asked.

Whippet glanced at her. "Sorry, what?"

Her mother shot her a look. "Your grandmother remembered you in her will," she said.

Whippet perked up. But Gran hadn't left her ready cash; Gran had left her a building. Whippet wasn't sure what she was going to do with a building in downtown Normal. Main Street was hardly the retail mecca of the Midwest. Whippet half listened as the attorney explained that she couldn't do anything with her inheritance right away, something to do with contracts and tenants. But it was nice Gran had remembered her.

Hopper Spickett said he'd take care of the transfer of ownership and kindly offered his assistance if she ever needed help. After a couple of signatures, Whippet was out the door, no richer than when she'd walked in.

They all went back to Miss Lily's House for dinner.

"After careful consideration, I've decided to extend our stay," Whippet told her mom as they sat down for dinner. She could see Tucker rolling his eyes from across the table. "My job isn't worth returning to, and Everly could continue school here just as easily as in Texas."

"You didn't get fired, did you?" her mother asked. She was a regular psychic. "You won't ever get ahead if you don't stay at a job long enough to make something of yourself," she said. "Weren't you on track for management?"

Whippet glanced at Tucker who was regarding her with raised eyebrows. "Not exactly. My boss really had a hard time—"

"Keeping his hands to himself," Tucker muttered under his breath.

"Delegating," Whippet said over him.

Her mother remained grim-faced through the rest of dinner. Whippet fervently hoped the subject was closed.

"Wait a minute. Tucker." Her mother turned her attention to her son. "Didn't your receptionist just go on maternity leave?"

Tucker's fork froze on its way to his mouth. "Yes, but my nurse is—"

"Couldn't Whippet work for you?" Her face brightened. "Oh, this is a great idea! Whippet, you can ride to work with Tucker every morning. How convenient is that?" Good old Mom. Taking over as usual. "Let's see. We'll have to get Everly registered for school right away. I'll call over there in the morning. And darling, I think you should stay with me at Shep's house." The old farmhouse where Mom lived and managed Emma's B&B had once belonged to Miss Lily's foreman, Shep. Even though he'd retired and moved away years ago, they still referred to it as "Shep's house."

Whippet felt a shiver of panic at the thought of living under the same roof as her mother. "Oh, I don't know. There's plenty of room here, right Tucker?" she said through gritted teeth. "And I wouldn't want to get in the way of your guests, Emma."

"Nonsense!" her mother said before Emma could respond. "You can help out too. You're a wonder in the kitchen," she said with a self-satisfied smile. "See how things are working out? It's like it was meant to be."

"I guess so," Whippet said weakly, looking at Tucker. He was shaking his head.

After dinner, her mother went upstairs with Everly, and Emma went into the kitchen to take a business call. Tucker followed Whippet out onto the front porch where she stood quietly, looking out across the acres of Madsen land that curved in a swath of green toward the old stone wall that bordered the highway. She did love it here. And she knew she should be grateful to her mother for making things easier for her. But she felt trapped.

"She means well," Tucker said, bracing his arms against the railing.
"You think so? I think she just wants me to do things her way."
"Yeah, that too." Tucker paused. "She loves you. And she's proud of you."
"See, I heard neither of those statements come from her mouth."
"Subtext," he said.

Whippet ran her finger over the porch rail. "I don't belong here, Tucker. Y'all are like a bunch of bright and shiny new dimes. I'm just an old, rusty penny."

Tucker slung an arm around her shoulder. "You belong, Whip. And I love pennies."

Whippet looked up at him. "Can you think of anything I can do to get Mom to calm down?"

Tucker eyed her. "You could go to church with us," he suggested.

She knew this was going to be a sticking point. Last Sunday, Whippet had slept in. Her bed was gloriously comfortable, and the shutters blocked out the rising sun. Why get up? Then Everly had come in and jumped up on her bed, shaking her awake. She said Grammy was taking them to church and would Whippet please go with them?

Ha! No, thank you. Whippet's faith had been shaken years ago. Her father's death, her catastrophic marriage, her unhealthy addiction to alcohol. Where had God been during those moments? She hadn't set foot in a church in years. She was a little afraid she'd get struck by lightning if she did. So she'd begged off that morning, telling Everly she had a headache. When Whippet had opened her eyes properly, her mother was standing there, dressed and ready for church, disapproval radiating from every pore.

Tucker slid his arm around her. "I don't think she'd worry so much if she didn't care."

"Maybe. Do you really want me to fill in for your receptionist? I mean, how long will she be out?"

"Three months. And I'm fine with it. Barb was going to do double duty until Lise came back, but the job is yours if you want it." Tucker looked at her. "Can you handle full time?"

She rolled her eyes. "Yes. Despite all reports to the contrary, I am a fairly competent individual. The only reason I lost my last job was because—"

"Yeah, don't tell me anymore about that. It makes me want to hunt down your boss and drop him. You should have told Mom the truth though. It wasn't your fault you lost your job." Tucker scratched his head. "Well, at least she didn't ask about your car."

"Guess that's a silver lining." Whippet sighed. "I could really use my car."

"Two more weeks. You'll make it," Tucker reassured.

"If you say so."

# CHAPTER SIX

"I don't want to do that," Erica Allen said, crossing her arms across her chest and chewing her gum. Sam looked at Whit Coleman who held up his hands in surrender before walking away. Didi Bradley, the station's administrative assistant, leaned forward and propped her arms on her desk, waiting to see what Sam would do next.

"Excuse me?" Sam asked, not sure he'd heard his new recruit correctly.

"I don't want to do that. That's not why I became a cop. Writing parking tickets is basic."

"Basic," Sam repeated, glancing again at Didi who put a hand over her mouth, probably to keep from laughing.

Erica nodded. "It's not meaningful."

How Officer Allen had made it through the hiring process was still a mystery to Sam. She'd passed all the necessary exams. She'd gone through extensive interviewing by both the mayor and himself, but somehow they'd both missed the fact that Erica Allen had no desire to be a police officer.

Sam took a deep, long-suffering breath. "Officer Allen, you and Officer Coleman are on patrol this morning. It's nice out. When the weather is good, folks come out of their homes and get creative with their parking. People speed through town on their way to Branson. It makes the good citizens of Normal feel better knowing we're out there maintaining order. That is about as meaningful as it's going to get today. So, if you'd like to keep your job, please exit the building, and join Officer Coleman in the squad car."

Erica kept chomping her gum and gave Sam a look his grandmother would have termed "salty." Finally, common sense prevailed, and she scooted her chair back and ambled out the door.

Sam was not having a good day. His ex kept texting, insisting they needed to talk. He was on edge because Sharon O'Neil had left another message, and Erica's little stunt hadn't helped.

Didi turned to him as soon as Erica was gone. "She told me yesterday that the only reason she became a cop is because her boyfriend thinks it's 'hot.' You should fire her, Sam."

"Can't. The mayor is concerned about affirmative action within the municipality."

"Is that a fancy way of saying she needs to keep a woman on payroll?"

"Correct."

"Well, she's a terrible cop," Didi said.

No arguing that.

"Maybe she could fill in for me after I have the baby." Didi smoothed a hand down her perfectly flat belly.

"You'd trust her on the phone?" Sam asked.

Didi's expression turned thoughtful. "Probably not the best idea, on second thought," she said.

Sam went into his office to attack the mound of paperwork on his desk. He'd just logged onto the computer when Didi's voice came over the intercom. "Tucker Madsen is on line one for you."

Sam picked up the phone. "Beaufort here."

"Hey, Sam. How's it going?"

"Can't complain," Sam lied. He could complain all right. It just wouldn't do any good.

"Well, I guess that's good. Hey, I was wondering if there would be a way for my sister to get into her car. My niece is starting school here next week, and they need to get a few things out of the trunk."

Ah, yes. The kooky blond with a lead foot. He'd almost forgotten about her. Good to know she'd be sticking around. Forewarned was forearmed.

"Sure, that should be fine. We don't actually have the car at the station. Cam Buckman keeps impounded vehicles behind his garage over on Mitchell Street. I'll call over there and tell him to look for you."

"Thanks. I appreciate it," Tucker said.

Sam hung up and dialed Buckman Auto. As the line connected, Sam was grateful it wasn't him who'd have to deal with Doc Madsen's quirky sister.

\* \* \*

Her mother hit the blinker and slowly turned right onto the highway. "It seems like your car has been in the shop for an awful long time, Whippet."

"Oh, well, they had to order a part. It's coming from Detroit, I think."

"Hmm." Her mom slowed as she got closer to town. "I didn't want to mention this earlier," she said, "but I'm pretty sure Tucker and Emma are trying to get pregnant. That's why I think it would be best that you stay with me."

"Ya know, I could have gone my whole life without knowing that," Whippet said.

The family had spent the last twenty-four hours getting her and Everly set up at Shep's house, conveniently located just down the road from Miss Lily's House. The two of them would share the attic room. It was still April, and while there were a few guests booked at the B&B, Emma blocked out their upstairs room for the next couple of months. Demand would pick up soon, and Whippet felt guilty for costing Emma money.

"It's fine," Emma had insisted. "We just opened last summer. And since Nina quit doing PR for me it's been kind of slow. Denver! Why would she take a job in Denver?" Nina was Emma's best friend who'd taken a job in Colorado. Whippet would have bet it was for the usual reasons: money, career advancement, and, judging from what she'd seen of Normal, maybe boredom.

Her mother drove past Grimm's Market and through the roundabout. They went past the courthouse and that darn police station before taking a left on Mitchell. She pulled up in front of an old gas station with pumps that looked like they hadn't been operational since 1955. The small parking lot was littered with cars. The sign above the garage said Buckman Auto.

Whippet started to get out of the car. Her mother picked up her phone and pushed back her seat. "Aren't you coming with me?" Whippet asked.

"I'm sure you can handle it, and I'm in the middle of reading the book club book for this month. I haven't been able to get into it yet. Call me if you need me." Her mother waved her away.

Whippet walked toward the office attached to the garage and pushed through the front door. A man stood behind the counter, phone against his ear.

"It's definitely the differential," he said into the receiver. "Yeah, I know."

Whippet stood next to the window, the smell of oil and exhaust bringing back memories of the days when she'd take Cal his lunch at work.

Cal's football career had ended abruptly when he tore his MCL his junior year of college. He'd refused to believe he'd never play again at first and spent most of his time after surgery trying to rehabilitate his left knee. But it was never the same again. Inexplicably, he was angry at Whippet, claiming if she hadn't gotten pregnant—evidently, she'd done that all by herself—he would've been able to focus on football. Discouraged and bitter, he'd dropped out of college and eventually found his way to a trade school and had become a mechanic. He put his football dreams behind him and picked up a bottle instead.

Ah, the good old days.

Whippet took a seat. The mechanic searched for a piece of paper and wrote something down. When he turned, she got her first good look at him. He had a sort of boy-next-door look about him. His disheveled brown hair kept falling across his forehead, which he pushed back with fingers black with grease. For some reason she found the gesture quite appealing.

He finally looked up and did a very flattering double take when he saw her sitting there. A slow grin spread across his face. Whippet looked down, but not before she smiled too.

"Ben, I'll call you when your truck is done. Yep. No problem. Talk to you soon." He hung up, braced both arms against the counter and asked, "And how can I help *you* today?" His tone was friendly, and Whippet wondered for a second if he was flirting.

She stood up and walked to the counter. "My name is Whippet Moran, and I'm—"

"Whippet? Like the dog?"

"It's my nickname," she clarified.

Whippet had a sentimental attachment to her nickname. Family lore said that as a baby, she had run before she walked, a source of pride for her dad. "Look at her!" her father had once exclaimed. "She's whippet fast!" The rest, as they say, was history.

"See, now, if I was trying to come up with a nickname for you," he said, grinning, "I would have gone with something cheerful, like Sunshine or maybe Daisy."

Definitely flirting.

"Well, thank you. Um, I'm here to get some things from my car. It's, uh, been impounded."

"Oh, right. Chief Beaufort called over this morning. The thing is—"

"Hello, Daphne," a familiar voice came from behind and Whippet turned to see Officer Grumpy Pants standing there. There was no denying the man was attractive. Too bad his disposition wasn't.

"Daphne? I thought you went by Whippet," the mechanic said.

"I do, it's just—you know what? It's a long story." She turned to the cop. "Why are you here? Afraid I'll make a run for it?"

He raised an eyebrow at her before turning and ignoring her completely. "Hey, Cam," he said to the mechanic. Cam. That was a nice name.

Officer Unfriendly tossed a set of keys onto the counter. "Sorry about that. Must have pocketed them when I brought the car over."

"No problem," Cam said affably, "I'll get her taken care of."

Chief Beaufort nodded and turned back to her. "Have a good day," he said so firmly she felt like she'd been given an order. He'd just reached the door when he added, "Ma'am," with a nod.

Whippet scowled as she watched him leave then turned to Cam and smiled. "All set?"

Cam walked her out behind the garage and unlocked a set of high chain link gates. "Your car has Texas plates. How'd you end up here?" he asked.

"My grandmother died. I'm here visiting my family."

"Oh, man. I am so sorry. Wait, it wasn't Miss Lily, was it? You're her granddaughter?"

"I am."

"Well, that makes you cool by association. Miss Lily is, I mean was, a firecracker. I'm gonna miss her. She was my Sunday School teacher when I was five years old."

"Was she?"

"I was shy back then. Hated being away from my parents even for a second. She'd have me sit next to her every week until I got used to the other kids."

Gran, ever the champion of the underdog. During their summer visits, Tucker would take off with Emma and leave Whippet behind. Gran knew she felt left out, and she'd turned their time together into something exclusive, for just the two of them. "That sounds like Gran all right."

Cam nodded. "Great lady. Well, here we are." Cam popped the trunk for her. It was a little embarrassing, having her whole life crammed into the back of her car. She rooted around and managed to find a box of Everly's clothes. Whippet moved a couple of boxes out of the way and found Everly's backpack and the laundry basket. The thing about packing in a hurry was that everything tended to get shoved in whatever was handy at the time. She dug around in the basket until her hand closed around cool glass, and just like that some of the tension she'd been dragging around with her for the last week melted away. Risking a lightning strike, Whippet said a quick prayer that she'd be able to keep the bottle hidden from her mother.

"Um, there's a little more here than I thought. Would you mind carrying that box to my mother's car? I'll grab a couple more things and follow you out."

"You bet," Cam said as he hoisted the box into his arms and walked back toward the garage. Acting quickly, Whippet grabbed the bottle and shoved it into Everly's backpack. Whippet knew her mom would go through her stuff later; she just hoped she'd have time to stash the bottle somewhere before her mother went on the hunt. She flung Everly's backpack over her shoulder and grabbed the laundry basket. Blowing the hair out of her eyes, she closed the trunk with her elbow and followed Cam out of the impound yard.

Her mother saw them and scrambled out of the car to help. "Hey, Cam," she said, taking the laundry basket from Whippet, "How are you?"

"Great. Thank you, ma'am." Now that was a completely appropriate use of the word "ma'am." Cam loaded the last box into her mother's car and closed the trunk.

"Well, it was nice to meet you," Whippet said. She kept a tight grip on the backpack as she held out her hand. "I appreciate your help, Mr.—" she realized she didn't know his last name.

He took her hand in his. "Buckman."

"Oh. Is this your place then?"

"Sure is. And if you ever need anything, anything at *all*—you give me a call." He nodded, still holding her hand.

Whippet felt a smile threaten. "Thank you," she said, looking back at him as she got into the car.

Maybe Normal wouldn't be so bad after all.

# CHAPTER SEVEN

The first couple of days working for her brother went well enough, for the most part. Tucker's nurse, Barb, gave her a short training on how to answer the phones. She showed her how to book appointments, set reminders, and make entries into the billing program. "Lise is going to do all the medical transcribing and insurance stuff from home, thank heaven, but if you can keep the office afloat until she gets back, we'd all be grateful."

Easier said than done, as proven by a call she'd received on her first morning.

"Lise?" A raspy voice came over the line.

"No, this is Whippet Moran. I'll be filling in for Lise while she . . . hello?"

The phone rang again five seconds later.

"Dr. Madsen's office, can I help you?"

"Lise?" It was the same gravelly voice on the other end of the line.

"No, I'm sorry. Lise is on—hello? Hello!"

The phone rang again. This time she answered right away. "Don't hang up!" Whippet said in a rush.

"Who is this?" the voice demanded.

"This is Dr. Madsen's receptionist. Lise just had a baby, and I'm—"

"She had the baby! Well, why didn't you just say that? Congratulations!"

"Uh, thank you? Can I help you with something?"

"This is Victoria Welles; can I get an appointment with the doc for this afternoon?"

Victoria? Whippet would have bet double or nothing she'd been speaking to a man.

It was a busy office for a small town, and Whippet felt like she'd been thrown in the deep end. Her brother saw patients of all ages and circumstances, and she had to refer to the patient files a lot, but Whippet was grateful to have the job. Any job.

After work, she was able to go home and focus on Everly, who seemed to be having a hard time with their sudden move. Her daughter hadn't said anything outright, but Whippet could tell something was wrong. She'd tried asking Everly what was bothering her last night, but her daughter had just shrugged and gone back to watching TV. Whippet felt guilty about all the adjustments Everly had been forced to make over the last year. What was worse, Whippet didn't really have a plan. It was very likely that their stop in Normal was temporary, and Everly would be forced to adjust again.

"Have you seen your brother?" Barb poked her head around the corner. But before Whippet could answer, Barb disappeared with the next patient.

Barb was great at her job and answered Whippet's questions in a way she understood. Whippet was happy to be working under her.

Most days.

Some days Barb was stressed or was trying to lose a little weight or hadn't gotten enough sleep, or all three at once, heaven help her. On those days, Barb could be a bit waspish. And today seemed like it might be one of those days.

Barb stormed back into the reception area. "Where is your brother?" Barb asked sharply.

Whippet looked up from the computer screen. "Uh, I don't know. When he dropped me off, he said he had an appointment and would be in later."

Barb hefted fists onto her substantial hips. "Well, he's half an hour late for his first appointment," Barb said, like it was Whippet's fault.

Whippet reached for the phone. "I'll call him."

"You think I haven't already called him five times?"

Whippet put the phone back, bent her head, and picked up a stack of mail, planning to wait out hurricane Barb.

She'd just begun sorting the letters when the door burst open, and a woman rushed in, dragging a sobbing child behind her.

"I need to see Doctor Madsen right now!"

Barb muttered something about Mondays and full moons and showed the mother into an exam room. A gentleman who'd been waiting patiently started to grumble.

Whippet offered him an uneasy smile and said, "Sorry," before returning to sorting the mail.

Minutes later, Barb stuck her head around the corner of an exam room. "I need you to come in here and help me," she said.

"I'm not a nurse," Whippet protested.

"Gee, then I guess I won't ask you to stitch up the kid's arm then."

Whippet went pale.

"Relax," Barb said. "I just need you in the room while I examine the kid. Mom had to leave so she could drop her other kids off at the babysitter. There's no one else to help."

"Fine," Whippet mumbled as she pushed away from the relative safety of her desk. She turned and grabbed a few suckers from the container on her desk before going into the room.

"Whippet, this is Josh Carter. He took a spill at the park this morning and managed to find a broken bottle without even looking for it."

"Hey, buddy," Whippet said, sitting down in the chair next to the kid.

He turned a tear-stained face her way. "When is my mom gonna be back?" he asked between hiccups.

"Soon, I bet." Josh gave her a doubtful look. "Oh, I promise," Whippet said, trying to distract him. "I'm a mom, and I can tell you, we don't like leaving our kids for very long. Especially when they're hurt. But I bet your mom trusts Barb here a lot. You know how I know that?"

"How?"

"Because she wouldn't leave you with just anyone. Barb is a nurse, and she's going to fix your arm, okay?"

The kid sniffed and nodded. Barb gave her a look before holding up a menacing looking syringe filled with clear liquid. So much for earning the kid's trust.

"Uh, here, buddy," Whippet held up the bouquet of lollipops. "You want one of these?" she asked, then breathed a sigh of relief when the kid's frazzled mom came into the room.

Whippet had just closed the door when little Josh started to wail.

\* \* \*

Sam glanced at the clock and then out the window. It was a beautiful day. The sun was out. The flowering dogwoods behind the station were in bloom.

The phone rang.

Even if caller ID hadn't already identified the source of the call from Normal Elementary, Sam would have recognized the principal's molasses-in-January accent. Miss Arnetta Winslow was a transplant from Louisiana and spoke with slow authority.

"Hey, Sam. How you doin'?" she asked.

"Fine," he said, getting the niceties out of the way. A call during school hours wasn't social.

"We have a little situation over here," she drawled. "Just the teensiest bit of an emergency. It seems one of our students has gone AWOL."

Sam stood up. "Any idea where they are?" he asked, already heading out the door.

"No. Video surveillance suggests she just kind of wandered off. We searched the school grounds, but I don't have the resources to stop the day and look for her. Could you help us out?"

"Sure. You have a name and description for me?" Sam started his squad car and pulled out of the parking lot.

He heard the rustling of paper. "Her name is Everly Moran, she's about four foot—"

Sam rolled his eyes. "Yeah, I got this," he said. "I'll let you know when I find her." He hung up.

He started down Main Street in the direction of the school. He slowed when he got to the roundabout. The school was two blocks away, and he had a hunch Everly Moran would be heading over to the doctor's office where he heard her mother worked.

Sure enough, he spied Everly a second later walking down the sidewalk, backpack dragging off one arm, shoulders slumped. He flipped a U-turn and slowed down. Sam rolled down his passenger-side window. "Nice day," he called, keeping pace with her as she walked.

Everly looked at him but said nothing.

"Great day for a stroll," he added conversationally.

"I guess so," she said glumly.

"Just got a call from Principal Winslow over at the school. She said to be on the lookout for an escapee. You wouldn't know anything about that, would you?"

"Escapee from what? School or stupid Missouri history?"

"Missouri history is stupid, huh?"

The girl shrugged. "Don't see the point in learning it."

He kept driving beside her as a car with Illinois plates breezed past him going over fifty. More lost revenue. "Why's that?"

Everly stopped and turned toward him. He hit the brakes. "Because in another couple of months I'll be back in Texas or somewhere else. I won't need to know any of that stuff then," she said.

"You might have a point," Sam said, and she started walking again. "Can I give you a lift back to school?"

"No, thanks. I'm gonna go see my mom at my uncle Tucker's office."

"And she's okay with you skipping school?"

The girl shuffled to a stop. "Prob'ly not." Everly glanced at him. "Are you gonna make me go back to school?"

"It's only one-fifteen. There's still a lot of school left. Besides, the principal is worried about you," he said, hoping to appeal to her sense of responsibility. "How about I give you a ride back?"

The girl looked down the street to where her mother worked then back at him. For a minute she looked like she might make a run for it. She must have thought better of it and walked to his car. "Fine," she mumbled and threw her backpack into the back and climbed in.

"Seat belt," he reminded her. Everly complied and then slouched against the door, her forehead pressed against the window.

"This town is so small," she said.

"Yes, it is," Sam said, pulling away from the curb.

"I miss my old school. I had a lot of friends there," Everly said.

He felt for the kid. Starting over wasn't easy. "That's rough," he said, "But you should give us chance. Folks around here are pretty nice."

"Uh-uh. Today Kara Warren asked me if it was true that everything is bigger in Texas, and when I said I didn't know, she said, 'Because that would explain the size of your nose.'"

It always surprised him how mean some kids could be. "Your nose is fine."

"I know. Kara is just trying to act cool," Everly said.

"So what did you do?" Sam asked, genuinely curious.

"I walked away," she mumbled.

"Impressive. I bet that was hard to do."

"Gramma Fancy—she's my grandma back in Texas—she always told me 'The hard thing to do is usually the right thing to do.'"

"Grandma Fancy is right," Sam said, looking at her through the rearview mirror. "Do you miss her?" Sam felt a twinge of sympathy for the girl.

"Yeah," Everly said and went quiet.

Sam hoped he wasn't making things worse by bringing up her grandmother. He cleared his throat. "Well, she'd be proud of you. You were the better person."

"Yeah, except everyone in my class still laughed." Everly went back to staring out the window. "I wish I had a dog. Everything would be so much better if I had a dog."

"I have a dog. Well, sort of," Sam said, absently.

"Sort of? How do you sort of have a dog?" Everly asked.

"He just kind of showed up one day and stayed."

Everly perked up. "That's so cool. I wish that would happen to me." She paused. "What's your dog's name?"

"Don't know. I haven't given him one. Right now, I just call him 'dog'."

"You haven't named your dog? I have a whole list of names for when I get a dog."

"A list?"

"Well, yeah. I figure I'll have to get to know the dog a little before I give it a name."

Sam nodded. "Good idea. Maybe that's what I'm doing."

"Or you're just lazy," Everly offered.

"There could also be that," he said as they pulled up in front of the school. "Here we are." Sam turned around to look at her. "You want me to go in with you? Maybe arrest Kara Warren?"

"Really?" Her face brightened.

"No."

"Oh. Well, no thanks then. I hope no one sees me. What would Kara think if she saw me getting out of a cop car?"

"Cool," Sam said. "She'd think you were cool."

Everly opened the door, then hesitated. "You won't tell my mom, will you? About me skipping out? She'll just get worried and then mad and then she'll ground me, which wouldn't be so bad because I don't have any friends anyway."

Sam chuckled. "You're laying it on a bit thick, don't you think?"

"Is it working?" Everly asked, voice hopeful.

Sam looked at her for a second. "How about a plea bargain?"

"A what?"

"A compromise. If you promise never to skip school again, I won't tell your mom."

Everly tapped her chin like she was thinking. "Okay," she said. "You've got a deal." She stuck her hand out, and they shook on it. She got out of the car and swung her backpack over her shoulder. "Thanks for helping me. And don't worry, I didn't believe any of the horrible things my mom said about you when you took our car," she said and ran into the school.

# CHAPTER EIGHT

SHE'D JUST TAKEN A SEAT after showing the Clarkes into exam room three. Identical twin girls with identical cases of the flu. With all that coughing in unison, she was glad there were no other patients in the waiting room.

Her phone pinged with a text.

*Question for you.*

She didn't recognize the number. Her brows came together as she picked up her phone.

*Who is this?*

*Cam Buckman.*

Oh! The cutie from the impound yard.

*What's your question?* She held her phone a little tighter. Maybe it was about her car.

Oh, how she missed her little car and the freedom it represented. Her Cobalt was a heap of junk, but it got her around. Everly was anxious for the car's return as well. Last week she'd cut and stapled together a paper chain to count down the days until the car's liberation.

*Hope you don't mind, but I took a look at your car. Figured I might as well since it was here.*

Oh, dear. That didn't sound good.

*Why do I think you've got bad news for me?*

*Smart and beautiful.* She smiled. *It's not too bad. The brake pads need to be replaced. Thought maybe I'd get your car in fighting form while it's here. What do you say?*

*Hmm . . . I say, how much?* she texted.

While she waited for Cam to respond, Tucker's next appointment walked through the front door. She checked him in and took him back to an exam room. When she sat down again, she had a text.

*What if we say dinner and call it even?* Oh, goody! A date. *Your mom says you're a pretty good cook. Thought I'd put that to the test.*

Whippet grinned.

*Sounds like I'm getting the better deal,* Whippet texted.

*I don't think so. It's been a while since I've had a homecooked meal. You'd be doing me a favor.*

Whippet thought for a minute.

*How about Saturday?*

His answer came lightning fast.

*Perfect.*

Whippet put down her phone, already cobbling together a menu in her head. She picked up her phone again. Maybe she should check with Cam to see if he had any food allergies. She hesitated. Nah. Their flirty texts were enough for today.

The door crashed open, and Officer Beaufort pushed inside, his arm around a man who was bent over and moaning.

"I need to see Doc Madsen, now!" the police chief barked.

Whippet came to her feet. "Do you have—what's wrong with him?" she asked in alarm. The man in question looked up at her, his face pale and sweaty. He lifted a trembling hand to show her. His thumb was bloody and mangled, a nail protruding from the center.

It was the last thing she remembered.

*  *  *

When she came to, she was on the floor and Sam Beaufort was leaning over her holding an ice pack to her head. Not exactly the stuff of dreams.

"You again?" she said, squinting. For some reason, it really, really hurt to open her eyes. She tried to sit up.

"You say that like you're not happy to see me," he said, gently pushing her back down.

"Ya think?" Whippet said and gave up, melting into the floor. "What happened?"

"I brought in Milt Walker. He shot a ring shank roofing nail through his thumb—"

Whippet groaned.

"And you, uh, passed out. Your brother wants me to keep you immobile until he can take a look at you. You hit your head on the chair on your way down. He's concerned you might have a concussion."

She closed her eyes again. "Great."

They were silent for a blessed moment. Maybe if she kept her eyes closed, he'd magically disappear.

No such luck.

"So does this happen a lot?" he asked.

She cracked an eye open. "Does what happen a lot?"

"This," he said, gesturing down her prostrate figure. "Seems like maybe this job might not be a great fit. You're kind of squeamish."

She sat up. "I'll have you know I love this job." She put a hand to her head. "I'm giving back to the community. I'm—" The door to the exam rooms opened and her brother came into the lobby, Milt at his side. The man's hand was bandaged, and his color was much better.

"You're all set," Tucker said, slapping Milt on the back. "Glad Sam brought you in."

"Thanks, Doc." Milt nodded at her brother. Sam unfolded from the floor and pushed the ice pack into her hand. "I'm his ride," he said. "You take care, now."

Whippet heard the door close and leaned against the wall. Tucker walked over and squatted next to her. "Barb will be back in a few minutes. How are you?" He took the ice pack and looked at her head. "Sam said you lost consciousness. That's not a good sign. Any confusion? Headache? Vision okay?"

"I'm fine. I feel a little foolish, that's all," she said.

"Mmm." Tucker sat down next to her.

Whippet rubbed her head and glanced over at her brother. "Just say it, Tucker."

"Say what?"

"This job might not be the best fit for me," she said echoing Sam Beaufort's words.

"Okay. This job might not be the best fit for you."

"Tucker!"

"You said it first. It was just temporary, anyway. Maybe you should try to find something you actually enjoy. It's not great PR having you pass out when patients come in."

He was right. "Well then, I guess I'm handing in my resignation," she said, her voice a little thick. She might not love the job, but she felt bad for quitting. What would she do now? She swallowed hard and pushed down the panic.

Tucker slung an arm around her, and she put her head on his shoulder. "I accept your resignation," he said gently. "It'll be okay, Whip. Things will work out. You'll see." He gave her shoulder a squeeze.

"I hope so." Whippet said, trying not to cry. "Tucker, I'll only quit on one condition."

He looked at her. "What's that?"

"You have to tell Mom."

\* \* \*

Tucker clocked out early and took her home. When she walked inside, her mom was busily wiping down the tables and chatting with someone on the phone. Everly was at the kitchen table doing her homework. Good girl. Neither of them seemed to notice her go upstairs.

Whippet went into the room she shared with Everly and closed the door behind her. She walked to the bureau next to the window. The top two drawers belonged to her; the bottom two were Everly's. She knelt and pulled the bottom drawer out as far as it would go then reached behind it. Her hand closed around the cool glass bottle she'd stashed there.

In moments of crisis, her mother would pray. In contrast, Whippet's modus operandi had always been to take a drink.

She would bet hard money her mother searched her room while she was at work. Sniffing mouthwash bottles, looking in the closet, in between the mattress and box springs. Once an alcoholic, always an alcoholic. Her mother was right. Whippet rotated the hiding spot for her unopened bottle of Ketel One, switching it from the toilet tank to the air vent to its current hiding place, behind her daughter's sock drawer.

Did she want a drink? Absolutely. Was she going to take one? No way. She hadn't had a drink in over seven years, and she wasn't going to start just because she couldn't hold down a job. She gave the bottle a squeeze and closed the drawer.

In Texas, she'd had a wonderful therapist, a woman who'd helped Whippet along her path to sobriety. *Alcohol is a coping strategy. When faced with a stressful situation, find another way to relax or distract yourself until the temptation passes,* her therapist's voice encouraged.

Blessedly, the room, while small, had an en suite bathroom with a beautiful soaker tub. Whippet got the water running and then set her iPhone to play her favorite rainy-day music: opera. It wasn't everyone's cup of tea, and she couldn't really explain the appeal. She'd started listening in high school when she had to study for a test. It was one of the few habits her mother encouraged. "Your father used to listen to opera," her mom would say wistfully.

Whippet heard raised voices coming from downstairs. One of them sounded like it was Tucker's. He'd probably come in to tell their mother the glad tidings.

She heard a knock. After a pause, Everly's voice came through the door.

"Aunt Emma, do *not* go in there. Mom's listening to opera. She only listens to Andrea Bocelli when she's upset."

Whippet quickly turned off the water and opened the door. "Okay, missy. Go downstairs and help Grandma."

"With what?" Everly counted off on her fingers. "Grammy wants me to unload the dishwasher; she wants me to peel the potatoes; she wants me to finish my math homework."

"Better go do it then," Whippet said, pulling Emma into the room.

"Which one?" Everly asked.

"All of them. You're a good girl. Love you!" she said, closing the door behind her.

"Sometimes you two seem more like sisters than mother and daughter," Emma said.

"That's because Everly helped raise me," Whippet said. "What's going on downstairs?"

"Your mom is yelling at Tucker," Emma said.

"Why?"

"She's mad at him for firing you."

"He didn't fire me. I quit," Whippet insisted.

"I know. I was there when he told her, but I think now she's worried you'll leave town," Emma said, grinning. Suddenly, Emma's face collapsed, tears threatening to spill.

"Hey!" Whippet said, alarmed. She pulled Emma over to Everly's bed. Whippet sat down across from her. "I promise you I'm not going anywhere. I can't. I don't have a car."

Emma gave a little laugh. "It's not that. I mean, I'm glad you're staying . . . or at least I hope you're . . . it'd be really nice if you'd—" She took a deep breath. "Sorry. It's just . . . well"—she looked at Whippet—"Can I ask you something?"

Whippet moved to sit cross-legged. "Of course."

Emma played with the edge of Everly's blanket. "How long do you think it should take to get pregnant?"

Oh boy. So her mom had guessed the truth.

"I have no idea. Everly certainly wasn't planned, and I spent most of my marriage trying *not* to get pregnant."

Emma plucked at the blanket, the tears coming fast and silent. "We've been trying for a year and a half," she whispered.

"Have you seen a doctor? I mean, I know you're married to one, but—"

"I have. There doesn't seem to be anything wrong with either of us." Emma dashed a hand across her eyes. "I guess I'm just frustrated. I'm thirty-one. I think it gets harder to get pregnant the older you get."

Whippet sat back. She'd never pictured herself with just one child. She'd wanted at least two, maybe three, close together so they could play and fill the house with their happy noise. She'd approached Cal once about the idea of another child when Everly was about two. He'd looked at her as if she were crazy. "One's enough!" he'd barked at her and gone back to working on his car. End of discussion.

"I don't know what to do," Emma confided. "Part of me wants to give up."

Whippet chose her words carefully. Through so many of the disasters in her life, people had tried to help her with advice and pithy little sayings which, after hearing them all roughly five hundred times, had kind of lost their punch. *Things will work out. What doesn't kill you makes you stronger! Everything happens for a reason. Good things are coming!* And Whippet's favorite, *The same heat that softens the potato hardens the egg.* Whippet had spent an inordinate amount of time trying to figure out if it would be better to be the potato or the egg.

"Don't give up. You're an incredible human being. And beautiful and talented and all the things a mom should be. Getting pregnant might take some time, that's all." Whippet bit her lip, hoping she didn't sound like an idiot. She wasn't good at this stuff.

Emma nodded. "Tucker's not worried. He says he's happy even if it's just us." Emma's eyes filled again. "But I want kids." Emma hesitated. "The doctor wants to start me on Clomid. We have an appointment next week."

"Oh, wow. You know what? I say go for it. Good things are coming, I can feel it." Okay, time to stop talking.

"Would you mind, I mean . . . would it be okay if we talked once in a while? I don't want to be a pain, but sometimes I just need a woman's perspective."

Whippet's heart expanded in her chest. "Yes! Emma, of course." The thought of getting closer to Emma was, well, nice. "I would love that."

"Okay, I'm done being a drag." She sniffed. "Thanks for listening to me." Emma hopped off the bed and walked to the door. Whippet followed. With her hand on the knob, Emma turned and pulled Whippet in for a hug. "I'm really glad you're here," Emma said.

Those words meant everything to Whippet.

# CHAPTER NINE

Her mother was very supportive of Whippet's decision to quit working at Tucker's practice. Very, very supportive. She must have told her at least a half dozen times that first night how supportive she was. Whippet thought that meant her mother would leave the subject alone.

It had been too much to hope for.

"Have you prayed about it?" her mom asked as soon as they'd dropped Everly off at school the next morning. "About what you should do next, I mean."

Whippet turned her face to the window and kept quiet. Her mother's faith was strong. Whippet's was not. It didn't stop her mom from pushing though.

Gran's old King James Bible had miraculously materialized on her bedside table. Subtle, her mother. Everly was still going to church with her family. Whippet smiled and waved at them as they drove off each Sunday before she headed back to bed, enjoying the luxury of an empty house.

Whippet's mother turned right on Main Street. "What do you think about getting your education?"

Whippet looked at her mom. She must have read something in Whippet's expression because she looked back at the road and said, "Well, maybe now isn't the time to talk about it."

Living near family wasn't all bad. Emma was a bonus. The night Whippet made dinner for Cam Buckman, Emma came over and spent an hour helping her figure out what to wear. Some of her wardrobe was still in boxes in the back of her car, but they managed to find a pretty pale-yellow sundress with daisies twining down it. She'd thrown on a cardigan, put her hair up in a messy bun, and charmed the man with her grilling prowess. The weather cooperated, and she and Cam spent the evening outside getting to know each other.

Cam was unexpected. When she'd offered to make him dinner, she'd been prepared for an evening of conversation about car parts and pneumatic tools, but Cam had surprised her. He was polite and interesting. He'd asked about her life in Texas, what it was like to be a mom, and what her plans were now that she was here. When the conversation had turned to him, she'd learned that he had a degree in automotive technology. When he decided to buy the garage with his brothers, he went on to minor in business.

It had been a nice night, and when she'd walked him to his truck, he'd asked if he could see her again.

Life was settling into a pattern. Whippet got up early each morning to prepare breakfast for the guests at the B&B. Emma might own the business, but as far as Whippet could tell, her mother had carte blanche on how she managed the place. Most days after they dropped Everly off at school, she and her mom ran errands for the B&B.

Which was why they were in town this morning.

"Would you do me a favor?" her mother said as they pulled up in front of Grimm's Market. "Would you mind walking down to the library and returning the books in the back seat?"

"Sure. Is the library open?" Whippet asked, reaching for the stack of novels.

"No, but there's a drop box on the side on the building closest to the park."

The biggest advantage of a small town was that everything was close. Grimm's was in the newer section of town, an area of buildings constructed after the end of World War II. The grocery store was a squat, cinder block building with large plate glass windows displaying posters with the week's specials. An imposing marquee sat on the store roof, announcing in large green letters "Grimm's Market." The place hadn't been updated since the fifties, but maybe that was part of the novelty, shopping in a time capsule.

Whippet headed north past the elegant courthouse into her favorite section of town. Dubbed the historic district, this end of Main Street was lined with charming two-story brick storefronts sporting wide display windows, old stone cornice pieces, and carved parapets. Next to the courthouse was a park with towering maples, a stark white gazebo, and a line of short shrubs that separated the playground equipment from the park benches. The library was just on the other side of the park.

She dropped the books through the box as instructed and took a little detour. She crossed the street again and looked back. A couple of doors down from the library, next to a vacant lot, was Whippet's favorite building, a gracious pale-brick building with large black-paned windows. The second story sported high arched windows and a recessed balcony protected by a scrolled wrought-iron balustrade. Old-fashioned apothecary letters spelled out "Aldridge Sporting Goods" across the sign band. Whippet had loved this place as a child, maybe because when she was little it had been the candy store, its windows alive with glass jars full of colorful confections. That cute store was long gone. Now the beautiful windows held a small tent, a camping stove, and mannequins dressed in fishing gear.

Whippet turned and headed back toward the market.

Meacham's Diner, with its metal lines and glass brick corners, came into view. There was a "help wanted" sign propped just inside the front window. Whippet slowed to a stop. She'd waitressed her fair share over the years. She didn't necessarily like the work, but at this point a job, any job, would be great if it would get her out from under the careful scrutiny of her mother.

Whippet stood there for a full minute, trying to decide whether to go in.

She closed her eyes. Her mind conjured a tall, broad-shouldered image of a man standing next to her, asking her why she was doing this, because of *course* he would take care of her. There was no reason to debase herself by working as a waitress. Whippet snuggled up to the daydream.

Occasionally, she would indulge in elaborate rescue fantasies where the man of her dreams would materialize just in time to save her from the consequences of her bad choices. The rich, handsome, thoughtful guy would step in and provide her with rent money, food, and a new car to tide her over until they could be married. Then she would have the life she'd always dreamed of. Everly would have more for a father than a man who petitioned a judge to have the fact of his paternity scrubbed out by a court order. In lucid moments, Whippet knew it was ridiculous, but sometimes fantasy took away the sting of reality.

A car honked and she opened her eyes. She squared her shoulders. Time to slay her own dragons.

Whippet took a deep breath, pushed her self-doubt down deep, and opened the door. She walked past a glass display case showcasing a couple of old prom dresses and a rhinestone tiara. A frazzled looking waitress paused while refilling a cup of coffee to shove the hair out of her eyes and tell Whippet to seat herself.

"Um, I'm actually here about the job," she said, and the waitress's eyes got round. She set down the coffeepot and pulled Whippet behind the counter, through the swinging door, and into a cramped office that smelled of stale oil. The woman told her to stay put as she went searching for her boss.

Meacham's Diner was one of the only eating establishments in Normal. Whippet herself had been here a handful of times as a child, her dad bringing the family into town on Saturday mornings for silver dollar pancakes and warm maple syrup.

The door swung open, and Whippet moved her legs to avoid being hit.

"Sorry," came a voice. A stunning woman walked in. With her curves, white-blonde hair, and wide blue eyes, she could have passed for Marilyn Monroe's younger sister. Whippet ran a hand over her hair and pulled on her wrinkled cotton shirt, suddenly self-conscious.

"Hi," the woman said. "I'm Luna Meacham." She held out her hand and Whippet took it. "Jan told me you're here about the job."

"Yes, I am."

"Oh, good." Luna collapsed in the chair. "I'll be honest, I'm kind of desperate. One of my waiters quit without notice and until school is out, the daytime shift is slammed. Do you have any experience?"

"I do. I was passing by when I saw the sign. I can email you my resume when I get home," Whippet offered.

"That would be great, but why don't you tell me what you've done in the past."

Whippet filled her in on her previous employment. Everything seemed to be going okay until Whippet revealed that she didn't have a car.

"That could be a problem." Luna's brow furrowed.

"I promise it won't be," Whippet said. "My family will be happy to get me to work."

"Right. Except one of your duties would be running deliveries around town."

"Really?" Hadn't these people heard of DoorDash?

"It's only for a few people, a handful of elderly customers. Actually, now that I think about it . . ." Luna trailed off, obviously considering something. "The weather has turned nice; maybe you could use a bike."

"A bike," Whippet repeated.

"The furthest you'd have to go is about a mile from here. When do you think you'll have your car back?"

"Next week, fingers crossed," Whippet said.

"Well, fingers crossed, we won't get rain. When can you start?"

# CHAPTER TEN

"The diner," her mother said as if a skunk had just crawled onto her lap. "Don't you think you should have held out for something more promising?"

Whippet grabbed her purse. It was her first week at work, and she didn't want to be late. Arguments with her mother tended to be time consuming. "Lest we forget, mother, I am an adult and get to make my own choices."

Blessedly, Emma pulled up in her old truck and tapped the horn.

"Gotta run," she said, kissing her mother on the cheek. "Don't frown. It causes wrinkles."

Emma had very generously offered to drive her into town today, which was advantageous since she was also hauling the yellow beach cruiser they'd found in the garage last weekend. Tucker had grumbled about cleaning it and reinflating the tires, but it was in decent shape. The bike even had a basket, which meant she didn't have to maneuver the mean streets of Normal with takeout bags hanging from the handlebars.

"Hey," Emma said as Whippet climbed into the truck.

"Good morning. Thanks for doing this."

"Of course!" Emma said, pulling away from the house. "So I hear your mom doesn't approve of your new job."

"Seriously? She told you that?"

"No. She told Tucker that. I just happened to be in the room."

"What did Tucker have to say on the subject?" Whippet asked.

"He told her that he was proud of you for finding a job without any help from the rest of us," Emma said.

Her heart gave a little tug. "He did?"

"Yep. He was worried your mom might try to—"

"Oh, she has."

"Really?"

"Um-hmm," Whippet said. "She left a brochure for a low residency business program on my bed last night," Whippet said.

"I'm sorry."

"She means well, I think." Whippet shrugged.

"Well, I'm excited that I'll run into you at the diner," Emma said.

"Oh, please. You told me you never eat there."

"Maybe I'll start."

Emma had worked at the diner back when she was in high school, and evidently the scars from that time ran deep. From what Emma said, Luna Meacham had been her nemesis in high school, torturing Emma every chance she got. Whippet didn't know her new boss very well, but it seemed like Luna's mean-girl days might be behind her.

Emma pulled up in front of the diner. "I'd offer to help you with the bike," she said, "but I think that might be for you." Emma nodded toward the sidewalk where Cam Buckman was standing. Whippet grinned at her sister-in-law and climbed out.

"Hey, stranger," she called as she went to the rear of the truck and opened the tailgate.

"Hey, yourself," he said, sauntering over. "So it's true," he said. He lifted her bike and set it on the sidewalk.

"What's true?"

"You're working here. Your mom told me yesterday when she brought her car in for an oil change. She sounded a bit—"

"Disappointed?" Whippet supplied.

"Surprised. She sounded surprised."

"Oh. Well, a job's a job. I think it'll be fun." She shrugged.

Cam smiled and stuffed his hands in his pockets. "So I thought I'd stop by and say hi. Think we could grab lunch, or dinner?"

Whippet beamed at him. "I work through lunch, but dinner would be lovely."

Cam's smile grew. "Later then?"

Whippet nodded. "Text me," she said as she locked her bike to a parking meter.

She walked to the diner and saw Jan, the waitress she'd met the other day, motioning her inside.

"You're late," the woman rasped as soon as Whippet was through the door. Whippet glanced at the clock above the juke box. She was right on time but didn't argue.

Jan handed her two take-out orders. "This one is for Clive Martinson, the other for Edith Kane."

"Edith again?" Edith lived at the end of an ancient cobblestone street a couple of blocks from the diner. Whippet had delivered breakfast there yesterday. The uneven road had made the ride bone rattling.

"Yes," replied Jan tersely. "And this time, don't stay so long."

Whippet flushed at the chastisement. Yesterday, when she'd taken the old woman her meal, Edith had noted that the French toast was cold. She hadn't been complaining, just making conversation. "That's what I get for not making my own breakfast!" she'd said cheerfully. When Whippet had offered to warm it up for her, the woman's face lit up. They'd spent the next few minutes getting acquainted. Whippet had liked her so much that she'd stopped by after work with some day-old pie that Luna had been about to throw out.

"I won't," Whippet replied diplomatically. She wasn't sure if she and Jan were going to be friends, which was a shame considering it looked like it was just the two of them working the day shift.

\* \* \*

"Sam, thank you so much for coming by," Edith said, watching him work. "I couldn't get it to budge. I'd have the most wonderful breeze if you could get it open." Sam suspected Edith had more nefarious motives for calling him over today. She kept running her eyes over him with an appraising gaze that made him feel like a steer being judged at the county fair.

"Not a problem, Mrs. Kane. I'm on my lunch break anyway," he said, taking a putty knife from the toolbox he kept in the back of his truck. The window was sealed tight, a hundred years of paint had it glued shut.

"Mm-hmm," Edith said distractedly, looking expectantly out the window. Sam had the distinct feeling she was waiting for someone: a niece or daughter or some other eligible relative who was about to be offered up as a prospective date. It happened a lot. The matronly set of Normal heard the word "single" and thought it meant "lonely." He jammed the putty knife between the sash and frame and cranked a little harder.

"You're a good man, Sam. So thoughtful." He saw her glance out the window again. "Do you like it here, Sam?" she asked, absently. "Not a lot of crime in Normal."

"And I'm glad of it, ma'am," he said as he replaced the putty knife with a screwdriver.

"Well, we think you're wonderful. We're lucky to have you," Edith said, and Sam braced for what was coming next. "What you did for the O'Neil family. So brave. No one will ever forget it."

He hoped that wasn't true.

Sam saw movement in the driveway, probably the mystery woman Edith wanted to set him up with. He'd hoped to be out of here before whoever it was showed up. He tried the window. Still stuck. Maybe he could nod to whoever it was and keep busy. He heard the back door open.

"Hey, Mrs. Kane. I have your order right here," came a female voice. "Let's see, three BLTs. Wow, did you mean to order so many? And there's a side of fries. Does that sound right?"

Sam shoved at the window. If he got it open, maybe he could jump out.

"It looks wonderful, sweetheart. Thank you for bringing it," Edith said politely. Sam heard shuffling footsteps behind him. "Have you met our chief of police, dear?" Edith asked, ushering the girl into the front room.

Sam turned. It was Doc Madsen's sister. Great.

The smile she wore dropped like a lead weight when she saw him. "Oh, it's you," she said.

Edith looked between them. "You know each other?"

"What are you doing here?" Whippet asked.

"Sam is very handy," Edith said, still trying to make the sale.

"Just helping out," he murmured.

"Four more days and my car will finally be out of bondage," Whippet said, hands on hips.

"Good to hear." He paused. "Did you drive over here?" he asked, raising an eyebrow.

"No, I did not *drive* over here," she said testily. "Thanks to you, I'm making deliveries on a bike."

It was on the tip of his tongue to tell her that her lead foot was responsible for her trouble, but he didn't see the point. He pushed up on the window frame, and hallelujah, it opened. "There you go, Mrs. K. You need anything else?" he asked.

"Thank you so much, Sam. Why don't you sit down and join us for a minute?" Yep. A set up. She needn't have bothered. Once upon a time he'd been married to a beautiful virago. He wasn't looking to repeat that experience.

"No thank you, ma'am." He nodded politely and headed toward the door. "You take care, Mrs. K. Call if you need anything." He paused for a moment and said, "See you around, Daphne."

# CHAPTER ELEVEN

WHIPPET THREW HER PURSE INTO the car and got in, shoving a piece of toast in her mouth as she shut the door and jammed the key into the ignition. She had her car back! Cam had shown up a few days ago at the behest of the police chief and surprised her, dangling her keys from one hand, and offering her a bouquet of daisies with the other. The two of them had hopped into the car and did a victory lap around town, all without so much as a speeding ticket.

She didn't feel quite so victorious this morning. She was late for work, again. She'd just made it to the end of the drive when her phone started to ring. She leaned across the seat, fumbling to retrieve it from her purse. She could hear it, but she couldn't find it. Sighing, she pulled over to the side of the road and pulled her bag open. Her phone was buried under her wallet, a packet of tissues, and a half-eaten package of goldfish crackers. Her annoyance turned to alarm when she saw it was the school.

"Hello?" she answered cautiously.

"Hey, Mom," Everly's voice came across the line, and Whippet felt a rush of relief.

"What's up, sweetheart?" she asked, pulling onto the road.

"I forgot my lunch."

"I thought I saw you leave with a brown paper bag."

"No. I didn't even pack my lunch. You must be thinking of yesterday. Can you please bring me a lunch?" Everly begged.

"Honey, I'm already late for work."

"Please, Mom. If I don't eat lunch, I. Will. Starve." Everly delivered each word with so much drama, Whippet wondered if the girl might be suffering from early-onset puberty. Then she remembered the parenting book she'd been reading, the one that said children should suffer natural consequences for their mistakes.

"I'm sorry, hon, but I'm late for work," she said calmly. "You'll have to eat school lunch today."

"But I don't like school lunch," Everly moaned.

Whippet pulled into the alley behind the diner. "I have an idea. Tonight, we'll pack your lunch for tomorrow so this doesn't happen again."

"Fine," Everly said and hung up.

Whippet tossed her phone into her purse and got out of the car. She rushed inside, jerking on an apron as she charged through the swinging door into the dining area. Luna raised an eyebrow at her, but Jan wasn't so subtle.

"You're late," the woman rasped. Whippet gave her coworker a stiff smile. Today Jan sported magenta streaks in her graying hair. "Number five is ready to order," Jan informed her, nodding at the booth. The new hair color was a bit jarring as it bounced against her sunken cheeks.

Whippet zipped over, took the family's order, and watched as Jan disappeared out back for a smoke break.

"Order up!" Chuck called from the pass-through window, and Whippet hurried over to grab it. She looked at Chuck, a question in her eyes. "Treemontons' table," he muttered. She mouthed "thank you" and whirled through the dining room to lay the Treemontons' breakfast in front of them.

"Chopped pepper and bacon omelet, Mr. Treemonton, and a single stack with a fruit plate for you, ma'am. Will there be anything else for you folks?"

"No, darlin'. This looks wonderful. Thank you," Alice Treemonton said.

One of the tables flagged her down on her way to the kitchen and asked where their order was.

Whippet pushed through the swinging door to the back. "Table six is waiting on an order of hash brown patties, Chuck," she said, stretching against the confines of her polyester uniform.

"Whaddo I look like to you? Huh? What've I told you a million times?" Chuck grumbled.

"Check the timer," she muttered.

"Check the timer!" Chuck said at the same time.

"Timer says 'zero,' Chuck," Whippet informed him.

"What?"

Whippet walked over to the fryer and pointed. "Zero."

"Impossible," Chuck muttered. He rapped against the display with his knuckles. "Huh," he said setting the fry basket to drain.

Whippet rolled her eyes. "So can I have those hash browns now?"

She and Jan managed the morning rush, moving between the dining room and the kitchen, a dance that kept them busy and afforded little opportunity for conversation. Thank goodness. Luna manned the cash register and took phone calls.

Things died down at around ten, and Whippet was able to move on to her other duties, namely all the grunt work Jan avoided by taking long breaks out back. Whippet filled the salt and pepper shakers, wiped down the counters, and checked the restroom, making sure everything was tidy. She liked her job. She did. Luna was a fair boss and very kindly ignored the fact that Whippet didn't always make it in on time.

"Hey, Whippet," Luna said coming up behind her. "Do you have a minute?"

Uh-oh.

Whippet leaned over and refilled Mr. Mackerly's coffee. There was a couple she didn't recognize in the corner booth, holding hands, so wrapped up in each other they hadn't even started to eat. Other than that, the diner was empty.

"Sure," she said, following Luna's lead and taking a seat in the booth next to the window.

Luna seemed a little tense. "About this morning," Luna began. "I know it's—"

"I'm sorry," Whippet blurted. "I know I was late. I was on my way to work, and my daughter called me from the school. She forgot her lunch."

"Right, well, I know the whole single-mom thing is tricky. I'm in the same boat myself."

Whippet's head jerked. "You are?" Huh. Luna was a single mother but managed to make it to the diner by seven.

"I am," Luna said, clasping her hands on the table.

"I guess I didn't realize that."

Luna pointed to herself. "Twice divorced."

Whippet grimaced in empathy. "Lovely, isn't it?"

"So lovely," Luna said. "So about this morning . . ."

"Right." Whippet gave her boss her full attention.

"I told Jan I would talk to you. She said you've been late every morning this week."

Yikes! She didn't think that was true, but—

"Of course, it'd be hard for Jan to tell since she spends half her shift out back having a smoke. Just be mindful, okay?" Luna finished.

Whippet agreed, and Luna got up. She paused by the table. "Is everything okay? With your daughter, I mean. It was tough on Max, moving here."

Whippet shrugged. "She's adjusting."

Luna nodded. "Well, if there's anything I can do, let me know. Everly is in Max's class. Maybe they could study together sometime. He comes in after school every day and does his homework at the counter. Everly's welcome to join him."

Whippet smiled at her boss. "Thanks, I'll talk to her about it."

She noticed the couple from the corner booth were at the counter ready to pay, so she went over to their table and collected dirty dishes and took them into the back while Luna rang them up. Whippet returned to the dining room just in time to see Jan walk over to their booth and pocket the tip. Nice.

"Whippet," Luna called from behind the counter, holding the black cordless phone. "It's for you."

"Thanks," she said, taking the phone. "This is Whippet," she said into the receiver.

"Ms. Moran? It's Kathy Hicks. Secretary over at the school. Not sure how to tell you this but, your daughter is missing."

* * *

Sam Beaufort wandered into the station after a budget meeting with the city council. Trying to figure out how to run the police department on fairy dust and fumes was always a great way to start the day. It gave him a headache.

"Sharon O'Neil called," Didi said as he walked in.

Sam felt his spine stiffen. "Thanks," he muttered.

"You're looking grumpy this morning. Guess the mayor didn't unclench the budget."

"She did not."

"So no increases?" Didi asked.

"Not this quarter."

"Terrific. Maybe I'll put 'volunteer' on my resume."

"You're not allowed to quit, Bradley."

"Oh, relax. I know this place would implode without me."

He wished that weren't true. He might be in charge, but Didi had a way of making things happen. If he needed something done fast, he gave it to Didi. Maybe he should have sent *her* to the budget meeting. He walked into his office and froze.

Behind his desk, sitting in his chair and twirling in circles, was Everly Moran. Sam looked at the clock on the wall then poked his head out of his office.

"Anything you want to tell me, Didi?"

His assistant looked up from her computer. "Like what?"

He opened his door wider so she could see inside. Didi's mouth opened in surprise. "Uh, I guess I'll call the school," she murmured, picking up the phone.

Sam turned back to his office, hands on his hips. "Everly, what are you doing here?"

The girl's head tilted to one side. "Whaddya mean?"

Sam took a seat across from her. "I mean, shouldn't you be in school right now?"

"But you told me if I needed something I should tell you," she said.

"That's true, but I didn't mean—"

"Where's your dog?" Everly asked.

"What?"

"Your dog. The one with no name." She gave another spin in his chair. "Where is he?"

Sam scratched his head. "At my house."

"Oh." Everly sounded disappointed. "I thought maybe you were training him to be a police dog."

"Right now, I'm just trying to train him to go outside to use the bathroom," Sam said.

"My mom won't let me have a dog. She says I'm enough work as it is."

Sam leaned forward. "Do you think she might have a point?"

"Why? Because I'm not in school?"

He gave her his sternest look.

"I know I should be in school." Another spin. "But I have a good reason for skipping today."

"Oh, really?" Sam could hardly wait to hear this.

Everly nodded. "They're having hotdogs for school lunch today."

"And?"

"And I hate hotdogs."

Sam leaned back in the chair. "Is that so?"

"It is so. And when I called my mom, she refused to bring me lunch."

He paused before asking, "How is school going, Everly?"

She looked down. "Uh, fine, I guess."

"Everything all right with Kara Warren?"

Everly shrugged. "She and her friends just kind of ignore me now. They don't tease me as much." She looked at him then. "Sometimes it stinks though. I don't have anyone to sit next to in the lunchroom."

A frantic voice drifted in from the lobby. "Hi, I'm Whippet Moran. Is my daughter here?" Sam glanced back at Everly, but she'd disappeared. This one was part ninja. "Everly?" he called.

"Don't tell her where I am," she whispered from under his desk.

"Come out from under there," he said.

"No. She had to leave work. She's gonna to be mad."

Sam rubbed the back of his neck. A budget meeting was cake compared to this. He walked out into reception.

"Mrs. Moran?"

"Yes?" she said meeting his eyes reluctantly.

"Can I speak with you?" He motioned for her to join him just outside his office so that Everly would hear. "This isn't the first time this has happened," he said.

"What do you mean?"

"A couple of weeks ago, I picked up your daughter walking down Main Street on her way to Doc Madsen's office."

Everly popped out from under his desk. "You promised not to tell!"

"All bets are off with repeat offenders," he said.

"You've done this before?" Whippet asked.

"A couple times," the girl said sheepishly.

"A couple times?" Sam and Whippet said in unison.

"Mom, what was I supposed to do?" Everly flung her arms wide. "Today you didn't feed me!"

Whippet turned uneasy eyes on him. "That's a bit of an exaggeration," she clarified. She looked down at her daughter. "You forgot your lunch at home. I told you to eat school lunch."

"But I wanted home lunch."

Sam walked over to his computer, entered the password, and opened the game app he'd downloaded. "Here," he said to Everly. "Play solitaire while I talk to your mother."

"What's solitaire?" she asked.

"You'll figure it out," Sam said. He walked into the conference room; Whippet Moran followed.

"What's going on?" she asked, moving so the table was between them.

"Everly is having a hard time adjusting to being in a new school," he said.

Whippet tugged at the hem of her polyester skirt as she took a seat. She rested her chin in her hand. "I know," she sighed.

"Do you know she's being teased at school?"

Whippet frowned. "She is?"

Sam nodded. "She mentioned it the day I picked her up."

"About that, shouldn't you have told me? I'm the mother," Whippet said tersely.

"I promised her I wouldn't if she never skipped school again."

"I don't know what to do. I have to work. She needs to be in school. Short of going in and sitting by her all day, I'm at a loss."

"I thought you should know."

Whippet nodded, got up, and moved to stand next to the door.

Sam followed her. Everly was a good kid, and at least her mother was concerned. That put Everly miles ahead of some of the things he'd witnessed in Chicago. He'd once returned a four-year-old kid back to his mother after she'd sent him to the corner store for smokes.

"I'm sure she'll be fine," he said.

"I hope so." She didn't look convinced.

They walked back to his office.

Whippet smiled at her daughter. "Get your backpack, Ev. We'll grab lunch at the diner, then I'll take you back to school."

Everly sprinted to her mother and threw her arms around her waist. "Thank you."

Problem solved. Sam pulled back his chair to sit down. He noticed Everly had closed out solitaire and opened Google. His computer screen was full of images of puppies.

"Maybe you should get her a dog," he suggested, earning him a beatific smile from Everly and a raised eyebrow from her mother as they left his office.

# CHAPTER TWELVE

"Mom." Everly's voice came to her over a sea of deep blue sleep. "Mom!" Stronger now. Whippet seemed to be rocking in her bed.
　Everly was shaking her. "Mom! I'm gonna be late for school!"
　Whippet shot up, squinting at her clock. "What? How?"
　"I turned off the alarm."
　"Why?" Whippet cried, stumbling to her feet. She looked at the clock again. She had twenty minutes to get to work. "Why?" she asked again.
　"I woke up with a headache and turned it off. I'm sorry."
　"Are you all right now?" Whippet felt her daughter's forehead and Everly nodded. "Okay sweetie, we need to leave in ten minutes. Hop to it, Ev."
　The next few minutes were a panicked blur. Whippet had been late to work yesterday. Not by much, but she knew she'd be in trouble this morning. The thought sent her into the bathroom where she pulled her hair into a high ponytail, managed some mascara, and smeared on a little lip gloss. "That's going to have to do," she told her frazzled reflection.
　They trundled down the stairs. Her mom was in the kitchen making breakfast for the single guest at the B&B.
　Mom handed Everly her lunch as she ran out the door, then turned to Whippet and muttered, "You're late."
　"Thanks, Mom. So helpful."
　Whippet shooed Everly into the car and made her way toward town, alternately speeding and slowing down, all the while looking at her rear-view and side mirrors to avoid getting a ticket from Officer OCD.
　Everly turned to her. "I don't think he has OCD, Mom. I think he's just doing his job." Oh, dear. Had she said that out loud?
　Whippet glanced at the dashboard clock. She was going to be late dropping Everly off at school, which meant she was going to be really late for work. She signaled, pulled up in front of the diner, and double parked.

"Mom." Everly cast a worried glance behind them. "I don't think you can park here."

"It's fine. I'll be right back."

Luna was standing behind the counter when Whippet walked in.

"Sorry, Luna," she said, slightly out of breath. "I'm going to be a few minutes late again today. Everly's out in the car and I've got to get her to school. Is that okay?" She waved at the Putnams sitting in the booth next to her.

"No, it's not okay."

"All right, then I'll see you—what?"

"It's not okay. You're late. Again. That's the third time this week," Luna said.

"But I thought—"

"Thought what? That being a single mom was a get out of jail free card?"

Ouch, this was not going the way she had envisioned.

"Whose car is double parked out front?" A deep male voice cut through the clamor in Whippet's brain. She turned to see Sam Beaufort standing just inside the diner door. His eyes scanned the dining room before settling on her. "Let me guess," he said.

It was the last straw.

"Can't you leave me alone?" she said a little too sharply. The smart part of her brain recognized that she should take it down a notch. Her mouth, however, seemed to have lost all contact with her brain.

"Excuse me?" he returned.

"Is there no crime in this town? Do you have nothing better to do than follow me around?"

Sam looked at her. Waited a beat and said, "Move your car," before he turned on his heel and stalked out.

The diner was oddly quiet. Whippet looked around. Everyone was staring at her. The Mosley twins were shaking their heads in unison. Mr. Taft was looking at her from under his bushy eyebrows. Luna leaned against the counter, order pad wedged under one arm.

"We don't do things like that around here. Sam Beaufort is a hero," said Tilly Mosley.

"A hero," her twin echoed.

Luna motioned for Whippet to follow her through the swinging door into her office.

"I'm sorry," Whippet said. She leaned against the door.

Luna was already shaking her head. "This isn't working. I need someone I can rely on."

"Wait," Whippet said, her mouth hanging open. "You're firing me?"
"I'm letting you go," Luna said, arms across her chest.
"It's the same thing." Whippet's heart thudded in her chest.
"You can use me as a reference," she offered.
"For what job?" Whippet asked, all desperation. "Normal isn't exactly a hotbed of opportunity."
Luna was silent for a moment, then said. "I'm sorry."

* * *

Whippet somehow made it to the school and dropped Everly off. She watched her daughter go inside, then continued to sit there, car idling. The crossing guard gave her a wary look, probably assuming, correctly, that there was something not quite right about the woman in the blue car.

Whippet leaned against the headrest and closed her eyes. When she was a girl, her father used to sit at the end of her bed and read her a story before he tucked her in for the night. Her favorite part of this little ritual came when he turned out the light and told her, "You're my smart girl, Whippet. You can do anything you set your mind to."

Those words did not seem particularly true today.

She couldn't sit in the drop-off lane all day, so she pulled out onto the road. Almost without thinking, she took a left on Pine Street. She wound her way around the post office and past the beautiful stone Methodist church. She pulled into a parking lot a couple of blocks down the street and sat for a moment looking up at the church.

It was funny that she'd driven here. Her grandmother had been religious, offering to pray for Whippet during various crises over the years. Their family had attended the First Christian Church with her grandmother when they visited. Her mother, Tucker, and Emma were carrying on the tradition with Everly.

She'd always called it the Little White Church because the white clapboard structure looked like a doll's house tucked into a grove of trees at the end of Pine Street. She remembered leaning against her father during church services, dangling her legs over the wooden pew, and wondering if her feet would ever touch the floor.

Whippet got out of her car and walked to the side doors. She was surprised to find them open on a weekday morning. "Hello?" Whippet called, not wanting to trespass. She walked through the lobby. She could hear a vacuum running somewhere in the building, but otherwise all was quiet.

The door to the nave stood open. Whippet slipped inside, glancing both ways as she walked down the center aisle. The deeply padded carpet silenced her footsteps. She stopped halfway, took a seat, and looked up.

Whippet had forgotten about the beautiful stained glass. The Tree of Life stretched across three panes, cascading flowers and climbing vines reaching through all the windows. She loved the way the glass caught the light. The windows were paradise floating above the pulpit. Looking at them now, Whippet remembered playing whispered games of *I Spy* with her father during lengthy sermons, noticing a bumblebee flitting between tree branches, an ant marching up a stalk of lilac, a butterfly resting atop an open rose. It was so beautiful; the perfect place to pray.

Whippet bowed her head.

"'Our Father, who art in heaven, hallowed be thy name,'" she whispered and looked around. There still didn't seem to be anyone around, so she continued. "'Thy kingdom come; thy will be done on earth as it is in heaven. Give us this day—' Okay, sorry, but that's all I remember," she murmured, looking up. "To be honest, I'm not sure if I should be here. You probably have Your doubts about that too." Whippet paused. "Maybe it's not cool, me showing up like this, all desperate and in a panic. We haven't talked in a while. To be honest, I wasn't sure you'd want to hear from me. I've, uh, made some significant mistakes. Broken a few commandments. But my grandmother—you probably know her; she's a recent arrival up there—anyway, she believed in You, and my mom believes in You too. I used to believe. But then my dad died. I don't blame You, but believing in anything since then has been hard." Whippet's eyes stung. "Gran always said that I didn't need to be perfect to pray. I hope that's true because I could use a divine assist right now." Whippet swiped at a tear. "I'm a little lost. Truth be told, I've been lost for a while, but now it feels like it's getting serious.

"I have a daughter. Thanks for her, by the way." Whippet cleared her throat. "I'd like her to be proud of me. I'd also like to give her a normal life. Well, as normal as I can. I mean, it's me we're talking about." Whippet knotted her hands in her lap. "If You could show me the way? Give me a hint? I'm not talking about parting the Red Sea here. Just point me in the right direction. I'd really appreciate it. Anyway . . . um, amen."

Whippet was quiet for a minute, waiting for inspiration to strike. Gran used to say, "God isn't a genie. You can't just say a prayer and expect Him to give you what you want. You need to be still so He can talk to you."

She waited.

Nothing. She felt nothing. Whippet sighed. She wondered, not for the first time, if God even knew she existed. She looked up at the stained glass. Maybe the things she'd done in the past were too bad to be forgiven. The thought made her heart hurt.

Whippet turned to retrieve her purse. A light touch on her shoulder made her jump.

"Oh, dear," a pair of kind blue eyes shone out of an old face. It was Edith Kane, the woman she'd met her first week working at the diner. "I didn't mean to startle you, sweetheart. I vacuum the church on Tuesdays and Fridays." Edith nodded at her. "Would you mind if I sat next to you for a minute?"

"Oh, of course, Mrs. Kane. It's nice to see you again." Whippet made room and Edith took a seat.

The two of them sat side by side for a quiet moment. Whippet clasped her hands together and twiddled her thumbs, wondering how soon she could excuse herself without seeming rude.

"My husband did the stained glass," Edith said.

Whippet's head came up. "He did?"

Edith smiled and nodded. "Oh, it was quite controversial when he finished the windows."

"Really? But they're so beautiful."

"They are, they are," Edith nodded. "But they're nothing like the windows they replaced."

"No?" Whippet listened with interest.

Edith continued. "A big storm blew through here, oh, my, it must have been fifty years ago. A storm of epic proportions. Sent hail like bullets through the old windows. After they cleaned up, the church elders voted to replace the windows with frosted glass. Can you imagine?" Edith's voice held a note of outrage. "Well, my Lonnie, he said he would replace them for the cost of the glass. He was a respected artisan back in the day. Won all kinds of awards for his art. He worked for over a year, and when the windows were finally installed, some of the congregants got their feathers in a fluff. You see, before the storm, the windows were kind of gloomy. All dour apostles and avenging angels." Edith chuckled. "But my Lonnie replaced them with the Garden of Eden, before that darn snake came along and spoiled all the fun."

Edith's expression turned wistful. "Lonnie had talent, that's for sure. He was a welder by trade. But all of that," she gestured to the stained glass, "all that beauty was inside of him just waiting to come out. People were shocked to be sure, but he liked that, doing something so unexpected." Edith looked at Whippet. "Makes you think, doesn't it, what potential might be locked up tight inside each of us? Something to think about." They fell quiet until Edith patted her arm. "I better scoot. My dog is home alone. Last time I left him for this long he unspooled a whole roll of toilet paper." She gave Whippet's arm another pat. "It was lovely to see you, dear."

"It was nice to see you too, Mrs. Kane." Whippet squeezed Edith's hand as she left the pew. "Thank you for sitting with me for a while."

Edith stood. "You stay as long as you like. I'm done with my work. Would you mind locking up when you leave? The pastor will be back in about an hour."

Whippet nodded and sat back, wondering if there was anything inside of her that was as beautiful as that stained glass.

Whippet looked at her phone. She should go too. She'd said all there was to say. Nothing had changed, but Edith's happy chatter had made her feel better. Maybe she'd keep up the praying. It couldn't hurt.

Whippet gathered her things and walked to the door, careful to lock the door behind her. Edith waved as she backed out of her parking spot and right into Whippet's bumper. Whippet's smile fell as she watched Edith drive away.

She walked over to her car. The dent wasn't bad, and it matched the one on the other side. She looked back at the church and shook her head.

That's what she got for praying.

\* \* \*

"About your job," Mom started, as she cut into a delicious looking lemon meringue pie.

Whippet froze. She'd been fired a mere eleven hours before. How did her mother know that she'd lost her job? "Mom, can we talk about this later?" she muttered. They were at Miss Lily's House for dinner and Whippet had kind of been hoping for safety in numbers. No such luck. Whippet glanced at Emma, but her sister-in-law just raised an eyebrow.

"I think it's a good thing," her mother said.

"You do?" Whippet asked, surprised.

"Sorry I'm late." Tucker came in through the back door. Whippet looked at the clock. It was after eight. Tucker hung up his jacket, headed straight for his wife, and kissed her. In front of everyone. They'd been married almost two years. You'd think they'd be over the PDA thing, but apparently not. "Mrs. Clements's water broke in the bread aisle at Grimm's," he said.

"Did you get to deliver the baby?" Emma asked, all enthusiasm.

"No. It's their first kid so it'll take a while. I checked her out. Everything seemed to be progressing normally. She's on her way to Springfield." Tucker sat next to his wife and looked at Whippet. "So I heard you cussed out Normal's finest today."

Whippet's mouth opened. "Who told you that?"

Tucker shrugged. "Small town."

"I did not cuss him out. I just asked him if he was stalking me." She thought for a second. "Maybe I was a little loud about it."

"Well, you need to apologize," Tucker said. "And if you want to have any kind of reputation in this town—I mean, other than the one you've got now—you need to do it soon."

"I have a reputation?"

"You do after the way you yelled at Sam Beaufort this morning."

"You yelled at Sam Beaufort?" her mother asked. "But he's so nice."

"Hey, a little loyalty please!" Whippet said glumly. "Every time I turn around, the guy is there, ready to give me a ticket or tow my car or something. It feels like profiling."

"Or maybe you're just particularly adept at breaking the law," Tucker suggested.

Whippet ignored her brother. "What's the deal with him anyway?" Whippet asked. "Everyone at the diner acted like he was the Dalai Lama, Mother Teresa, and Obi-Wan Kenobi all rolled into one."

Whippet didn't find him quite so angelic. Last week he'd pulled her over when she was on her way back from running an errand for Luna in Springfield. She had just passed the covered bridge when she saw flashing lights in the rearview mirror.

"Welcome to Normal," he'd drawled as he walked up to the driver's side window. "License and registr—you have got to be kidding me."

"I wasn't speeding," Whippet had insisted.

"Fifty-five in a thirty-five mile-per-hour zone," he'd said, already sounding exhausted by their exchange.

She'd scowled at him as she handed him her license.

"Think I should memorize this?" he'd asked as he took it.

"Ha, ha. Can you hurry? I have perishables in the back."

"All right," he'd said looking at her driver's license. "So Or—"

"Do not say my name out loud! Unless you want me to come after your firstborn like in that story . . . Rasputin."

"Rasputin?" he repeated. "You mean Rumpelstiltskin?"

"Whatever. I'm not big into fairy tales," she'd said.

"Or Russian history," he'd drawled.

At least he'd let her go with a warning.

"Sam is a local hero," Emma said. "A few months ago, there was a house fire out on Ridgeway Road. Sam saw it and called it in, but he was first on the scene. He went in—didn't even think about it. When the volunteer fire department showed up, Sam had already gotten Sharon and her boys out. The fire was bad, Whippet. The house was destroyed and Isaac O'Neil had to be life-flighted to St. Louis."

Whippet went still, suddenly feeling very small. "Wow," she mumbled. It looked like the comparison to Mother Teresa wasn't far off. "I guess I should apologize," she sighed.

# CHAPTER THIRTEEN

Sam had Isaac O'Neil slung over one shoulder. The relief he felt for finally finding him was outweighed by the fact that the house was about to collapse around them. The smoke was so black and dense, he couldn't see four inches in front of his face. He felt along the wall for the doorknob. But it was the oddest thing. Just as he grasped it, it moved. He seemed to be eternally stuck, fumbling along, trying to find it. Meanwhile, the O'Neils' fire alarm was going off. The persistent ping, ping, ping annoyingly similar to the text notification on his phone.

Sam jerked awake and sat up. Disoriented, he grabbed the phone and pushed at the screen, thinking he was deactivating the smoke alarm. But no, that wasn't right. He squinted and sure enough, he had seven new texts waiting for him. His brows came together when he saw who they were from. Emory. He chucked his phone back on the nightstand and collapsed against the pillows. A second later there was another ping. He opened one eye. If he didn't respond soon, she'd—his phone started to vibrate.

"Yes, Emory?" Sam mumbled.

"You're avoiding me."

"We're divorced. It shouldn't be this hard."

"Ha ha. You haven't responded to my texts. I just want to make sure you're okay."

No, she didn't. This had been her tactic since they'd parted ways. She'd disappear for a couple of months, and just when he thought they were finally through, she'd call, text, or—heaven help him—show up, telling him she still cared, still thought about him. It was like Russian roulette with emotions.

"I'm fine. Actually, thanks for the call. In another five minutes, I would have been late for work. Gotta go. See you later." He winced. Why had he said that? He hung up before any more stupid came out of his mouth.

He swung his feet to the floor where they landed on a bed of fur. "Dog, you need to find a better place to sleep," he muttered. The animal looked up at him with soulful black eyes. "And maybe next time, wake me up when I'm having a nightmare," he suggested. The dog whined and lowered his head.

Last night's dream was courtesy of Didi Bradley. He'd been on his way home after work yesterday when she'd called.

"Sharon O'Neil called again," Didi had said when he answered the phone.

"Thanks for letting me know," he'd said.

"You ever going to call her back?" she'd asked before he could hang up.

"None of your business," he'd said brusquely.

"Coward."

Sam had sighed and reminded her, "You do know I'm your boss, right?"

Sam showered, dressed, and headed downstairs to the kitchen.

He should be used to it by now. Sharon called almost every week. Usually she just checked in, but sometimes she left messages.

*Isaac is off the ventilator.*

*They've moved Isaac to a burn center.*

*The skin graft operation was a success.*

Each message felt like a punch in the solar plexus. Few things caused Sam anxiety, but messages from Sharon did the trick. He had trouble breathing after hearing them.

Sam looked around his kitchen and tried to focus on something else.

The cabinets were in. The countertops were not. The subcontractor who was doing the work had measured incorrectly and there would be another delay before they could go in. That was okay. Sam had the appliances installed regardless. He was now the proud owner of a stainless-steel fridge that sat mostly empty except for a half gallon of orange juice and a pint jar of huckleberry jam Bette Watts had given him last week for helping her change a flat tire. He walked over to the card table where his toaster sat and threw in a slice of bread. His toast had just finished when his phone started to ring. He approached the device with caution, but his shoulders relaxed when he saw it was his mother.

"Hey, Mom," he said, jamming the phone against his shoulder. He could hear his mother opening and closing cabinets, the clanking of glass.

"The gutters need cleaning."

Sam smiled and spread jam onto his toast before taking a bite. "Is that so?" he asked. His mom made announcements like this all the time to guilt him into coming home, he guessed.

"It is so. Stuffed with leaves from last fall. Mark my words, they'll overflow the next time it rains."

"And what does Dad say about it?"

"Your father? How should I know? It's May. Baseball season has started. He's watching last night's game on the DVR. He fell asleep in his recliner before it was over." His mother made a huffing noise. "I swear, it doesn't matter which team is playing—explain that to me, why don't you? We're from Chicago. Seven generations going back before Mrs. O'Leary's cow knocked over the lantern. You'd think he'd show a little loyalty and root for the Cubs," she said loudly, for his father's benefit, he was sure. "I won't see him until October. You know how he is. The house could be on fire, and he wouldn't budge from that blasted recliner."

Sam flinched a little at the word "fire."

"Oh, sweetheart," his mom said, realizing what she'd said, "I'm sorry."

"Mom, I'm fine." He cleared his throat. "And if memory serves, you're the one who bought Dad that recliner."

His mom gave a little chuckle. "I guess that's true. No one to blame but myself."

"I've got to run. Be nice to Dad. Maybe you can use the baseball thing as leverage to get those gutters cleared out."

He got off the phone and stood staring out back.

The night of the fire, Sam had been working on his house, stripping seventy years' worth of paint off the stair rails. It was monotonous, repetitive work, and a couple of hours into the job he'd had enough. Sam had grabbed his keys and headed out, thinking maybe he'd just drive around town and let the good citizens of Normal know he was out there.

The roads were clear, and it had been a quiet night until, in his peripheral vision, a smudge of light had caught his eye. When he'd turned, there had been no mistaking that burnished glow filtering through the trees. He couldn't tell exactly where the fire was, but as he'd headed in that direction, he'd seen it was the O'Neil place.

Isaac O'Neil had become one of Sam's few friends in town. He'd been fixing up his century-old farmhouse over the past year, and he and Sam often commiserated about the pitfalls of owning an old home. When the new golf course in town had been built, they'd started playing a few rounds together some weekends. Isaac always beat him by a couple of strokes.

The second Sam had stopped outside the house, he was out of his cruiser and calling in the fire. Sam was police chief and an EMT, but he'd had exactly zero training on the protocol of entering a burning building. He knew he'd need back up, but it couldn't wait. He had to get in there and fast.

He'd run around to the back of the house to the kitchen, where the fire hadn't reached yet, and elbowed a glass pane in the door so he could reach inside and unlock it. The air in the house was murky with smoke.

Racing toward the stairs, he'd grabbed a blanket off the back of the couch and covered his mouth as he made his way to check the rooms upstairs. Flames licked the walls at the end of the hall. He'd kicked open the first door at the top of the stairs. Bathroom. He'd raced to the next closed door and kicked it in. Two twin beds sat against the wall, and Sam blindly grabbed at the boys and got out of there. The youngest boy groaned as Sam snatched him high, then started to wriggle until Sam got them both outside.

"Stay with him," he'd instructed the older boy. "Do not move from here until I get back. Do you understand?" The boy had looked up at him, his face tear streaked and wretched. "Mommy," he'd cried.

"I'm gonna go get her, but you have to stay here." The boy had nodded, and Sam had shot back into the house. Flames now engulfed the ceiling in the hall. He could hear the wail of sirens in the distance, the volunteer fire department making its way up the hill. Sam had pulled his jacket up over his face. His eyes had stung. He'd kicked in the door at the end of the hall. Sharon must have roused at some point. She was on the floor, coughing so hard she couldn't move. He crouched down next to her and slid his arms under her legs.

"Let's get you out of here," he said. She pushed against him and shook her head.

"My boys," she rasped.

"They're already outside." He headed to the door, his lungs screaming with every breath. The fire was starting to make its way into the bedrooms. In another few minutes, he wouldn't be able to make it back upstairs. He set her on her feet at the top of the stairs. "I've got to go back for Isaac. Can you make it down yourself?" he asked. Sharon was coughing and sobbing, but she nodded and started down.

When he'd burst into the room again, everything was on fire. Flames moved in waves across the wall. "Isaac," Sam called, covering his face with his arm. He'd moved deeper into the room. When he made it to the bed, he realized part of Isaac's pajama top was on fire. Sam had thrown the edge of the comforter over him to smother the blaze. He'd tried to rouse Isaac, but he was out cold. Sam yanked him upward, supporting his weight with his arm as he dragged him out of the room, trying to find the stairs. He was coughing and lightheaded, Isaac heavy in his arms. When he'd reached the top of the stairs, a figure clad in turnout gear materialized, the yellow reflective stripes the most miraculous sight Sam had ever seen.

Sam woke the next day in the hospital, hooked up to an IV, a nasal cannula delivering sweet, clean oxygen. A nurse delivered the news that Sharon and the boys were fine. Isaac had been intubated for respiratory failure and life-flighted to St. Louis.

Sam was discharged and went back to work the next day. The media picked up on the story, and a news station out of St. Louis wanted to interview him. Didi answered the call, took one look at Sam, and had correctly assumed he didn't want to talk about it. "No comment," she'd said, and hung up. The fire marshal made a statement on the evening news, commending Sam's quick thinking. Since then, he'd been regularly slapped on the back and congratulated for being a hero. He didn't feel like a hero. Isaac had been in and out of a burn center for months, and the O'Neils had lost their home.

Sam felt something nudge his leg, and he was back in the kitchen again. He took a deep breath, shook off the memory, and glanced out the window. It looked like it might rain. The dog looked up at him with those big black eyes. Maybe he was crazy, but it seemed like the animal understood.

* * *

A low-pressure system moved across the valley, dragging a spring storm with it. There was no shutter-rattling wind, no drama at all. Just gray skies and a light drizzle. In a word, perfect.

Baking weather.

No one was up yet, so Whippet threw open the kitchen window to let in the smell of rain. If only she could bottle it. She went to the pantry and pulled out the flour and sugar, tied an apron around her waist, and set to work. She made cinnamon rolls, kneading a bit of her soul into the dough as she pushed it across the board. By the time the rolls were done, the kitchen was vibrant, warm, and sweet. She let them cool, then covered them in plastic wrap. She picked up a towel and wiped down the counter. Whippet slowed as she reached the end of the island. There sat a small white box tied with twine. This cute little box was full of goodness, but it had been sitting there since last night, and if she waited too much longer to deliver it, the deliciousness would go stale. Apology brownies. That's what they were. Meant for Sam Beaufort because, yes, the tale of his heroism had affected her.

Before she could talk herself out of going, she grabbed the box and her keys and headed out to her car. How hard could it be to apologize? "I'm sorry for being as condescending to you as you've been to me," she said out loud as she turned onto the highway. Hmm, probably not the best approach. Tucker very helpfully suggested she lead with, "I apologize for being a twit." She turned onto the gravel drive that led to the Beaufort place and slowed down.

Truthfully, she had another motive for apologizing. She had always wanted to see inside the Beaufort house. It was the stuff of fantasies! That beautiful, gleaming stack of bricks rose through the trees like a fairy castle. She'd wandered up here once as a child, equal parts enchanted and curious. A lethal combination it turned out. Harlan Beaufort had been outside and spied her through the lilac bushes. He'd actually hissed and shaken a stick at her as if she were a snake. She'd been so frightened, she'd run all the way home, galloping into Gran's house and up the stairs into the cupola where she'd stayed until dark.

Whippet parked on a wide cobblestone drive and grabbed the box. She hurried up the stone steps where tapered columns supported an arched portico. Gathering her courage, she knocked.

And waited.

Maybe he hadn't heard her. She stepped back. The closest windows were several feet away. She thought about peeking inside, but with her luck she'd get caught and possibly arrested for trespassing. She raised a hand to knock again, then noticed a knob in the center of the door. It was one of those old-fashioned doorbells. She twisted it and heard a ring. It sounded like the bell she'd had on her bicycle when she was a kid.

The door opened and there was Officer Beaufort, in uniform and wearing his gun, for crying out loud. "Do you wear that thing to bed?" she asked.

"I was just leaving for work," he said, hands on his hips. "Can I help you?"

"This is a very impressive pile of bricks you have here," she said, clutching the box to her chest and standing on tippy-toes trying to get a look inside. Lots of lovely dark wood in there.

"Do you always start conversations like this?" he asked.

"Like what?"

"By being insulting." He looked at his watch.

"I wasn't insulting you," Whippet insisted.

"You just called my house a pile of bricks."

"No, I called your house impressive," she clarified.

Sam looked at her for a beat. "Can I help you?" he asked again.

"Are you going to invite me in?"

Sam raised both eyebrows but said nothing.

"Okay," she said and extended the box. "Here."

"What's this?" he said, reluctantly taking it from her. "A bomb?"

"No. It's an apology. Well, it's actually brownies. But they're meant to be an apology." She took a deep breath. "I shouldn't have yelled at you the other day at the diner. I'm sorry."

His eyes narrowed on her. "They told you about the O'Neils, didn't they?"

Whippet put her hands behind her back. "Um, yes, maybe," she said.

"So these are guilt brownies," he said, cracking the lid to look inside.

"I guess. But I am sorry. I don't usually act that way," she said.

"Really? That hasn't been my experience."

Whippet's smile flattened. "Be nice. I brought you chocolate."

Sam closed the box and Whippet took advantage of the momentary distraction to slip inside.

"Hey! Brownies don't give you a free pass!" he said, but it was too late. She was already in the wide foyer.

"This is amazing! Oh, my gosh. It echoes in here."

"That's only because there isn't any furniture," Sam said.

"Wow, this is pretty," Whippet said running her fingers over the ornately carved mahogany mirror that stood floor to ceiling.

"It's an old pier mirror I picked up in Chicago last summer."

"Is that original?" she asked pointing at the curved staircase that twisted to the second and—oh wow—third floors.

"Yes—where do you think you're going?"

"Sorry, but I've wanted to see inside this place since I was little. This room is lovely," she said taking a left. "Huh. No furniture in here either."

"It's a big house. It's going to take a while to outfit it the way I want to."

Whippet walked in the opposite direction before stopping in her tracks. "Wow. This is interesting," she said taking in the flocked, olive-green wallpaper in a large velveteen fleur-de-lis pattern. It made the room look like the parlor of a French bordello.

Sam scratched his head. "You can say it. It's hideous. It, uh, used to be the dining room."

"Cool built-ins, but really, what were they thinking?" There was a ladder leaning against one wall. The wallpaper had been stripped away on one side of the room. "Are you doing the work yourself?" she asked.

"I am."

"Well, you're doing a nice job. Where's the kitchen?'

"At the back of the house." Sam eyed her. "And that concludes our tour," he said stepping in front of her and gesturing toward the front door. "I've got to get to work."

They walked back to the entry. "You have a beautiful home," she said. Sam opened the door, and she stepped outside. "I really am sorry about what I said at the diner. And at the garage." She looked at him. "And at the police station that first day." She might have been imagining it, but she thought she saw the beginnings of a smile.

"Does that cover it, you think?" he asked, his voice dipping low, causing a corresponding flutter in her stomach.

"I, uh—I don't know. Maybe I should apologize in advance. You know, to cover whatever I might do next?" Whippet felt her face heat.

"How 'bout we call it good?" he said and smiled for real this time.

It was a really nice smile. The kind that transforms someone's face. And it made him look even more handsome. She needed to get out of here.

"That would be great," she said. "Uh, I'll see you around."

She hurried to her car and gave him a small wave before she drove down the hill.

# CHAPTER FOURTEEN

WHIPPET HAD JUST SNUGGLED BACK into bed after taking Everly to school. She had big plans today: reading the morning away, relaxing, taking full advantage of her current employment status.

Someone pounded on her door.

"Whip, you up?" Tucker hollered. He didn't wait for an answer and came charging in. "C'mon. Let's go," he said.

She eyed him with suspicion. Tucker had been texting her reminders lately, particularly about the number of days she had left to file a harassment claim. She knew he meant well, but it was annoying. She'd do it when she was ready. Spending a day with him would be anything but relaxing. "Go where?" she asked over the top of *Jane Eyre*.

"Strawberry fields," he answered.

If you were a Madsen, you had farmer's blood running through your veins, and that meant work. The digging in the dirt and planting things type of work. It made Whippet want a transfusion.

Tucker recruited their mother too and drove them out to a lovely patch of land, one of the few remaining plots of Madsen land reserved for growing things. In this case, strawberries. The family had a "U-Pick" venture that was very popular with locals and tourists alike.

"So," Tucker said as he worked compost into the soil. "You and Cam, huh?"

Cam had come to dinner last night and endured her family's endless questions and her mother's over-cooked pot roast. Whippet sat back on her heels and looked up at her big brother. "Is this your attempt at small talk? Bringing up my love life?"

"We could talk about the job search," Tucker suggested.

"Yep, I'm dating Cam. Ask me anything," she said, and Tucker gave a laugh.

"How *is* the job search going?" her mother asked.

"Walked right into that one, didn't I?" Whippet stabbed at the dirt. "The answer is, slowly. Mom, do you know anything about the property Gran left me? Maybe I could sell it."

"Hopper gave me a file when we left his office that day. The information is probably in there. I'll look for it when we get home," her mother said before heading back to Tucker's SUV.

"You shouldn't sell, Whip," Tucker said, leaning against his shovel. "I don't know which building you own, but Hopper said you've got a good tenant in there. It'll be a great source of passive income."

"Yeah, but will it be enough to live on?" Whippet sat back and looked down the hill at her grandmother's house.

Gran would have told her she was in a pickle, and that she needed to get down on her knees and pray. Whippet had started to do just that. Quietly. Secretly. So far there had been no flashes of inspiration. She wasn't sure God was listening.

Tucker waved away a fly. "Have you thought about talking to Luna? Seeing if she'd give you your old job back? I hear she's short staffed during the day."

Cam had made a similar suggestion last night. Evidently, Luna had hired seventy-year-old June Burton to take Whippet's place. Cam had been there two mornings ago when June suffered a bout of arrhythmia that sent her to the hospital in Springfield. Evidently, she'd phoned in her resignation the next day.

"You wouldn't really consider going back, would you, Whippet?" their mom walked up behind them carrying a flat of strawberry starts. "Don't you think you should set your sights a little higher?"

Whippet yanked another weed. "Sure. I think I'll run for mayor."

"Sarcasm is the lowest form of humor." Mom set the flat between them.

"I'm serious," her brother said.

"I don't know, Tucker," she said, jabbing at the hard ground. "Luna said I was unreliable."

"Were you?" he asked.

"Probably."

"So promise to do better. Throw yourself on her mercy. Bake her a cake."

"Bake her a cake?" Whippet laughed.

"Yes. The one you made last night was amazing. That cake was front and center in my dreams." Tucker's expression turned wistful.

"Really?" she asked.

"I'm just saying, you take Luna a cake like that, and I bet all will be forgiven."

Whippet shook her head. It hadn't been anything special. Just an ordinary vanilla bean cake with seven-minute frosting, but one bite and Tucker had waxed poetic, telling her it was the best thing he'd ever eaten.

"I guess I could take her a slice and see how it goes."

"You can't," their mother said as she patted soil around a strawberry plant.

"Why not?" Whippet asked.

Her mom's expression turned sheepish. "Because I ate the last piece for breakfast."

The three of them worked until noon. Tucker drove them back to the B&B, and her mother ran into the house to find the file from the lawyer.

"Here you go," she said, handing Whippet a bulky envelope with her name on it. "I picked it up when you left it on the lawyer's desk." Her mother gave her a pointed look before going into the kitchen to get a head start on dinner.

Whippet went out onto the porch swing, opened the envelope, and pulled out the folder. The terms of Gran's will were laid out in a letter paper clipped to the inside of the folder. Whippet sagged a little as she read. Even if she wanted to, she couldn't sell the building. She had a tenant. His name was Ed Aldridge, and his lease didn't expire for a year and even then, he had an option to renew. Rent money was deposited directly into an account set aside for expenses on the building. After six months, half of the rent would be paid directly to her. The other half would continue to go into the account for insurance, taxes, and upkeep. Not quite the windfall she'd been hoping for.

She'd just opened a smaller envelope when a key fell into her lap. Attached to the letter was an old photograph. Was that . . . ? Her eyes went to her grandmother's letter.

> *Darling Girl,*
>
> *If you're reading this, then I finally decided it was time to join your grandpa Jack. It also means you now own that pretty little shop on Main Street. When you were younger, we used to call it the Sugar Plum Castle. You were convinced fairies lived in the basement.*
>
> *You were a cute little thing. So full of dreams and possibility. I think that girl is still inside of you, Whippet. Find her again. Use your inheritance as a start.*
>
> *You can do it. And always remember, I love you.*
>
> *Gran*

Whippet was off the porch like a shot. She got in her car and headed north, not needing the address scrawled on the file folder. She knew exactly where she was going. She parked across the street, just so she could get a better look at her building. *Her* building. She owned a piece of property. She, Whippet Madsen Moran, who had always lived like a new plant in loose soil, owned something that had been around since 1892.

She owned her favorite building in downtown Normal. Happiness, a feeling that had only played a supporting role in her life lately, welled up inside. She closed her eyes and whispered, "Thank you, Gran."

She tucked the file under her arm and crossed the street, practically skipping to the door. Whippet turned the knob, walked inside and jerked to a stop.

It wasn't like she remembered. It seemed smaller. And ugly. She hadn't been inside the store for a couple of decades, but she remembered it well enough to know that the sweet little wedding cake of a shop from before was long gone. The outside was all nineteenth century glory. Inside, fake wood paneling, an acoustic tile ceiling, and beige paint created the backdrop for racks of clothing, most of it bright orange or camo. She walked deeper into the store. Against a paneled wall were shelves of sporting equipment all stacked haphazardly. Some of the displays looked like they might topple over at any moment. She dodged a pyramid of unopened boxes that were blocking an aisle. A musty smell enveloped her the farther she went into the store, and she found herself wondering if she could get a job here. Maybe she could help clean and organize the place. As she explored, the wood floors creaked beneath her feet. At least those were original. The sound alerted the sales guy standing next to a case of fishing lures.

"Be with you in a sec," he said, then went back to helping a customer.

Whippet continued to wander. Behind the cash register was a marquee advertising adventure packages ranging from guided fishing trips to hiking tours.

The sales guy came up behind her. "What can I help you with?" he said politely. He seemed friendly enough. Whippet glanced his name tag and noticed it said "Ed."

"Oh. Are you Ed Aldridge?" she asked.

The guy gave a nod. "The same."

She thrust out her hand. "I'm Whippet Moran. My grandmother, Miss Lily, owned this place."

Ed nodded, unsmiling. "She was a great old lady. Actually used to come in here for crankbaits."

Crankbaits? "Oh, well, that's nice. Anyway, she left this place to me. Would you mind if I had a look around?"

"I guess so." He scratched his chin. "You, uh, aren't planning to kick me out, are you?" He gave an uneasy laugh. "I have a year left on my lease."

"Oh, no. I just wanted to ask a few questions," she said.

"Okay," he said cautiously.

"What's the square footage here?"

"Uh, I don't really know." He stuffed his hands in his pockets.

"What's upstairs?"

"Nothing." He shrugged.

"Nothing? Don't you use it for storage?"

"No, we keep surplus inventory in a warehouse somewhere else. Why are you asking so many questions?"

"I'm just curious," Whippet said.

Ed braced his arm on a rack of yoga pants "Because it kind of sounds like you're making plans for the building."

"No, I was—"

"You should know, I've got a clause in my contract that says you can't raise the rent. And I have the option to renew my lease next year." Ed advanced on her, forcing her to take a step back. "I think it might be best if you dealt with my lawyer. He's got a copy of the contract I signed with your grandmother. Thanks for stopping by." He nodded and Whippet was out on the sidewalk before she knew what had happened.

Later that night, Whippet lay in bed, eyes wide open. She turned and jammed her hands under the pillow, trying to get comfortable. She glanced over at Everly who was sprawled across the mattress, covers bunched at her feet, mouth slack.

Well, at least one of them could sleep.

She couldn't seem to turn her brain off tonight. She needed a job. Soon. Whippet turned onto her back, looking at the ceiling. Lying here wasn't helping.

Easing from the bed, she crept downstairs to the kitchen where the microwave read 1:27. She went to the fridge and opened it. Then closed it. Then opened it again and grabbed a container of yogurt. She slid into the chair next to the big picture window that overlooked the side yard. Tall pines were smudges against the night sky. It was so quiet. Maybe that's why she couldn't sleep.

Her mind turned to her beautiful building on Main Street and the ornery Ed Aldridge. She wondered if the key to her future might just be within its walls. If she could just get in there and look around maybe she'd . . .

Whippet tossed the empty yogurt container in the trash and padded toward the stairs, wide awake now. She tiptoed into her room and changed into a pair of yoga pants and a T-shirt. Then she grabbed her phone and keys and headed out the door.

# CHAPTER FIFTEEN

Just once he'd like to make it through his work week without answering a call involving Whippet Moran. Yet here he was in the alley behind Aldridge Sporting Goods in the middle of the night, refereeing a disagreement between owner and tenant.

"She was breaking and entering," Ed insisted.

Whippet scowled, but Sam spoke before she could. "Ed, she owns the property," he said. "And she has a key."

"I don't care! She has no right to be in my store."

"I wasn't in your store. I was upstairs!" Whippet exclaimed.

Twenty minutes earlier, Sam had gotten the call that a silent alarm had been tripped at Aldridge's. When Sam arrived, he'd seen a light inside bouncing off the second-floor windows. He circled around to the back, where he'd discovered everything unlocked and the door at the top of the steps ajar. He'd drawn his gun and gone in, only to have Whippet Moran scream and drop her phone—which was on flashlight mode—and nearly blind him. Ed Aldridge had slammed out of his car moments later dressed in sagging sweatpants and wrinkled shirt, hair sticking up at odd angles.

"Ed, hang on for just a second." He turned to Whippet whose arms were folded across her chest, eyes shooting darts at her grumpy tenant. "Why were you in the building at this time of night?" He looked at her. "Dressed like a cat burglar."

"I am not—" She broke off as she glanced down. She was wearing black yoga pants, black flip-flops and a black T-shirt. "I got dressed in the dark," she muttered.

"She's been skulking around my store lately," Ed insisted.

"I've been in your store once, and that was, what? Ten hours ago?" Whippet said, tightly. She turned to Sam. "I inherited this building from my grandmother. I just wanted to check it out, see inside, get an idea of the square footage, and see what's upstairs." She jabbed a finger toward the second story where Sam had found her. "I asked Mr. Aldridge to show me around yesterday, but he refused," she said.

"I'm the tenant," Ed said through gritted teeth. "I have a signed lease, and she has no right to go nosing around in a building that I pay rent for!"

"Right." Sam sighed.

"Excuse me," Ed muttered, plowing between them. "I'm going to check the till. I didn't get to the bank last night." He shot Whippet an accusatory glare as he passed.

"Did he just accuse me of stealing?" she asked.

Sam stood there, arms folded. Whippet wouldn't look at him. She bit her lip and studied the ground. When she did open her mouth to say something, he held up a finger.

"Do you have something against me getting a full night's sleep?" he asked.

"No," she said.

"Then why would you decide to come into town at two in the morning to investigate your inheritance?"

She kicked at the ground. "I, uh, couldn't sleep."

"You couldn't—okay, that's it. I'm gonna have to arrest you."

"What! Why?"

"For being the most bothersome citizen in Normal." Sam ran a hand through his hair.

"I'm sorry!" she exclaimed.

They stood in silence for a moment, watching Ed through the door as he checked his inventory to make sure she hadn't absconded with a camping stove.

"Sorry I pulled a gun on you," he said reluctantly.

"Sorry I set off the alarm. I didn't know—"

"Yeah, yeah, yeah. We're good. You better head home. I'll wait for Ed to finish counting his pennies."

"I didn't take anything!" she insisted.

"I know, I'm just messing with you. Goodnight, Daphne."

"I'm really sorry," she said, glancing back at the store. "I hope you get some sleep."

But sleep wasn't in the cards. A scant five hours later, Sam made his way up the shallow steps to the station and swung the door open. He was bleary-eyed and sleep deprived but managed a nod to Didi who was busy typing at her desk. He was almost to his office when his phone vibrated with a text. He glanced down and shuffled to a stop.

It was Emory again. What was with all the texts?

Sam deleted the text without looking at it and walked back out to Didi's desk. "Where's Whit?" he asked.

"Out making the streets safe for old women, small children, and the biker gang that rolled into the Rusty Nail last night."

The Rusty Nail was a dive bar west of town known for its watered-down drinks and lack of ambiance. It was also a great place for folks to show a complete lack of judgment. The bar wasn't within Normal city limits, but the owner called in once in a while when county police couldn't be bothered.

"Is there a problem?"

"Rusty found someone out back when he was opening up this morning. He just wanted the authorities to come out to see if the guy was dead or alive."

Didi went on typing.

"And?" Sam asked.

"Sleeping like a baby," she said, still not looking up. "Whit made sure the guy was sober before sending him on his way. Evidently there's a Bikers Against Child Abuse convention in Branson this weekend."

Terrific.

"Sharon O'Neil call *me* this morning," she said. "Evidently your voicemail is full. Better get to it."

"Yes, ma'am," Sam said with raised eyebrow before going into his office. Sam had just turned on his computer when Didi appeared in his doorway.

"Nuisance call from the Thorntons. The Mathers are fighting again."

"Okay," he sighed, reaching for his keys.

"Lyla Mathers called in herself, right after the Thorntons did."

Erica Allen poked her head around the breakroom door. "Can I come?" she asked.

Not one to discourage the junior officer from doing actual work, Sam agreed.

They rode in silence, pulling onto the gravel lane, then up the hill to park next to the Mathers' little ranch house. Lyla was outside sitting on the porch steps.

"Lyla? You okay?" Sam asked.

She looked up at them, eyes swollen. "Oh, just peachy."

There was no sign of her husband, but Sam could hear the sound of children crying coming from inside the house. "Did Clay hit you?" he asked.

"No! I didn't call you because he hit *me*. I called because if you don't get him out of here, I'm gonna kill *him*."

Sam walked closer. "What happened?"

"He lost another job! That's what happened. That man can't hold a job to save his life. Not that it matters. He drinks away half of his paycheck anyway."

"Where is he?" Sam asked.

"Inside," Lyla muttered.

"Mind if I talk to him?" Erica interjected.

"Ha!" Lyla spat. "Good luck."

Erica went inside. Sam could hear her talking to the Mathers kids in calming tones, and soon the crying stopped.

He turned his attention back to Lyla. This wasn't his first call to their house. He came out here every once in a while, usually when the neighbors couldn't stand the noise anymore. Clay wasn't a mean drunk, but he could be belligerent when intoxicated. Sam had warned him on several occasions to clean up his act, but the advice fell on deaf ears.

Sam folded his arms. "Is the drinking getting worse?"

"I don't know," Lyla said. Fresh tears leaked from her eyes.

"You don't have to stay with him. If you need help, I have some great resources through the county. I'd be happy to make some calls," Sam offered.

The screen door flapped open, and Erica shooed Clay outside. Lyla made a show of irritation by coming to stand next to Sam. Clay staggered over the threshold, squinting at the sun and holding onto the porch post before sliding down to sit on the first step.

"Lyla, you don't have to put up with this," Sam said.

"Hey!" Clay winced at the sound of his own voice and grabbed his head.

"Ma'am," Erica spoke. "Maybe I'm speaking out of turn here, but my mother was an alcoholic. It put an awful burden on my father, raising me alone. I can only imagine what this is doing to you." Erica gestured at Clay, whose face had gone pale.

Lyla's chin came up. "You turned out all right."

"Thank you, but I had to learn how to take care of myself. It wasn't the same thing as having a mother."

"Aren't you glad your parents stayed together?" Lyla asked.

Erica was shaking her head before Lyla stopped speaking. "They fought all the time. I never felt secure. And I couldn't count on my mom."

Lyla took a step forward. "Do you hear what she's saying, Clay?" she spat. "She could be talking about you. Is this the example you want to set for our girls? You've got to get help or I'm leaving. I mean it this time."

Clay suddenly found the boards under his feet extremely interesting, but he nodded.

Sam put a hand on Lyla's shoulder. "If you're sure about staying . . ."

"I am," Lyla said.

"There's an AA meeting every Wednesday night in the basement of the Methodist church. Here's a card for the director," he said, grateful when Lyla actually took it. "There are other resources available through the community center—counseling and daycare, if you need a break. I can leave you the phone number and web address if you want."

"That would be wonderful," Lyla said before dissolving again.

When Sam was sure everyone was safe, he and Erica got into the squad car.

"Do you think he'll really get help?" Erica asked as they pulled away.

"Hard to say. Clay has made promises before," Sam said. Erica nodded and looked out the window.

"Hey," Sam said as he turned onto Main Street. "You were great with those kids."

"I know," Erica said. She shot him a look. "I mean, I like kids."

"And great job with Lyla." He paused. "Is that stuff you told her about your mom true?"

"Yeah," she acknowledged, but didn't say anymore. Sam guessed she didn't want to talk about it. He didn't blame her.

They both got out of the car and went into the station. Sam headed to his office. He paused before going inside. Erica stood next to her desk.

"You gonna head out on break?" he asked. It was almost noon, and she certainly deserved it. But Erica shook her head.

"Nah. I think I'll go out and write a few tickets." With that, she left, smiling as she went.

# CHAPTER SIXTEEN

Whippet was busy in the kitchen when she heard Everly burst through the front door.

"Mom!" she called.

"In here."

"Look at this!" Everly eyes were bright as she ran into the kitchen. She was shaking a piece of paper.

Whippet wiped her hands on her apron and came out from behind the counter. "What is it?" she asked, looking at the paper. A large circled "A" was scrawled across the top. "Ev! This is fantastic. I thought you said you didn't understand your math homework." She leaned down to give her girl a hug.

"I didn't, but Max helped me study last night."

"Wait, Max wasn't here last night," she said. Whippet was grateful that Luna's son, Max, had become Everly's friend.

"We FaceTimed. Remember? I borrowed your phone," Everly said. She threw her backpack on the floor and climbed onto a barstool.

"You got an A!" Whippet cheered and went into the pantry for more cake flour. She was on her second attempt at a cake for Luna: the vanilla bean cake Tucker had loved so much. Her first try had come out sunken in the middle.

"And guess what else? Kara Warren asked me to her birthday party next weekend. We worked on a project for our Missouri history unit, and she's being really nice to me now." Everly took a bite of the discarded cake. "There's only one thing that would make this day even better. A dog. If I had a dog, I would have something to come home to. Something to love me."

Whippet mixed the ingredients together. "*I* love you," she pointed out.

"It's not the same thing. Remind me again why we can't have a dog?" Everly asked.

"I don't think I could take care of another living thing right now," Whippet explained as she walked over to preheat the oven. She parked a hand on her hip. "You can either have a somewhat functional mother or a dog," she said.

"Well . . ."

"Those weren't real options, Ev!" Whippet laughed. "Now, scoot. Go do your homework."

"What are you doing?" Everly asked.

"Making a cake for Luna."

Everly's expression turned thoughtful. "Are you trying to get your job back?"

Very clever, her girl. "I am indeed."

"Hmmm." Everly hopped off the bar stool and grabbed her backpack. "Max said his mom likes chocolate," she offered helpfully as she ran up the stairs.

* * *

There were no close parking spots on Main Street. Whippet circled the block again until she found a spot outside the Clip N' Curl.

She threw the car into park, got out, and quickly went to the passenger side to retrieve the cake. She kicked the car door shut, smoothed her hair with one hand, and walked to the diner. She nodded at Eden Turner as she bustled past, and held onto the box with both hands as she dodged Helene Coleman chasing her toddler daughter.

She arrived at the diner and took a couple of calming breaths before gathering her courage and going inside.

Whippet spotted Luna across the dining room taking someone's order. She raised an eyebrow when she saw Whippet standing there.

"What's that?" Luna asked as she approached.

Whippet took a step closer and tipped the box so Luna could see inside. "It's an apology."

"Really? It looks like a cake."

"It is a cake. An apologetic cake." She took another breath. "I baked you this cake as an apology. I'm sorry I was so unreliable." Then she remembered yelling at Sam. "And for making a scene in front of half the town. If you're up for it, I'd love another chance."

Luna ignored that and said, "I don't eat sugary treats."

"I bet you do once in a while, when the day has been really long and you're tired and that will power of yours is running low."

Luna eyed the cake. "Well, today is not that day."

"That's fine. This isn't for you anyway. I thought you could sell it." She set the box on the counter and reached for the cake plate where a whole apple pie sat untouched. Everyone in town knew Luna couldn't bake. The pie would sit there until Harvey Tellis came in on Friday afternoon for a slice when it was marked down to half price—Harvey was too cheap to pay four bucks for a slice of pie. Folks around town figured Harvey's taste buds had stopped working long ago, so they didn't fault him for his poor judgment. Whippet removed the glass cover, slid the pie onto the counter and replaced it with the cake. "It's a four-layer vanilla bean cake."

Whippet noticed she had the undivided attention of the entire diner. Even Chuck was taking a break from his duties, arms hanging over the pass-through window, his expression wry.

"How much for a slice?" Lenny Hartley asked from where he sat at the counter.

Luna walked behind the counter. "Five dollars," she said, shooting Lenny a stern look, but he was more than happy to pay it and smiled appreciatively as Luna cut him a generous piece.

Luna replaced the glass dome and turned to Whippet. "I'll have to think about the job," she said.

"That's fair. You've got my number." Luna nodded, and Whippet made a hasty retreat, but not before she glanced at Chuck who gave her a wink.

A couple of hours later, Whippet sat on the porch swing, eyes closed, enjoying the feel of the sun on her face. Her cell phone sat beside her just in case the cake worked a miracle and Luna decided to call.

It had been a busy day. After dropping off the cake, she'd come home and made dinner. Emma joined them because Tucker was working late. Mrs. Rutt, one of the guests at the B&B, also joined them because her husband's fly-fishing expedition—led by Ed Aldridge—was running late too. Emma took Everly back to Miss Lily's House to continue their Marvel movie marathon while Whippet cleaned the kitchen and did the dishes. Now there was nothing left but to sit here and enjoy the waning sunlight.

She closed her eyes and leaned back against the cushion, feeling a little proud of herself. It was just cake, she knew that. But at least she'd done something.

Whippet opened her eyes and slowly reached for her phone. She touched the screen, opened her texts, and typed in Meggie's name. Whippet tapped out a short message, asking her if she was doing okay before telling Meggie that she was thinking about filing a harassment complaint against Anthony Bannon. Then she hit Send.

Whippet heard the crunch of tires over gravel and looked up to see Cam getting out of his truck.

"Hey there," he said, taking a seat next to her and swinging an arm over her shoulder. "How did it go with Luna?"

"I don't know. She didn't offer me a job. She actually seemed a little annoyed."

Cam nodded and smiled. "That's just Luna. Tough steel shell wrapped around a soft, sweet center."

Whippet pulled back and looked at him. "I guess I'll have to take your word for it," Whippet said, wondering how he knew so much about Luna. Maybe it was the whole townie thing. They'd known each other forever.

"Props for taking her the cake, though. That took guts. Did you, uh . . . apologize?"

Cam had never suggested she apologize to Luna, not once. Tucker was the one who beat that idea into the ground. Cam was far too diplomatic to suggest that Whippet might have something to do with her current employment predicament.

"I did," she said. "Fingers crossed that she takes it to heart and—" Her cell phone rang.

Cam looked over her shoulder. "That's Luna's number," he said.

Again, how did he know that? "Hello?"

"Your cake was gone in less than twenty minutes," Luna said without preamble. "How soon can I get another cake or two?"

"Wait. You want another cake?" Whippet asked sitting up straighter.

"Two. Soon. Like first thing tomorrow morning." Luna paused. "We can talk about the job when you bring them in."

Whippet turned to Cam and grinned. "That would be great! I'll see you right after I drop Everly off at school."

Whippet hung up and looked at Cam. "Luna wants two more cakes! And she wants to talk about the job. That's got to be good, right?"

Cam reached over to push a strand of hair behind her ear. "Sounds that way to me," he murmured before pulling her in for a kiss. She felt her phone vibrate with a text, but she ignored it. Soon all thoughts about cakes and jobs and her old boss floated away as Whippet sank deeper into Cam's arms. A loud rapping on the window behind them made her jump away from him. They both turned to see her mother standing on the other side of the glass.

"You two knock it off!" she said through the window. "Everly will be home any minute." The curtains swooshed closed.

Cam exhaled loudly. "Think Ed Aldridge would be okay with us having a little 'alone time' above his store sometime?" he asked with his cute sideways grin.

"I don't know," she whispered, reaching over for another kiss. "But I can ask him."

Cam pulled back a minute later. "I have to go," he said reluctantly. "My sister needs me to change her oil tonight." He stood up. "Way to go today. Let me know what you hear from Luna." She waved from the porch as he drove away.

Whippet took a deep breath and settled into a feeling of satisfaction.

She picked up her phone, suddenly remembering she'd missed a text.

It was from Meggie. Just three little words.

"Go for it."

# CHAPTER SEVENTEEN

WHIPPET SHADOWED CAM AS HE took measurements and scribbled them down on a notepad. They were upstairs in her building. Cam's off-the-cuff remark about 'alone time' yesterday had given her an idea.

On the night Whippet snuck into her building and tripped the alarm, she'd had about seven minutes before Officer Beaufort showed up and traumatized her by pulling a gun on her. In those seven minutes, she had been able to see that the upstairs had once upon a time been an apartment. It hadn't been lived in for years, maybe decades. The ceiling was water stained and drooping. The fixtures in the bathroom were rusted and the sink looked about a hundred years old. There was no shower, and except for the rickety walls separating the bathroom, everything was wide open. It was a disaster, but Whippet saw potential. And that left her with one question: Could she convert the space into an apartment for herself and Everly?

She'd called Hopper Spickett, and he told her he'd be willing to release some of the funds Gran had set aside for repairs and improvements on the property. "An apartment upstairs definitely qualifies," he'd said.

She had her job back, so she'd have the income to cover utilities, and she hoped, down the road, furniture. She didn't want to jinx anything, but it kind of felt like maybe things were falling into place.

"For real?" Everly asked, eyes alight when Whippet broached the subject that morning. "Could I have my own room?"

Following Cam now, Whippet crossed her fingers on both hands because she'd hate to let Everly down.

"Yeah, I can do it," Cam said, as his tape measure retracted.

"No, no. I wasn't asking you to do it. I just wanted to know if it could be done."

"It can be done. Luckily the door is centered on the wall so I'm thinking bedrooms over there, kitchen against this wall." He pointed to the wall she shared with her neighbor. "It'll save some money if you keep the plumbing where it is in the bathroom. Washer and dryer can go in there too. The plumber will have to run a supply and drain line over against that wall to plumb the kitchen." Cam went on, talking about vent lines, junction boxes, and circuit breakers. She didn't understand any of it, but the words filled her with excitement just the same. "It'll be nice up here," he said. "I can start this weekend if you want. We can get everything roughed in before you need permits."

"Cam, really. You don't have to do this. You're busy. I can hire a contractor."

"Uh, no you can't. Not on your budget. I can do most of this at cost, and I have a couple of subcontractors who owe me a favor or three. They'd do the electrical and plumbing for a song or, in your case, maybe a cake." He winked at her. "But it'll be slow, Whip. I work full time at the shop, and a lot of folks around here rely on me to do odd jobs on the weekends. I do good work, but I don't work fast."

"That's fine. That's great! I mean, I haven't told my mom about this anyway, so slow is probably best. Thank you, Cam." She stood on tippy-toes and planted a kiss on his cheek. "So what's next?"

The first thing she did was warn Ed Aldridge. She asked if Cam could run an extension cord down the stairway and use the outlet outside Ed's door. He agreed only after Whippet told him she'd pay his electric bill until she got power turned on upstairs.

Cam took care of drafting the floor plan, while Whippet downloaded permit forms, gathered the necessary paperwork, and headed down to the courthouse to submit everything and pay her application fee.

Now she just had to tell her mother.

Whippet had asked her mom to join her for lunch at the diner. It was Saturday, and she hoped the weekend crowds would discourage her mother from making a scene. She dragged Everly along and had tried to recruit Emma, but she was busy at The Barn, the events venue she owned and managed.

They stood in line, waiting. A table opened up in the middle of the dining room. Perfect. Nice and surrounded. Jan showed them to their seats.

"So, Mom," Whippet started as soon as Jan had collected their menus. "I, uh, have something I wanted to talk to you about."

Mom looked up. "Well, that sounds ominous," she said. "Everly, sweetheart. Your glass is too close to the edge of the table. What do you want to tell me, Whippet?"

"Right. Uh, the thing I wanted to talk to you about . . . it's not. I mean it's . . . well, it'll mean a change, for sure." She fumbled around for the right approach. Whippet sat up straighter. "Um, a couple of days ago, Cam and I were looking at the space above the sporting goods store."

Jan was back in record time. She slid their order onto the table, and Whippet sat back in her chair. "Will that be all?" Jan asked glancing over their heads, clearly not thrilled to be serving her coworker.

"Yep. Thanks." Whippet's smile was lost on Jan, and she trundled off.

"Mom!" Everly exclaimed. "Sam's here. Can I go talk to him?"

"Sam?"

"Yeah, Sam. The police officer." Everly turned and pointed to where every member of Normal PD stood in line, chatting amiably, Officer Beaufort towering over them all.

"Oh, honey. I don't know. He looks busy."

"He's not busy. Please, Mom? I want to ask him about his dog," Everly begged.

Whippet looked back at the police chief. "Go ahead. But come right back, okay?"

Sophie tsked as they watched Everly go. "Her lunch is going to get cold."

"Oh, well. It's only grilled cheese. Anyway. About the store—"

"What store?" her mother asked as she cut into her chicken-fried steak.

"Cam and I were looking at the building Gran left me. Aldridge Sporting Goods is downstairs, but the upstairs is vacant."

"Um-hmm," her mother said, savoring a bite.

"Cam worked up some plans, and then I talked to the attorney."

"Uh-huh," her mother said absently.

"Hopper is going to release some of the funds in the account Gran left me. Cam is going to remodel the space upstairs into an apartment for Ev and me. So we'll be moving out. Soon." She blurted. "Well, soon-ish."

Sophie froze. "What did you say?"

Whippet swallowed. "Everly and I will be moving out. Not for a few months, but . . . yeah," she finished weakly.

Sophie put down her fork. "Why?"

Everly ran back over and plopped down in her chair. "He hasn't named his dog yet," she said breathlessly. "He asked me to think up a couple of names. Isn't that cool?"

Whippet looked over, and Sam nodded at her. "That's great, Everly," she said as she looked at her mother's pinched face.

The rest of their lunch was a bit strained.

As soon as they pulled up in front of the B&B, her mother shot out of the car.

"What's wrong with Grammy?" Everly asked.

"I think maybe she's tired," Whippet answered as they went inside.

Everly ran upstairs, and Whippet went to the kitchen. Her mother was standing at the sink, hands encased in plastic gloves, attacking the morning dishes.

Her mother looked up when Whippet walked over. A pan clattered in the sink.

"Mom, I didn't—"

"This was supposed to be my time," her mom said, scrubbing furiously.

"Your time? Time for what?"

"Time with you. Time with Everly. You spent years in Texas with that woman."

"What woman? You mean Cal's mother?" Whippet asked.

"After Cal took off, I was packed and ready to drive out to that silly town and bring you home," her mother said. "I was halfway through Arkansas when you called to tell me you'd moved in with Francine. Francine! Who spent a year dragging you to grief counseling and filling your head with a lot of nonsense about you not trying hard enough in your marriage before *kicking you out*!"

It was true. Her mother-in-law had signed them both up for a support group right after Cal vanished. Francine had dragged Whippet along every Wednesday night to meetings held in the basement of the First Baptist Church. Those meetings had made Whippet squirm. She'd felt like a fraud sitting there, surrounded by people who were *really* grieving, just because her husband had run off with the checkout girl at the Corner Mart. She wasn't grieving. Ticked off? You bet. Cal had cleared out their checking account before he left. But she'd mostly been embarrassed. A secret part of her rejoiced at being free of the bully she'd tied herself to in holy matrimony. Francine, on the other hand, had been heartbroken and was deeply disturbed that Whippet didn't share the sentiment.

"Mom, I didn't know."

"I know you didn't! You never asked for help. You didn't want to come home. You turned your back on your family." Her mother was doing some robust scrubbing.

Whippet was still for a moment. Her mother was right. Whippet hadn't called. She hadn't asked for help. But it wasn't because she'd chosen Cal's family over her own. No, she'd simply followed her lifelong pattern of taking the easiest path.

Whippet walked over and slid an arm around her mother and leaned her head on her shoulder. "I'm sorry, Mom," she said gently.

Sophie turned to look at her, and her eyes filled again. "I love having you here," she said with a sniffle. "It's been nice to feel needed again. And I've never had this much time with Everly."

"Mom, I'm staying in Normal. I'm putting down roots, sort of. We're just moving into town. You can see Everly all the time, and me too if that's what you want," she said, and her mother nodded.

"Okay, good. You can help me decorate the apartment," Whippet promised, hoping to coax her mom into a better mood. "I've never had my own place before. It'll be fun."

Her mother reached for a tissue. "I would love that."

# CHAPTER EIGHTEEN

"That'll be five bucks even, Mrs. Turner," Whippet said cheerfully as she took the woman's credit card.

"You're happy this morning," Eden said in a tone that indicated she didn't share Whippet's mood.

She shrugged. "Maybe it's because the sun's out today."

Eden gave her a look. "We're having a heat wave. The sun's been out every day this week." She walked away muttering about the heat index.

Whippet chuckled. She *was* in a good mood. She had her job back. And her daughter was happy because school would be out in a few days. Everly had made more friends and now ran around with a little gang that included Max, whom Whippet suspected might just be her daughter's first crush.

The permits for the apartment had come through. Her family had helped with demo, hauling away a dumpster's worth of trash, including the ancient toilet and sink. She'd been hanging out with Cam a lot lately, mostly on weekends when her mom was home and could watch Everly. Last Saturday, she and Cam had removed the warped paneling from the south-facing wall and high-fived each other when they had uncovered brick. Cam was anxious to get started on the framing, but Whippet hadn't gotten around to having the electricity turned on.

Whippet had just finished taking the Jensens' order and handing it to Chuck when Cam's voice came from behind her. "Hey, there." She turned around just as he took a seat at the counter.

"Luna, can I have a couple of minutes?" Whippet asked.

Luna had taken over at the cash register and was trying to teach their new hire, Jared Scott, how to ring up an order. From the way she was frowning, it didn't seem to be going too well. Luna looked up, eyes glancing off Cam before they came to rest on Whippet. "As long as you don't leave. Lunch rush starts in fifteen."

Whippet nodded and took off her apron. "Hi," she said, coming to sit next to Cam. "You hungry?"

"I'm good. I came to grab the key. The lumber is being delivered this afternoon."

"Don't you have work? I can see if I can get off early to let them in," Whippet offered.

"No, I got it," he insisted.

Luna walked over to retrieve an order pad. Cam glanced at her and started fiddling with a napkin holder, spinning it around and around, color high on his cheeks. Luna turned sharply, her elbow dislodging an empty pitcher. She righted it quickly, eyes trained on the floor.

Whippet watched her boss fumble to get the cash register open. She'd never seen Luna so flustered. "I think the key might be in my purse. I'll go check." Whippet got up and impulsively leaned over and kissed Cam's cheek before disappearing into the kitchen.

She fished around in her purse and found the key. On her way back to the dining room, Chuck asked her to check the fryer. She turned off the timer and set a basket of fries to drain.

Whippet pushed through the door and stopped short. Cam was laughing, grinning up at Luna. Her boss wore an almost bashful smile. Seemed like the two of them were only awkward around each other when she was near.

"Here you go," Whippet said, holding up the key.

Luna jumped and turned, wiping her hands on her skirt. "Right, well, good to see you, Cam," Luna said, giving him a half smile before walking back to the cash register.

Cam cleared his throat. "You too, Luna."

"Luna, can I walk him to his car?" Whippet asked.

"Uh, sure," Luna said, suddenly consumed with checking the receipt paper. Whippet had replaced it this morning.

Cam held the door for her. "What was that all about?" she asked when they were outside.

"What was what all about?"

"In there, with Luna. You two seemed weird around each other."

Many a man became tongue tied around Luna. But Cam was *her* boyfriend. He was supposed to be immune to Luna's charms.

"There was no weirdness. I've known Luna a long time. Just haven't talked to her in a while." Cam tapped Whippet's nose like she was a child. "You're imagining things," he said, taking the key from her fingers and getting into his car.

"I hope so," she sighed as he drove away.

\* \* \*

Nope. It was not her imagination.

The next day Cam came into the diner for a late breakfast and asked if she could take her break. It was Saturday and crazy busy. Luna was mysteriously absent, which meant Whippet was doing double duty. Cam waited patiently while she buzzed around seating customers, taking orders, and running the register. At a quarter after ten, Luna swung through the kitchen door pulling her hair into a ponytail.

"Sorry I'm late. My hot water heater exploded this morning," Luna explained, then froze when her eyes landed on Cam.

"Can I place a takeout order?" a woman asked Whippet just as she heard Cam ask, "What's up with your water heater, Luna?"

Luna glanced at Whippet before heading toward Cam. Soon they were embroiled in conversation. The noise in the diner made it difficult for Whippet to eavesdrop, but she did manage to make out the words, "flood" and "disaster," as she rang up the next customer.

"Uh, that'll be two seventy-three," Whippet said, casting a surreptitious glance toward the end of the counter while she waited for Neely to hunt through her coin purse for exact change.

"I have seventy-three cents. I know I do," Neely murmured.

Whippet's irritation grew. It sure would be nice if Luna would take over at the register for a minute so she could take a break and maybe sit with her boyfriend.

"Here you go," Neely said, handing her a warm pile of quarters, nickels, dimes, and pennies. Rather than count it, Whippet decided she'd make up the difference herself if the till was short tonight.

"Thanks, Neely," Whippet said, wiping her hand on her apron. "Have a good day."

Myrna Hudson was next in line, but she was too preoccupied with the man behind her to pay her bill. Whippet braced one hand against the countertop and slapped the other on her hip as she waited.

"Good morning, Chief," Myrna said.

"Hello, Mrs. Hudson," Officer Beaufort replied, then glanced up at the blackboard advertising the day's specials.

"Have you given it some thought?" Mrs. Hudson asked him. Whippet leaned against the counter, blatantly eavesdropping.

Sam glanced at her then back at Mrs. Hudson. "Have I given what some thought?"

"My granddaughter. Lovely girl. She's seeing someone right now." Myrna waved a dismissive hand. "But no one likes him. I'd be happy to introduce you." Whippet watched Myrna turn a speculative eye on the chief of police.

"I'm, uh, seeing someone in Springfield," Sam Beaufort muttered.

Huh. So the good officer had a social life. That was hard to believe. Still, Whippet felt a twinge of . . . something at the news.

Myrna's eyes narrowed. She harrumphed her disapproval, paid her bill, and bustled out.

Whippet raised an eyebrow at him. "Can I help you, or should I offer my matchmaking services as well?"

"That won't be necessary. I phoned in a takeout order about twenty minutes ago."

Whippet went to check the window. Nothing there. "Chuck?" she said, poking her head into the kitchen. "You got a takeout order for Beaufort?"

"Give me a minute, will ya?" Chuck called as he flipped a line of flapjacks.

"Chuck, I can feel you weakening. One of these days you're going to admit you like me."

"Don't hold your breath, sweetheart," he rasped.

Whippet shot the old guy a grin and returned to the counter. She picked up a rag and started to wipe it down. Every now and then she'd steal a glance at Cam and Luna, still chatting away. For crying out loud! How long did it take to talk about a broken water heater? She'd overheard Cam offer to stop by later. What else was there to say?

"Hello? Earth to Daphne." Sam Beaufort waved a hand in front of her face.

Whippet blinked. "Oh. Sorry. Let me check the window."

She found the white sack with his name on it. "Here you go," she said, thrusting it at him. Sam took it. "Thanks," he said, looking at his phone. "Didi just texted. She wants me to pick up a muffin," he said, shifting his focus to the display case.

Sam's eyes were blue. Huh. She'd never noticed that before. But they were blue. Really blue, actually. Maybe it was the color of his uniform that brought out the—okay, she was staring. Any second now he'd look up, catch her and, yep—busted.

"What?" he asked, raising an eyebrow.

"Blue . . . uh, the blueberry pie is really good today," she said lamely.

His eyes flicked to the pie stand. "That looks like cherry."

"Right. That's what I said."

"Uh-huh. Can I get one of those poppy seed muffins?"

"Will that be all?" she asked.

"Yep." Sam gave her his credit card then casually glanced down at the end of the counter. She rang up his bill and gave him back his card. He took it before saying, "You have a good day, Daphne."

* * *

Later that night, Sam pulled up behind Whippet Moran's Chevy Cobalt and sighed. This should be fun. He stretched his neck and scratched his head. He got out of the cruiser and walked toward her car.

He rapped lightly on the window and motioned for her to roll it down. Whippet obliged, giving him one of her trademark do-I-really-have-to-talk-to-you looks.

"What are you doing?" he asked.

"Nothing. Just sitting here," she said, gripping the steering wheel and looking straight ahead.

Sam braced one hand against the roof of her car. "Any particular reason why you're parked on Grant Avenue at eleven o'clock at night?"

"Seemed like a good spot to sit and contemplate," she said.

"Really? Contemplate what?"

"Would you believe Einstein's theory of relativity?" she asked squinting up at him.

"No."

"Yeah, me neither." She sighed.

"What's going on, Daphne?"

"I don't want to tell you." She studied the back of her hand.

"I'm sure you don't, but Helen Butchard just called in a suspicious vehicle loitering outside her house, and I have a professional duty to find out what said vehicle is up to." Sam looked up at Helen's front window and saw the lace curtains swish closed. "You need to move your car."

"I'm not loitering. I'm just sitting here."

"Which is the textbook definition of loitering. Tell me what's going on."

"Fine," she said, looking at him. "Luna's water heater is broken."

Sam looked across the street to the Meacham place, the 1980s ranch home that Luna had moved into a few years back when her parents retired to the Gulf Coast. "And?"

"And that red truck parked out front happens to belong to my boyfriend."

Ah. Everything began to click into place.

Sam thought for a minute, then crossed to the other side of the vehicle, tossing a wave in Helen Butchard's direction. He opened the passenger-side door and got in.

"What are you doing?" Whippet sputtered.

"You're worried because Cam is helping Luna."

"Yes," she said, eyes wide.

"Why?"

Whippet didn't answer right away; she just stared at him, arm braced against the steering wheel. And even as she sat there, shooting daggers straight into his chest, he acknowledged that there was something different about Whippet Moran. Was he attracted to her? Sure. Was he going to do something about that? Not in this lifetime.

Finally, her shoulders sagged. "I seem to have a magnetic pull when it comes to cheaters," she said, biting her lip and glancing up at Luna's house.

"Cam isn't cheating on you," he said.

She turned to look at him. "How could you possibly know that?"

"Because you spend enough time around a person you get a sense of who they are."

"You think so?" Whippet didn't seem convinced.

He gave her a slow nod. "You've been around him more than most. Think about it for a minute. Do you really think he's the kind of guy who would cheat?"

Whippet's expression clouded as she looked out the window. "You're probably right," she whispered. "But Luna's so beautiful and I—"

"You're every bit as beautiful as Luna. You've got nothing to worry about." He needed to stop talking. This was none of his business anyway. Still, Whippet seemed to relax a little in her seat. "Are you good now?" he asked.

"Yeah, I think so. Thanks," she said, eyes flicking to his and then away again.

Sam opened the door. He could still see Helen Butchard, silhouetted behind her front window. "Move your car, will ya?"

Whippet gave him a little smile. "Yes, sir," she said, with a mock salute.

Sam stood in the street as she drove away, watching until she disappeared around the corner.

# CHAPTER NINETEEN

June blew in on a late spring storm. When the rain moved on, the humidity stayed.

Luna moved Whippet back to the morning shift once school was out. And now that tourist season was upon them, the diner was humming. Whippet had just cleared away breakfast for a family of five. There was maple syrup everywhere. At least tips had increased, even if work was a little repetitive.

Someone knocked on the window next to the table she was clearing. Whippet looked up and saw Cam motioning for her to come outside.

"Gonna take a break, Jan," she called.

"Whatever," Jan said in her gravelly, pack-a-day voice.

Whippet rolled her eyes and went outside. "Hey."

"I just stopped by your place," Cam said. "The electricity's been turned on. Did you do that?"

"Yeah, I called a few days ago. Really? It's on? They told me it would take a week."

"I can start framing this weekend, if that's okay."

Finally! "That would be fantastic."

Cam grinned at her and raised his hand for a high five before walking to his car. He raised his chin at her as he pulled away from the curb.

Huh. Her boyfriend had just high-fived her.

She turned just in time to find Luna watching Cam drive away. Whippet's eyes narrowed on her boss. She pulled the door open and stalked inside. "You know, you get a look every time he comes in," Whippet said.

"No, I don't," Luna snorted, then walked through the swinging door into the kitchen.

Whippet was hot on her heels. "Yes, you do," she insisted. "Is there something going on that I don't know about?" she asked, tracking Luna all the way to her office.

Luna sat down at her desk and flipped open her laptop, briefly closing her eyes before turning to face Whippet. "We dated in high school," she admitted.

Whippet's head jerked back a fraction. "Oh."

"I was an idiot and broke up with him. I was kind of a brat back then. I cared more about being prom queen and what a boy could do for *me* than appreciating—" Luna stopped. "Look, I made a lot of mistakes when I was younger. That's why I keep my old pageant dresses out front. To remind myself that I'm not that sad, shallow girl anymore." Luna's eyes clouded. "Sometimes I wish—well, never mind. It's no big deal. Just—" Luna paused. "Cam is a good guy. Don't forget that, all right?"

Whippet didn't respond right away, still stunned by Luna's confession. "Uh, I won't," she said, trying to ignore the sick feeling that had settled in her stomach.

The next night, Cam suggested they go out to celebrate the beginning of construction on her apartment. It was a quiet drive to Springfield. Whippet was in her head too much for conversation.

She'd fretted about Luna and Cam all day: the way Whippet had seen Cam lean into Luna when they were talking, like every word that came out of her mouth was gold. Clearly her boss regretted breaking up with Cam. She'd hinted as much in her office yesterday. And what was that saying about hindsight? Maybe after two failed marriages Luna finally realized what she'd let go. The whole thing made Whippet a little queasy.

By the afternoon, she'd decided she needed to figure out how Cam felt about *her* before she got too involved. Luna was right. Cam was a good guy. It would be better to find out the truth now rather than end up with a broken heart.

After they were seated at the restaurant and the waitress had moved out of earshot, Whippet gathered her courage. "You like Luna," she said, keeping her voice level so as not to sound accusatory. She even managed a smile.

Cam leaned back in his chair, playing with the saltshaker. "She's good people."

"No, I mean, it seems like you *like her*. Like you have feelings for her. Like—"

Cam held up a hand in surrender. "I get the idea." He shrugged and said nothing, which seemed like an answer in itself. Whippet sagged in her chair, a little deflated at having her suspicions confirmed.

"Luna and I dated our senior year in high school," he said, still fascinated by the saltshaker.

"I heard," Whippet replied sotto voce.

Ah, the power of first love. Not that Whippet had a clue what that was like. She'd married her first love, and he'd cheated on her within six months of the "I do's."

"So why'd you break up?" she asked.

A funny little smile showed up. "I really love small town life," he said. "I'd always planned on taking over my uncle's garage. It was enough for me."

"But not for Luna," Whippet guessed, and Cam shot her with a finger pistol.

"Luna had big plans back then. She was itching to get out of Normal. She broke up with me and was gone a month later. She married some guy from Pensacola about a year after that. I thought I'd never see her again. I moved on."

"Well," Whippet said, picking up her drink and fiddling with the straw. "She's back now."

Cam's expression turned thoughtful. He pushed the saltshaker away. "It wasn't a good break up. I was kind of a jerk about it. Might have burned a bridge there."

Whippet shook her head. "You were, what? Eighteen?"

Cam nodded. "About that."

"Well, there you go. No one is rational at eighteen. I should know. I got married at eighteen."

Cam was no dummy. "What's this about, Whip?" he asked.

She picked up her napkin and folded it in half and then in half again. "My marriage was miserable. My ex cheated on me more than once. He made it clear that I wasn't what he wanted in a wife. When I got divorced, I swore I'd never be in a relationship with someone who didn't want to be with *me*." She paused and looked down. "I'm sensing that might be the case here."

"I like you, Whippet," Cam insisted.

"I like you too." Before she could think about what she was doing she said, "But I think maybe you like Luna more."

"I don't think she—"

"I think she does," she interrupted.

"You girls been talking?"

Whippet shrugged. "She hasn't said too much, but I think she has regrets."

Cam's eyes narrowed even as his good-natured smile appeared on his face. "I smell a trap," he said.

Whippet took a deep breath. "I think you'd be good together."

Cam retrieved his napkin from his lap and made a show of wiping his mouth, but he didn't look at her. "I don't know about that. Besides . . ."

The pause went on too long, and Whippet's hopes of having him make some kind of declaration were fading fast. "Yes?" she coaxed.

He shrugged. "I'm fine with you."

Whippet froze. As declarations of love went . . . Okay, that wasn't a declaration of love. It wasn't even a declaration of middling affection. He'd basically told her he was content, or worse, settling.

Whippet's therapist in Texas had a saying, "If you keep doing what you're doing, you're going to keep getting what you've got." She liked to trot it out whenever Whippet struggled with making a decision. Whippet needed to be decisive now.

She took his hand. "Cam. You're a great guy."

"Uh-oh," he said. "What's going on?"

"I think we should stop seeing each other." It wasn't what she'd planned to say at all, but once the words were out, they felt right.

"Whippet, I—"

"No. It's okay. It really *is* okay. We both deserve more than 'fine,' don't you think?"

The poor guy didn't speak, didn't move. "I thought we were going out for a nice dinner together," he said a little helplessly. He was quiet for a minute. "Whippet, I think you're one of the prettiest girls in town. And one of the sweetest. You're a good person."

"But . . ."

To his credit, he looked regretful. "But I've been in love with Luna Meacham since the fifth grade."

The drive home was lighter somehow. Conversation flowed pretty freely for two people who had just ended a relationship. Maybe friends was a better fit.

Cam generously offered to keep working on her apartment. "If you're okay with that," he said. She'd have been a fool to say no.

"I'll get started in the morning," he promised as he dropped her off in front of the diner. "You okay from here?"

"I'm good," she said, grateful there wasn't a parking ticket on her windshield because, yes, she'd parked in a two-hour zone. Perhaps Normal PD was all tucked in for the night.

She waved at Cam as he drove away, maybe in the direction of Luna's place, she couldn't tell. She was okay with it. Or at least she would be.

She got into her car and sighed. Another failed relationship.

She sat there for a minute, processing what had happened. Cam had a good heart. Failed relationship or not, at least her choices were getting better. There was hope in that. Whippet started her car.

She drove north before turning into the roundabout so she could lay her eyes on her soon-to-be home. It never failed to lift her spirits.

Just as she rounded the corner, she saw something odd. A trail of smoke was coming from the upper floors of Aldridge Sporting Goods.

Her apartment was on fire.

\* \* \*

Sam stretched in his chair, rubbed his eyes, then turned off his computer. He'd stayed late trying to get caught up on paperwork.

His phone vibrated with a text. He ignored it. Emory was on a no-holds-barred text campaign. The last one he'd read said: *You can't avoid me forever.* Wanna bet?

His phone started to ring. He looked at the display and answered it.

"Hello, trouble," Sam said, greeting his sister as he walked out to his car.

"Hello there. I'm calling on behalf of our mother. She wants me to pry sensitive information out of you."

"What kind of sensitive information are we talking about?" he asked.

"Mom says she hasn't heard from you in a while. Last time there was a communication blackout, you ended up marrying the harpy. She's worried you haven't called because you're dating someone horrible." His sister's voice dropped to a whisper. "Are you?"

"Dating someone? No. Busy with a full-time job and remodeling a house? Yes."

Sam got into his car, hit speaker and pulled out of the parking lot, heading out to do his customary cruise up and down Main Street before going home. "I appreciate the concern," he said. "Aren't you supposed to keep Mom busy with all those wild animals you call children? She shouldn't have time to worry about me, Lanie."

"You know how she is. Last week she was scouting out one of Rosemary Tuckett's daughters at church. She thinks she can get you home for good if she can find the right girl."

"This is all your fault. You set an impossible precedent." His sister had been happily married for the last five years. His mother brought it up every time she called.

"You're right," Lanie replied. "I should have married a jerk."

"So help your brother out. Fight with the guy once in a while. Run home to Mom. Then maybe she'll get off my—" Sam slammed on the brakes just as he cleared the roundabout. "Sorry Lanie. Gotta go."

He hung up and jerked to a stop in front of Aldridge's. Smoke poured out of the second story windows. Adrenaline kicked in, and he was out of the car and trying the front door. Locked. He called the fire department as he circled around the building to the back entrance. The door stood ajar, light spilling across the parking lot. He went inside and looked through the glass door into Aldridge's. No fire. It must not have spread yet. He glanced up the stairs. Whippet Moran stood there, hand poised over the doorknob.

"Don't!" he barked. She jerked back, turning startled eyes on him. He stomped up the stairs. "You might burn yourself." He reached her side and put a hand on her arm, intent on getting her out of there.

She shook him off. "I saw smoke!"

"And where there's smoke . . ." He grabbed her hand. "C'mon."

"Wait," Whippet said, pausing. "Do you hear that?"

Sam heard a deep rumbling. It increased in pitch, building into a clanking. The very walls seemed to vibrate, and it sounded like the building was about to come down around them. "What is that?" Whippet asked.

"I don't know. And I don't care to find out either. Let's get you out of here." He curled his arms around Whippet, not touching her but forming a shield, herding her down the stairs.

The clanking turned into a hiss and they both looked up. An ancient sprinkler head coughed and burst to life, water pouring down and soaking them.

"I don't believe it!" Whippet looked up at Sam, grinning. He didn't share her mood and dragged her down the last few steps before pushing her out the back door and into the alley. She ran to the front of the building, and he followed her out into the street. One of the panes in the arched window upstairs was broken. Char marks fanned out on either side. No flames were visible, and pale smoke poured through the opening. It looked like the sprinklers had done their job.

A car skidded up to the curb and Ed Aldridge tumbled out. "No, no, no!" He ran up to the storefront, his hands on his head, and Sam felt a flash of empathy for the guy. It was raining inside his store.

Ed turned on them. "She did this. She's been nothing but trouble since she showed up. I guarantee she's the one who set the fire," he said shaking a finger at Whippet.

"There is no fire," Sam and Whippet said at the same time.

"There was a fire," Sam explained. "You should be happy the sprinklers came on, Ed."

But Ed wasn't listening. "Look at that! Gallons of water flooding my store—my inventory will be ruined. You're going to pay for this!" Ed focused his wrath on Whippet. Sam watched her shrink. "Can't you override the system?" Ed turned desperate eyes on him.

Sam shrugged. "The fire department has to do that. I'd unlock the front door though. That way they won't have to bust it in. It'll save you the cost of a new door at least."

"*I* won't have to pay for a new anything." Ed shot Whippet a pointed look before he stormed off.

"He's going to sue me," Whippet whispered, tears threatening.

Moments later, the county fire department showed up. The water was turned off, and Ed stumbled inside, wailing over his soaked store. Whippet tried to move around Sam, but he held up an arm and said, "No."

"But I just want to go upstairs and—"

"No," he said again, firmer this time.

An hour later Whippet stood, white-faced, listening as Stu Jacobs from the county fire department explained what had happened.

"Normally just a couple of sprinklers are activated when they sense heat. Your system is either faulty or out of date. Every head came on."

Sam could probably get her statement later. He'd really like to get out of here. It smelled like smoke, just like the O'Neil's house had that night. But Whippet looked a little weepy as the firefighter talked to her, and Sam felt funny about abandoning her.

"We won't know for weeks what really happened, but if I had to guess, I'd say the wiring was faulty. I'm guessing this place hasn't been updated in a while."

"No." Whippet's voice sounded raspy. She cleared her throat. "We were working on it."

Sam watched Whippet's eyes fill with tears as she said, "So this is my fault? For turning on the electricity?" she asked.

Her tears worked their magic, and Stu gave her an awkward pat on the back. "Don't worry, now. It'll work out. Accidents happen. It could have been a lot worse."

Whippet nodded and kept nodding. Sam felt an abrupt sense of protectiveness. "Thanks, Stu," he said. The other man waved and went back inside.

"Let's go," Sam said to Whippet. He gently guided her away from the building to where the air was clean. It didn't help. Her face was still pale, and she seemed brittle.

"Think you can drive home?" he asked.

"I—sure. Yes." She glanced at him briefly, then stumbled toward her car. She stopped, turned, and walked back toward him, her movements jerky. It seemed like she was going to say something, but then she shook her head and twisted the ring on her little finger.

"Are you okay?" he asked.

"This is bad, isn't it?" she whispered. "Really bad."

He didn't know what to say, and his silence raised a moan of distress.

Sam grabbed her hand, led her to her car, and opened the door. "Sit down, Daphne, okay?" he said gently. As she sat, he pulled out his cell phone and made a call.

"Hello?"

Sam was surprised the phone was answered after the first ring. "Uh, Madsen, I've got your sister here. I don't think she should drive. Can you come get her?"

"What's wrong?" Tucker's voice was instantly alert.

"There was a fire at Aldridge's tonight. It's a long story, but your sister is a little shook up."

Tucker Madsen pulled into the parking lot ten minutes later.

"What happened?" Tucker asked.

Sam jerked his head toward the building. "Not sure yet, but it looks like it might have been faulty wiring. It's not her fault."

"You okay?" Tucker asked his sister.

"I'm fine. I can drive myself," Whippet insisted.

"That's great. Get in my car," Tucker said, and his weepy sister complied.

"You need her for anything else?" Tucker asked, closing her door.

"Nah. Ed Aldridge is inside slamming things around. I'll make sure the building gets locked up. Your sister is putting on a brave face, Madsen. Ed was making all kinds of threats earlier. Take care of her," Sam said.

Tucker nodded. "I will. Thanks."

# CHAPTER TWENTY

Janet Huxley gave a dramatic sigh. "I told you I have celiac disease, and you still put croutons on my salad. I can't eat this now. Even if I pick them off, there might be cross contamination."

"I'm so sorry," Whippet said. "I'll make you another salad myself." Whippet scooped the plate off the table. "I'll be right back."

"Salad dressing on the side, dear," the woman called after her.

Whippet went into the kitchen. With unsteady hands, she threw away the offending salad and tossed together another one. As she swished through the kitchen door on her way back to the Huxleys' table, Luna lifted the salad from her hands. "Jan, make sure table four gets this." Before Whippet could say anything, Luna pulled her back into the kitchen.

Luna was going to fire her again. And who could blame her? Whippet had been distracted all morning: mixing up orders, leaving entrées at the pass-through window until they were cold.

She hadn't gotten much sleep last night. Every time she closed her eyes, she remembered the smoke pouring out of the apartment window. She shouldn't have turned on the electricity. If she hadn't, she wouldn't have woken up to a bundle of texts this morning from her irate tenant featuring words like "damage" and "liability" and "lawsuit." She'd stumbled out of bed and fallen to her knees. She'd tried to pray, but all she could manage were the desperate words, "please help me," repeated over and over and over again.

And now she was going to lose her job.

"Luna, I'm sorry," Whippet said, following her boss into the back.

Luna leaned against her desk. "Um, Cam came by last night," she said, not quite meeting Whippet's eye.

"Can we not talk about this right now?" Whippet begged. She had enough on her plate. She didn't want to do a postmortem of her relationship too.

"No . . . no, I just want you to know nothing is going to happen. I told Cam that last night."

"Well, that's stupid. I broke up with him so he could be with you." Luna started to protest but Whippet went on. "You like him, Luna. I can tell. And Cam and I are better off as friends."

"So the reason you're walking around here like a kicked puppy is because of the fire?"

Whippet paused before answering. "Yes. I mean, I am sad things didn't work out with Cam. But who's going to be able to compete with you, right?" she tried to joke, but she couldn't quite manage a smile.

"Whippet—" Luna looked stricken.

"I'm kidding. Well, mostly. But don't *not* date him because of me."

"Okaaay, but it's going to be weird between us, don't you think?"

"Nope. Zero weirdness, I promise. Besides, I've got my hands full with Ed Aldridge."

Luna nodded. "Okay. Just let me know if I can help."

Whippet nodded and went back to work. Her shift ended an hour later, and she drove home. Instead of turning down the drive toward the B&B, she continued up the hill to Miss Lily's House. Moments later, she was rifling through her grandmother's desk in the library.

"What are you doing?" Tucker asked from the doorway.

Whippet swiped at a rogue tear. "The water from the sprinklers ruined several thousand dollars worth of inventory at Aldridge's. The damage is technically my fault because I had the electricity turned on upstairs, and I own the stupid building. I might be financially responsible unless, by some miracle, the insurance policy covers it. I called Hopper. He says he doesn't have the paperwork."

Tucker came into the room. "Check the bottom left drawer. Gran kept files on each of her properties in the back."

"Thanks."

Tucker helped her search the library until they found the policy. Whippet made the call to the insurance company, and they promised to send an adjuster out that day.

"You've got a deductible," Tucker said flipping through the policy. "A thousand dollars. Mom and I can cover that."

"Tucker, no."

"Stop. Let us help you," he said, sliding an arm around her. She leaned into him.

"I guess we'll know more soon," she said as she walked to the front door, Tucker close behind. Her phone pinged with a text. It was Ed Aldridge letting her know he was taking advantage of the force majeure clause that allowed him to break his contract due to "extenuating circumstances" neither one of them could have anticipated. He wanted her to leave him alone until he was out of the building. "Look at this." Whippet handed Tucker her phone.

He read the text and ran a hand down his face. "I'm sorry, Whippet. But it's going to be okay. You'll see. Have a little faith."

Whippet gave a short laugh. "How can I? Every time I pray, something worse happens!"

Tucker was silent for a moment. "How can we help? Do you want Emma to take Ev for the rest of the day?"

"No, she's hanging out with friends." Whippet opened the front door and Emma jumped up from the porch swing.

"Hey, Whippet!" Emma said a little too brightly. "I'm heading to Springfield today. Any interest in coming along? We could go to lunch."

"No thanks. The insurance company is sending an adjuster out later. I need to be here. See you guys." Whippet went down the front steps, and Tucker followed.

"What if *we* spent the day together?" he suggested. "I'd like to be there when the adjuster comes. Maybe we could hang out until then," he suggested.

"Hang out? Don't you have patients to see?"

"I can cancel some appointments. We don't get to spend much time together. Or if that doesn't work, maybe you and Mom could—"

Whippet tilted her head. "Tucker, what's going on?"

"I don't think you should be alone right now."

"Why?" she asked.

Tucker looked at her for a long moment. "I don't want you to do something you might regret."

Whippet frowned. "Tucker, you don't—" No, surely not. She closed her eyes and took a deep breath. "You don't think I'm going to go on a bender just because—"

"Because your boyfriend dumped you, your building caught on fire, and you lost your tenant? It's a lot, Whip. It would be a lot for anyone, let alone someone who's . . ."

"An alcoholic," she finished for him. This day just kept getting better and better. "I might be an alcoholic, Tucker," she said, "but I haven't had a drink since Everly was two years old."

She glanced up at her brother who, to his credit, looked miserable. "I'm sorry, Whip. I worry about you. You haven't had it easy."

She stopped when she got to her car. "I'll be fine. But I'm not stupid, Tucker. I'm not going to toss seven years of sobriety because I'm having a bad week." She paused. "Okay, it's been a really bad week. But have a little faith in me." She yanked the door open.

Tucker's shoulders relaxed. "I'm sorry. You're right."

Whippet gave him a terse nod. "I'm heading to the building after I grab some lunch. If you want to meet me later, you can."

"I'll be there," Tucker said.

Whippet nodded, got into her car, and drove home.

* * *

Whippet loved the quiet of night. The stillness. Sitting next to the window, this was the most peaceful she'd felt all day.

The adjuster had met her as promised. There was still paperwork to be done, but after the deductible, the insurance company would pick up the tab for the damage to both the apartment and the store. So in that way, she might come out ahead. Tucker had been there acting as a human shield between her and Ed Aldridge. Sensing the possibility of a big fat check, Ed had calmed down considerably.

She could tell her brother was still concerned. And maybe Tucker was right to worry. A drink would be mighty fine right about now. Sometimes she missed the way alcohol made her feel, all golden and relaxed. Her ever-present anxiety would slowly drain away the more she had to drink. But the word "sober" represented days of blood, sweat, and tears—literally. She wasn't going to risk it. In fact. . .

When she was sure Everly was asleep, Whippet crept into the closet and pulled out her suitcase. She slowly unzipped it and retrieved her bottle of Ketel One Vodka. She cradled it to her chest as she slipped quietly down the stairs, pushed her feet into a pair of sandals, and headed out the door.

She walked up the hill past Miss Lily's House, striding into the woods. The clouds and trees blocked what little light the night sky offered, so Whippet swung her cell phone flashlight from side to side.

The clouds parted and then she saw it. The lake. As she walked out onto the dock, the old boards creaked under her weight. She kicked off her sandals and sat crossed legged, listening to the water move, a slight breeze lifting the hair from her shoulders.

It was a perfect night. The sharp scent of the evergreens came to her from across the lake, the sound of water gently lapping against the dock almost hypnotic. She glanced down at the bottle. She'd had it for years. She'd bought it the week after she had taken her last drink, keeping it "just in case," but she'd never opened it. A fact that gave her great pride. But every time she moved, it came with her. Hiding under a pile of old books, concealed in a box of laundry detergent, jammed under the driver's seat. The bottle was her plan B.

But it had become obsolete, and it was time to start working toward a future without it. A future that included a home of her own and a place with her family. She closed her eyes and breathed deep. It was time to let it go. From now on she would rely on herself, try to trust God, and hope her family's imperfect love would see her through the coming days in a way that the bottle could never quite manage.

Whippet stood at the edge of the dock and closed her eyes. She bowed her head and whispered the serenity prayer. Maybe it was sacrilegious to pray over a bottle of vodka, but she thought God would understand in this particular circumstance. She clasped the bottle against her chest before bringing her arm back, ready to—

"What are you doing?"

Whippet shrieked. She teetered on one foot, arms waving wildly, and braced for a midnight swim when a pair of strong hands wrapped around her from behind and pulled her back against a warm, broad chest.

Sam Beaufort steadied her before letting go.

"I was watching you make your way through the wood," he said.

"Watching me? From where?"

"I'm not stalking you," he said, eyes narrowed. "I was on my back porch." He pointed up the hill and Whippet saw a small rectangle of light in the distance. "I saw your flashlight and thought it might be some teenagers looking for a place to party. Underage drinking is against the law, you know." Sam shoved his hands in his pockets. "I see I was wrong about the underage part." He nodded toward the bottle clutched to her chest.

"Oh," Whippet said, looking down. "No, that's . . . no." She knew what it looked like. Single mother sneaking out for a drink after her daughter drifts off to sleep. Years ago, that assumption would have been spot on. Now, it hurt. She walked to the edge of the dock and sat down again, still clutching the bottle. She heard Sam come up behind her and pause before he sat down too.

He was quiet for a minute. "I'm not judging you," he said, looking out over the lake. "You've got a lot going on. And it's a nice night to come out here and—"

"Okay," she interrupted, "you're totally judging me, and you're way off. I didn't come out here for a drink."

Sam looked at her. "My mistake."

His comment surprised her. Was he really taking her at her word?

They sat in silence for a moment, the night air settling around them warm and sweet.

"I'm an alcoholic," she blurted. She could have smacked herself the moment the words were out of her mouth. What was she doing taking this man into her confidence?

Sam nodded. He waited a beat before asking, "So what changed?"

Whippet cast a speculative glance his way. "What makes you think anything has?"

Sam gave her a look. "Please. You've made up 25 percent of my work week since you moved here. Not one of those calls was because you were drunk and disorderly."

Whippet bit down on a smile. She didn't know what to say. Whippet was pretty sure that as far as he was concerned, she'd already been labeled a screw up. But he was listening, and he seemed interested.

"There was an incident," she said.

Sam was silent, but he didn't look away. She glanced at him and then shifted her focus to the water.

"I started drinking in high school. At first, I did it to fit in. But then it became, I don't know, more. I couldn't live without it. Couldn't stop. *Wouldn't* stop. I kept drinking right up until I found out I was pregnant with Everly. I stayed sober until she was about six months old and then . . ." she glanced at him. "Well, my ex-husband's girlfriend called the house one night, and I answered." Whippet shrugged. "It kind of set me off."

Sam sat listening.

"Actually, it was one of the few things my ex and I had in common. We used to get drunk together." She didn't know why she was telling him this. Maybe she was trying to shock him. "It made it seem like it was okay to be drinking at home late at night after the baby was asleep." She swung her legs out over the edge of the dock. "After a while, I decided that I operated more effectively when I was just a little buzzed." She closed her eyes for a moment, remembering. "It didn't stay that way, though. I started drinking more. Then one day the police knocked on my door wondering why my two-year-old daughter was walking down the street in nothing but a soggy diaper. She'd woken up from a nap, and I was passed out on the floor." She looked down. "I must have left the screen door unlatched. She could have been hit by a car or taken." Whippet shuddered at the memory. "Child Protective Services showed up the next day. I was only able to keep Ev because my mother-in-law moved in for a while. I sobered up after that." Whippet took a deep breath. It was her worst memory, but she counted it a miracle because Everly had no recollection of that day.

"Wow," Sam said, looking out over the dark lake.

Whippet went quiet. Waiting.

"You're really brave."

Whippet gave an unladylike snort. "Oh, please."

Sam shook his head. "Making a change like that is very brave. Brave and probably hard."

She raised the bottle. "I've kept this around as a security blanket. But Ev is nine now, and I don't think I need it anymore. I came out here tonight to get rid of it."

Sam smiled. "I like it. Let's do this thing." He stood up, held out his hand, and pulled her to her feet. "Go for it," he encouraged.

Her grip tightened on the bottle for just a moment, then she brought her arm back. She heard Sam yell something before she threw the bottle with all her might. It landed with a plop a few yards from where they stood. Sam sidled up next to her and they watched the bottle bob along in its own wake. Whippet made a noise of frustration. "It was supposed to sink!"

"I thought you were going to empty it into the lake," Sam said. "A full bottle isn't going to sink. Something to do with density and buoyancy."

"Thanks for that, but there's a bottle of vodka floating in the lake behind my brother's house!"

"It's fine. Eventually the bottle will make its way to the bank—"

"Eventually? My mom has book club coming over here for brunch tomorrow. *Leaves of Grass* by Walt Whitman. Afterward, they're going on a nature walk! I'll never live this down if my mother sees that bottle!"

Sam scratched his head. "I could go get my gun," he suggested.

She gave him a look. "You're awfully fond of that thing, aren't you? I think I'll pass. Gunshot just might bring my brother running, and I certainly don't want him to witness my stupidity." She raised an eyebrow. "It's bad enough that you're here."

"Me?" Sam held up both hands. "I'm just trying to help."

"Well, you can't shoot the bottle," she repeated.

"What do you want to do then?" he asked.

She looked around. "Do you see a stick or something?"

Sam hopped off the edge of the dock. He handed her a long branch a moment later. "Try this," he said and climbed back up.

She leaned over the water, extending the branch as far as it would go. It barely touched the floating bottle.

"Here, let me try. My arms are longer," Sam offered.

After a few tries, he had the bottle within arm's length. He reached out and pulled it out of the water, shaking it off before breaking the seal and handing it to her. "You do the honors," he said.

Whippet twisted the lid and upended the bottle over the lake, pouring out every last drop. Then smiling, she leaned over and pushed it into the lake, waiting for it to fill with water before she let it go. She watched it sink. "Bye," she whispered.

"Well," Sam said, a smile hitching to one side, "the lake is now eighty proof, but other than that, well done, Daphne."

She stood up and dusted off her hands. "Thanks," she said quietly. Sam nodded, and they started down the dock. The enormity of what she'd told him caught up with her. Before Sam got too far, Whippet put a hand on his arm.

"Hey," she said. "Um, nobody here knows my history. My family does, of course. I mean, I can't believe I told you, but I'd really appreciate it if you wouldn't—"

"Daphne," Sam said, taking her hand. "You don't even have to say it."

She paused. Sam's eyes were kind, understanding even. It was a little unexpected given their history, but somehow she knew she had nothing to worry about. "Thanks," she whispered, slipping her hand from the warm heat of his.

"Well, goodnight." She nodded and stepped off the dock, heading back in the direction of Miss Lily's House. She was at the edge of the woods when she realized he was following her.

"What are you doing?"

"Walking you home," he said, catching up to her.

"Why?"

"Because the job description says, 'protect and serve,' not 'listen, then abandon.' It's after midnight."

"You don't need to do that," she said and started walking again. "You're all the way up the hill that way, and I'm in the opposite direction. I'll be fine."

Sam kept stride beside her. "You sure about that? How could I live with myself if you were attacked by a rabid coyote or fell into a deep, deep hole, or—"

She stopped. "A hole?"

"Daphne, if there's a hole in these woods, you'll be the one to find it."

She gave a short laugh. "That's fair. Fine. Walk with me, but when we can see the house, you head home. If my mom sees the two of us coming from the—"

"You worry about your mom an awful lot."

Whippet sighed. "Yes, I do."

"Loosen up. Give people a chance," he said, and she wondered if he was talking about her mother or him.

They walked the rest of the way in silence. Whippet stole glances at him as they trudged along. Sam didn't seem to mind their nighttime walk. He kept pace with her, hands in his pockets, a half-smile on his face. And despite what she'd said, Sam delivered her right to the front door.

"Well, thank you," Whippet said turning and extending her hand.

Sam looked amused as he took it. He gave it a gentle squeeze then stepped a little closer. "Not a problem, Daphne," he said, his voice so low and warm, she felt it everywhere.

Whippet looked at him, suddenly grateful for the cover of night. It hid the blush burning its way up her neck.

She took a step back, muttered a quick goodnight, and rushed inside.

# CHAPTER TWENTY-ONE

A week later, Sam Beaufort nodded to Early Jackson as he left the courthouse. He glanced at the diner as he headed back to the police station. He'd been avoiding Meacham's lately. Childish? Yes. But he was giving Whippet Moran a wide berth, mostly out of a sense of self-preservation. He still felt a little off after their conversation on the dock.

Coming across her at the lake that night, all uncertain and—he hated to think it—vulnerable, had been a punch in the gut. He was used to her coming at him, eyes flashing. Everything about her a challenge. Finding out that all her bravado was just a tough-girl cover had upset the equilibrium in his life somehow.

Sam heard a shout of laughter. Luna's son, Max, and Everly were giggling and chasing each other outside the diner. It was a pretty fair assumption, then, that their mothers were inside. That was fine. He'd wait for a break and head home for lunch.

Sam went into the station, slowing as he passed Didi's desk. His assistant was staring him down.

"What?" he asked.

"There's a call holding on line two for you," she said, arching an eyebrow.

He went into his office but paused before picking up the handset. Maybe it was Sharon O'Neil. He mentally braced himself before punching the flashing light. "Officer Beaufort here," he said.

"Well, hello there, stranger." He froze at the sound of Emory's voice. "About time you picked up. I thought I was going to be on hold through the next lunar cycle. How are you?"

Sam sat down and ran a hand over his face. "Emory," he acknowledged. "How did you get this number?"

"No beating around the bush with you, is there?"

"Always the best tactic where you're concerned," he said.

"Tactic? You make it sound like we're at war," she said teasingly.

"What do you want, Emory?"

"Do I have to 'want' something to call?"

"In my experience, yes."

She was quiet for a moment. "I'll be out there next month. I have a client. In Branson. I thought we could—"

"No," Sam interrupted.

"—catch up. It's been a while."

"Has it?"

Emory glossed right over that. "You haven't returned any of my texts. I was concerned." She paused. "I heard about the fire. I wanted to make sure you were okay."

"I'm fine," he said. He kept his face blank and his tone neutral because Didi Bradley had magically appeared in the doorway.

"I ran into your sister at Bloomingdale's, did she tell you? She said you were remodeling your uncle's place out there. I could help. You know I have a knack for that type of thing." Yes, he did know. With her eye for design, they'd tripled their investment in their townhome by the time they split.

"Not necessary. I'm sure you're busy, and I've got to run. You take care now." He hung up and turned to Didi. "Can I help you?"

"She said she was your wife," Didi said. "Is she your wife? You've never mentioned a wife before."

He held up a hand. "Let me stop you right there before your imagination goes into overdrive, and I find myself with a month's worth of gossip to undo. Emory St. James is my *ex*-wife. We've been divorced for almost three years, so I'll thank you for keeping this information to yourself." He shot her a pointed look. "Please and thank you."

"Fine," Didi said, straightening. "Whit is out on patrol and Erica called in sick. Can you listen for the phones while I take my lunch break?" she asked, and he nodded.

Sam swung around in his chair and looked out the window. He was feeling on edge.

Emory St. James was a force of nature. Like a tidal wave or tsunami. Something destructive. She was beautiful, and he'd been hooked from day one. After their wedding, he'd walked around, strutting like a peacock, smug that she had chosen him.

He'd been a misguided twit.

A year and a half into their marriage, Emory had come home, out of breath and frantic. She'd found a place for them. A stand-alone townhouse in Bucktown. Emory was ambitious. She wanted to start a blog, maybe even a YouTube channel, and chronicle their journey turning the fixer-upper into a home. She'd finally be able to use her interior design degree.

He hadn't known it at the time, but it was the beginning of the end.

Emory began spending money they didn't have, turning the townhouse into a showplace. She'd posted idealized photos of the renovation, tripling her followers. Emory didn't just buy things for their home. She'd started filling her wardrobe with designer labels, insisting her followers had certain expectations about her appearance, and arguments had broken out almost daily.

The exposure on social media paid off. Within a year, she had more clients than she could handle, which meant she wasn't home much. When the two of them did manage to have a rare night alone together, she'd seemed restless.

Then one day Sam had been rummaging through the desk, trying to find a pen. Instead, he came across a receipt for a security deposit at a Gold Coast apartment complex. The tenant listed on the form was Emory St. James.

When she got home that night, Sam hadn't seen the point in stalling. "Are you leaving me?" he'd asked. Emory threw her purse onto the Louis XV armchair that had cost an entire month's salary and faced him. "Our marriage isn't what I thought it would be," she'd said.

*Me, either.* Sam had thought. But he'd been ready to call a marriage counselor, not file for divorce. It turned out that what he wanted didn't factor into the equation.

Emory got the house. Sam moved in with his parents. For months he walked around in a daze, feeling like he'd been sideswiped.

And now she wanted to get together for lunch like two old friends. Yeah, no.

A burst of noise came from Didi's desk. It sounded like Whit was back from patrol. Sam turned around, picked up a pen, and tapped it against his desk.

If he never saw Emory again that would be just fine. That chapter of his life was closed. Next time, he thought, he'd pick the right girl. Someone who wanted the same things he did: a home, a family, a quiet life. Someone who'd stick.

The next time, he'd go slow.

\* \* \*

It was a Hail Mary play for sure. But if there was one thing Whippet was an expert at, it was last minute desperation. And she was desperate.

Whippet watched Ed Aldridge and one of his employees load the truck parked in front of his store. Her spirits fell as one after the other, stacks of boxes disappeared inside. She breathed deep. It was now or never.

Ed's employee dashed back into the store, leaving him alone on the sidewalk glancing over some paperwork. It looked like luck was on her side for once.

"Hey, Ed," she said, pasting on her friendliest smile.

He looked at her warily. "I thought we agreed you'd leave me alone until I was out."

Whippet glanced through the empty display windows into the store and swallowed. There were still racks of merchandise on the floor. He'd be here for hours.

"I, uh, wanted to give you these," she said, pulling a box from her bag. He eyed the offering suspiciously.

"What's that?" he asked.

She opened the box to show him. "My specialty. Chocolate chip shortbread cookies."

"I'm low-carb," he said and started to move.

"Of course you are," she muttered. "Listen, Ed. You don't have to relocate. The repairs will be done soon and—"

"Look," he said, cutting her off. "I'm sure you mean well, but repairs take time, and summer is my busiest season."

"But your new store isn't on Main Street. You get more traffic coming by this location."

"I'll be fine," he said and turned away.

"Wait! Uh, what if I offered you some kind of incentive?" she blurted.

That gave him pause. "What kind of incentive?" he asked.

And this was where she choked. What could she offer? She took too long to answer, and Ed waved her away. "Face it. You're in over your head." He turned his back on her and strode into the store.

Whippet closed the box of cookies, stuffed them in her bag, and began walking to the diner. She'd be early for her shift, but she'd been late enough in the past that she figured she owed Luna. It wasn't even noon yet, but the stress of everything combined with the heat of the day made her polyester uniform chafe under her arms and stick to her legs.

Whippet tried to breathe past the knot in her chest. What if she couldn't find a new tenant? She'd be responsible for the taxes and insurance. She couldn't afford that, not with what she made as a waitress.

Luna was busy with a customer when Whippet walked through the door. She smiled at Chuck, who waved her off with a spatula as she pushed through the swinging door. She set down her bag and put on her apron before starting back out into the dining room. As she was about to push back through the swinging door, she made a last-minute decision, turned, and retrieved the box of cookies.

"Here," she said, sliding the box across the counter to Luna. "These are for you."

Luna opened it, her eyes brightening when she saw what was inside. She took a bite and closed her eyes. "Oh my gosh, these are so good. You're quite the little baker."

Whippet shrugged. "I bake when I'm stressed," she said, going to refill the coffeepot. "Or when I'm sad, or angry, or happy. Instead of eating my emotions, I guess I bake them."

"I'm so glad you do," Luna said reverently.

Whippet grabbed an order pad from behind the counter and greeted a family that had just seated themselves in the booth by the window. She took their order and went to the window to pass it to Chuck. Luna was still leaning against the counter, box of cookies in hand, her expression thoughtful.

"You okay?" Whippet asked, scooting around her.

"I'm fine." Luna looked at Whippet, slowly pulling a business card from her apron. She sighed before handing it to Whippet. "Here," she said.

"What's this?"

"Some lady came in yesterday. She saw your cakes and ordered a slice of each. She asked me to give that to you. She wants to know if she can order cakes for her restaurant in Branson."

"Seriously?" Whippet's mood brightened.

"Yes. But don't go getting any big ideas." Luna jabbed a finger in her direction. "I'm your first priority, right? Your cakes draw customers."

"Of course," Whippet responded.

"Okay." Luna relaxed. "Hey, will you take his order?" she asked, nodding toward the register before going into the kitchen.

Whippet turned and her face flushed. It was Sam Beaufort. She hadn't seen him since their lake-side chat. She wasn't sure if he'd been avoiding her, or it was just good luck, but she was grateful either way. The way she'd blabbed on and on and on that night made her feel humiliated now.

She bit her lip. "Um, did you want to place an order, Chief?"

He stood there for a moment. He really was cute with his hair rumpled. And his eyes were so blue.

"Hi," he said. He looked uncomfortable. "Ed Aldridge said you've been around today. He wants you to steer clear until he's out. Didn't you guys come to some kind of an agreement?"

Great. "We did. And as you can plainly see, I'm at work."

"He said you were at the store this morning." He paused. "Did you try to bribe him?"

"I offered him a box of cookies, not a stack of hundred-dollar bills!" She threw her hands in the air. Sam said nothing, and Whippet shook her head. "I asked him if he was absolutely sure he wanted to break his lease," she said more calmly.

Sam looked at her for a long minute. "You're sure that's all?"

"I'm positive."

Sam scratched his head. "Will you promise to leave him alone until he's out, please?"

Whippet took a deep breath and started to turn around, but he caught her arm. "Do you promise?" he repeated.

She glanced down to where his hand had hold of her and looked back up at him. He dropped his hand and took a step back. Pity.

"You haven't answered my question," he said.

"I know. I don't want to."

"Daphne—"

Whippet raised her right arm and made the Boy Scout sign—or at least what she thought was the Boy Scout sign. She couldn't remember if it was two fingers or three. "I, Whippet Moran, solemnly swear that I will steer clear of Ed Aldridge until he's out of my building."

Sam gave her a wry look. "Thank you." He headed for the door, but only took a couple of steps before turning around. "I'm sorry about this. Ed can be kind of difficult. Maybe having him gone will be a good thing." A hint of a smile showed on the police chief's face, and Whippet felt an unwilling tug of attraction.

What was wrong with her?

"Maybe," she said turning away. She didn't want him to see her blush.

# CHAPTER TWENTY-TWO

"I wouldn't recommend it," Tucker said, expression serious.

Whippet sat in a chair next to his desk. "But I can't afford insurance on the building without a tenant."

Tucker shook his head. "Letting the insurance lapse would be a mistake," he explained. "Especially after filing such a large claim. If there's another fire, or a broken pipe, or whatever, you'd be liable for the damage to your building and possibly your neighbor. Insurance is there to protect you. The monthly premium isn't that much, is it?"

"Well, it is when you don't make enough to cover it," Whippet said.

"You should have some money in the account Gran set up. Are you still doing the apartment?" he asked.

Whippet hesitated. "I'd like to. Why?"

"There's probably enough money in that account to cover the premium for a couple of months. That'll buy you some time."

"I hope so," Whippet said.

"You need to advertise." He looked at her. "Don't panic yet. Just try to get a tenant in there by the end of the summer."

"Yeah," she said. She surprised herself by managing to keep her voice calm. But inside, it was too late. She was already panicking. Catastrophizing had become her latest hobby.

Barb stuck her head around the door. "You've got patients lining up, Dr. Madsen."

"Okay. Be right there." He turned to Whippet. "Have you thought any more about filing a complaint? Time is ticking."

Whippet exhaled dramatically. Every time Tucker brought this up, she was reminded of that horrible moment when she'd been trapped in the storeroom with her old boss. It plucked at her already raw nerves. "I know that. And when I file, I'll tell you. But it's my business, Tucker."

"Whip, I—"

She put a hand on his arm. "My business," she repeated.

His eyes went all squinty as he studied her. "Look," he said, and Whippet made a noise of irritation. "Just listen! I think I have an idea. Can you come up to the house tonight?"

"Tucker—" she whined.

"I think you'll like what I have to say."

She looked at him for a moment. "Fine."

Whippet stood up and followed Tucker to the door. He paused before leaving his office. "Everything okay with you and Luna?" he asked.

"Yeah. Why wouldn't it be?"

"She's dating your ex-boyfriend."

Her head tilted. "How do you know that?"

"Everyone knows that. The question is, are you okay with it?"

"I'm fine."

"Fine? It must not have been love if you're 'fine'."

Whippet shrugged. "Probably not. He feels guilty though, which is why he's still working on the apartment. He's putting up drywall this week." Whippet walked out the door.

Tucker nodded. "Disaster averted there at least."

"For the moment, I suppose," she said and started down the hall.

*　*　*

He liked her. No doubt about it. Sam liked Whippet Moran. As in attracted to and a little bit hooked on the sassy waitress at Meacham's Diner. He found himself thinking about her at odd times. It was distracting.

Last night while he'd been sitting in the speed trap north of town, his mind wandered to how he'd found her that night on the dock, her arm raised over her head, ready to toss that blasted bottle into the lake before he'd come along and startled her. He still remembered what it felt like to pull her back against him, her soft hair brushing against his chin. Her hair had smelled like something citrusy. Oranges, maybe?

Sam had lifted his self-inflicted embargo on the diner. He'd eaten here almost every day for the past week. If it happened to be during Whippet's shift, so much the better. Although today it seemed that each time he moved into her orbit, she skittered away. She'd been behind the counter when he walked in. Now she was on the other side of the diner clearing a table.

Before he knew what he was doing, he left the line and headed straight toward her. She turned and seemed a little startled at seeing him standing there. That made two of them.

She shook her head. "Whatever it is, I didn't do it."

"Would you like to go out sometime?" The words left his mouth before he knew what he was saying. Maybe that was best. He was pretty sure that if he thought too long about it, he might question whether he wanted to get entangled with Whippet Moran and all her complications. Whippet's mouth hung open, and she glanced around the diner self-consciously.

"You want to go out with *me*?" she whispered. He didn't answer, just kept up the steady stare. It must have worked because a moment later she said, "Sure."

He nodded. "Friday night? I'll pick you up around seven."

"I—okay," she said, sounding a bit stunned.

Not nearly as stunned as he was. Sam made a hasty retreat, forgetting all about his lunch order.

\*\*\*

The Madsen family gathered around the dinner table at Miss Lily's House, joking and laughing and completely oblivious to the thoughts somersaulting in Whippet's head. Her mind was on the mysterious happenings at the diner this afternoon. Officer Beaufort had asked her out. Weird.

Aesthetically, the chief of police was very nice to look at. He wasn't an idiot, and even though she'd done her best to irritate him during past interactions, he'd always been polite. She used to think it was due to an overblown sense of professional courtesy; now she wasn't so sure. Maybe Sam Beaufort was a good guy.

Tucker went into the kitchen to help their mother with the dishes and Emma excused herself. There was an event at The Barn tonight, and she was short staffed.

"Let's play a game, Mom," Everly said. "Look at this!" Everly laid a dusty old box on the table. She took a deep breath and blew a cloud of dust into the air.

Whippet coughed and waved her hand. "Where did you find that?"

"Up in the cupola—you know, that secret room you showed me?"

"It's my old Scrabble game. I used to play this with your great-grandma." Whippet hugged Everly. "She beat me every time," she said with a laugh.

"Can you show me how to play?" Everly asked.

Fifteen minutes later, it was clear that her daughter had inherited Miss Lily's prowess with words. "Look Mom!" Everly pumped a fist. "Quack! And the "Q" is on a triple-word score."

"Whippet!" Tucker's voice boomed from the kitchen. "Come in here for a second, will ya?"

Right. Tucker's "idea." She pushed away from the table. "I'll be back." She pointed to the tiles on the table. "Don't cheat while I'm gone." She gave Everly a wink.

Whippet breezed into the kitchen. Tucker was seated at the table, tapping away on his phone. "Hey, can we make this quick? Ev and I are in the middle of a killer game of Scrabble."

"There's no such thing," Tucker said, kicking out the chair next to him.

"Great dinner tonight, Mom." Her mother stood at the sink loading the top rack of the dishwasher. Whippet looked at Tucker. "What's up?"

"Your brother has a great idea," her mom said.

"So he keeps telling me," Whippet said, taking a seat.

"I think I've come up with a solution to your problem," Tucker said, still texting.

"Which one?" she asked, picking an apple from the bowl on the table.

He finally looked up. "The empty building on Main Street."

"You mean besides burning it to the ground for the insurance money?"

"Whippet!" her mother chided.

"Haha. No," Tucker said, not smiling. "But I was thinking, maybe you should be your own tenant."

Her brows came together. "What, you mean like charge myself rent when the apartment is finished?" She took a bite out of the apple.

"No, I mean finish the downstairs, too, and use your talents to make a living."

"What talents?" Whippet frowned.

Tucker sighed. "I'm going to have to spell it out for you, aren't I?"

"That would be very helpful, Tucker." She nodded. "Mind reading is not in my skill set."

Tucker ignored her. "You're talented, Whip. Really talented. Nobody bakes the way you do. Nobody does 'cute' the way you do. Combine those two abilities and I think you could open a bakery."

Whippet sat back. "A bakery?"

"Yes. There isn't a bakery in town. You happen to own a beautiful building on Main Street. Outright. No mortgage. That's a huge advantage when opening your own business."

"My own business?" She seemed to have turned into a parrot. "It sounds like a recipe for disaster if you ask me. Pun intended." She gave an uneasy laugh.

"I think it's a wonderful idea," her mother said, taking a seat across from her. "You can do this, Whippet. You're so much smarter than you give yourself credit." Her mother patted her hand. "The Patriot Festival is coming up. You could rent a booth and sell some of your baked goods as a way of introducing yourself to the community. Show them what you can do."

Whippet's head was spinning. "But I-I don't have any idea how to run a business. Do you want me to go back to school? Is that what this is about? Because that takes money and—"

"That's not what I'm saying at all." Her mother looked at Tucker and he nodded. "I have some money saved," her mom continued. "I'd like to co-sign on a loan so you can remodel the downstairs, update it, and put in a kitchen. I'd be your partner." Her mother put up her hand before Whippet could say a word. "Silent partner."

This was all a bit dizzying. It would be heavenly. She'd be doing something she truly enjoyed. And once the apartment was finished, the commute would be a dream. She pulled out the business card Luna had given her earlier and slid it across the table.

"What's this?" Sophie asked, taking it.

"Luna gave it to me. That woman wants me to call her. She'd like to offer my cakes at her restaurant in Branson." Her mother shot Whippet an I-told-you-so look.

At that moment, Whippet remembered what Edith Kane had said to her all those weeks ago in the church. If God had unlocked the potential inside Edith's husband when he created the church's stained glass windows, might it be possible that that was what was happening here? She shrugged off the thought. Stained glass and cake were hardly comparable.

Whippet shook her head. "You *really* think I could do this?"

"Yes," her mother and Tucker replied in unison.

Whippet frowned. "I have no education, no business background. And it just feels too late. Like I should have had this figured out years ago."

"You're hardly at death's door." Tucker looked exasperated.

"I'll be thirty in two years!"

Her mother brought a hand to her heart. "Oh! The horror! And I'm starting to date again at fifty-eight. If I can figure out online dating, then you can run a bakery."

"You're starting to date?" Whippet asked.

"Not the point, Whippet." Her mom looked at her for a moment before getting up. "Convince her, Tucker," she said. "I'll go find Everly." She left the kitchen.

Whippet turned to look at her brother. "If I don't do this, she'll be disappointed in me."

"No, she won't."

"Easy for you to say, *Dr.* Madsen," she said pointedly.

"Please. Want me to name all the ways I've disappointed Mom?"

"Yes. I would like that very much," Whippet said.

Tucker turned his chair to face her. "Fine. I kind of ignored you guys during medical school. I was offered a residency close to home but chose to leave Missouri instead. Then I took a job halfway across the country and saw Mom maybe once a year."

"That was really selfish." Whippet nodded, enjoying the moment. "Why'd you do that?"

Tucker growled and brought his knuckles to her head for the world's longest noogie. She tried to wriggle away, but his arm held fast around her. "I'm sorry, Whip," he said, his voice so serious she looked up. "I should have done more for you."

She swallowed. "I don't think there's anything you could have done. You may not have noticed this," she wrinkled her nose at him, "but I tend to learn things the hard way."

"It'd be a great habit to break."

"Maybe," she whispered.

"Let us help you."

She'd never heard lovelier words in her life. "Thanks," she managed and turned to hug him. "Okay," she said, pushing away. "That's enough affection for one day." She looked at the kitchen door and shouted, "Did you hear that, Mom?"

"I did," came a voice from the other room. "It's about time!"

# CHAPTER TWENTY-THREE

"Where are we going?" Whippet asked.

Sam looked across the cab of his truck at her. "That's the third time you've asked me," he said. "Can't it just be a surprise?"

"I hate surprises," she muttered.

"Why?" Sam asked as he pulled out onto the road.

Whippet could tell him, she knew she could, but this one kinda wanted to stay locked inside. In her experience, surprises were linked to catastrophe. *Surprise! Your father's dead. Surprise! Your husband is leaving you for a nineteen-year-old. Surprise! You're fired.*

"Whippet?"

"It's just a personal preference," she said.

"Right." Sam was quiet for a moment, but he dropped it. "There's a restaurant in Branson I'd like to try if you're game?"

"Sure," she said. He turned onto the highway and headed south.

Everly was at Luna's tonight. Everly and Max were starting their *Harry Potter* film fest in Luna's backyard on a movie screen made out of a bedsheet. It meant Whippet was free for the night.

"I heard Ed Aldridge is out of your building," Sam said.

Whippet sighed. "Yes, he is."

He glanced at her. "Aren't you relieved?"

"I guess 'relieved' is one word for it. I'd feel better if I had a tenant moving in."

"Something will work out," he said.

Sam's cell phone rang. "Sorry," he said a little sheepishly, "It's a hazard of the job." Whippet nodded her understanding as he answered his phone. "Yeah," he said a little tersely. Whippet looked out the window. Rich, green farmland stretched out on either side of the winding road. "Whit is on call tonight," Sam said. A pause. "Seriously?" Sam hit the blinker and pulled over. "Yeah, yeah. I'll be there in ten minutes. Stay away from him if he's armed." Armed? How exciting. Whippet's interest was piqued. "He did? Well, that's something anyway. See you in a minute." Sam hung up and sat staring straight ahead for a moment. "I have to go back. Officer Allen needs backup. There's been an incident up at the Mathers place."

Whippet shrugged. "Okay."

He looked at her for a moment before saying, "It might take a while. The neighbors called in. Evidently Clay Mathers is drunk and causing problems."

"Okay," she repeated.

Sam hung one arm over the steering wheel. "Do you want me to take you home? We could try this another night. Sometime when—"

"No."

Sam raised an eyebrow. "No?"

Whippet nodded. "I'll go with you. It'll be interesting. I've never gone on a ride-along before." She smiled and inclined her head. "It might be nice, seeing you do something other than pull over unsuspecting single mothers for vague traffic offenses."

"Vague traffic offense? You were speeding. Then there was the time you—"

"I know. I'm a criminal. Hey, we should probably get going," Whippet said.

Sam chuckled and looked out the window. "Whatever the lady wants." He made a U-turn and headed back to Normal.

They rode in silence, and Whippet found that it was kind of nice being inside the big, rumbling truck with Sam. It was clear he was well-liked. She could tell by the way folks waved at him as they passed by. Not wanting to stir the gossip pot, Whippet slid lower in her seat.

Sam turned down a road Whippet didn't recognize. The homes sat on bigger lots out here. Forests of trees broken up by wide-open spaces. It was pretty. Sam pulled onto a gravel road and slowed down. They passed a mailbox, bent and leaning to one side. A little farther up the road there was a break in the trees, and they pulled up next to a little ranch house with a wide yard.

"What the—" Sam muttered. Whippet rolled down her window to get a better look, not exactly sure what to make of the scene unfolding before them.

Clay Mathers stumbled around the yard trying to evade Officer Erica Allen. Obviously drunk, he wore only unlaced hiking boots and a pair of American Flag swim trunks. Whippet felt for Erica. Clay was definitely not taking it easy on her. Whippet winced when he broadsided a tree and fell to the ground. Erica pounced on him, trying to finagle a pair of handcuffs onto his wrists. She got one on, but before she could fasten the second, he wriggled away and tried to climb the tree.

"Oh, he shouldn't do that," Whippet said absently. "That's a thorny locust tree."

Sam cut her a look then got out of the truck. "Officer Allen, what—"

"I've almost got him, Chief!" the beleaguered officer cried.

It did not seem that way to Whippet.

Whippet watched Clay Mathers fall to the ground, somehow still managing to evade both police officers. As he made a run for the front steps, he inexplicably fell backward. He got up, hurrying around to the other side of the porch, and scrambled over the railing into the backyard.

"His wife is out of town," Whippet heard Erica explain as they followed him.

"Terrific," Sam said.

Whippet leaned against the head rest. This really was a beautiful spot. The house was small but cute. The trees surrounding the property gave it a cozy, secluded feeling.

There was a rustling noise outside Whippet's window. She turned to see Clay stagger out of the trees. He tried to clear the low split-rail fence, but his foot slipped. He tried again, leaning a little too far forward this time. He barreled over and landed with a thud. Whippet scrambled out of the truck.

"Mr. Mathers," she said, coming to stand over him. "Are you okay?" She nudged him with her toe. He didn't respond. Instead, he turned onto his side and got comfortable on a bed of pine needles. Whippet reached down and brought one wrist next to the other and fastened the handcuffs. Clay mumbled something unintelligible and then started to snore.

"Sam!" Whippet called. "He's over here."

Sam and Erica rounded the corner.

"Did you cuff him?" Sam asked incredulously.

Whippet beamed. "Cool, right?"

Ten minutes later, Clay was in the back of Officer Allen's squad car. She apologized profusely for interrupting their evening before pulling away, taking Clay to the station.

Sam helped Whippet into his truck before crossing to the driver's side and getting in. It was quiet in the cab as he sat there, staring straight ahead. "I'm sorry," he said. "This is not how I saw the night going."

"I had a good time," Whippet replied honestly.

Sam looked up sharply. "What?"

She shrugged. "It was kind of fun."

"Fun," Sam repeated. He shook his head then looked at the clock on the dashboard. "Our reservation was for thirty minutes ago."

"Just out of curiosity, where were you going to take me?"

Sam scrubbed a hand through his hair. "The Château Grille in Branson. The restaurant is supposed to have great views of Table Rock Lake."

"Ah. Well, maybe some other time."

Sam nodded and started his truck. As they pulled back onto the main road he said, "I have an idea. Do you mind if we improvise for the rest of the night?"

"Okay," she said, glad the evening wasn't over yet.

Sam picked up takeout at the diner, and a few minutes later they pulled up in front of his house.

"A bit soon to be bringing me back to your place, isn't it?" she asked, raising an eyebrow at him.

"Hush, you," he said, putting the truck in park.

He showed her inside, and she was a little giddy as she walked through the house. She peeked into the wretched dining room she'd seen before. It was still a work in progress, but the kitchen looked like it was almost done.

"This is really nice," she said as she walked through a cased opening. "Did there used to be a wall here?"

"Yeah. Someday when I get furniture, this will be the family room."

Right now, it kind of had a frat-boy vibe with a futon facing a battered TV stand, a gaming console, and a flat-screen TV mounted to the wall. All the single-guy necessities.

Sam inclined his head, and Whippet followed him outside through a pair of French doors.

"Oh, wow," she said. They went down a few steps onto a patio surrounded by a low stone wall. Two Adirondack chairs sat facing the woods. Whippet took a seat, propping her feet on a brick firepit as Sam headed back into the house to grab their drinks.

Night began to settle in around her. The sun dipped low, and the air turned cooler. Fireflies flickered at the edge of the wood. Sam wasn't kidding when he said he could see Miss Lily's House from here. She could just make out the top floor. It looked like the light was on in Gran's room. Well, Tucker and Emma's room now.

Something nudged her knee and Whippet looked down. A black dog looked up at her, tongue lolling. Whippet let the animal sniff her hand before running it over its bony head. "Hey, pretty dog."

"You're insulting his manhood," Sam said from behind her.

"He's still pretty. Aren't you?" she crooned to the animal who planted himself beside her.

"Here you go." He slid a cold bottle of Pepsi into her hand and laid their takeout on the table between the chairs. "It was taco night at the diner. Hope that's okay."

"It's perfect," she said. She quickly discovered that tacos did not make great date food. She tried to eat carefully, but it was hard to look elegant with lettuce and tomatoes falling back into the container with each bite. They ate, serenaded by a choir of crickets as they watched the sun sink lower in the sky.

"This view is phenomenal," she said, setting her empty food container under her chair. Sam's dog gave it an investigatory sniff before lying down at her feet.

"Yes, it is," he replied.

"So you're fixing the place up. Are you planning to stay here, or are you going to sell it?"

"I like it here, and the house has been in the family for almost a hundred years." He shrugged and was quiet.

Whippet nodded. The patio faced southwest, and they were treated to a spectacular sunset, impressionistic streaks of pink and orange reaching in gauzy bands across the horizon.

"So," she said, brushing off her skirt. "What's your story?"

She'd caught him mid-bite. He paused, putting down the taco and setting his container on the table. "What have you heard?" he asked.

"Well, if I were to roll all the gossip I've heard about you together, you'd be a tragic widower superhero bank robber."

"Bank robber?"

She shrugged. "I made up that part to make you seem more interesting."

"I see." He brushed his hands together and settled back in his chair. "Well, I'm not a widower." He glanced out over the valley. "Divorced."

"Get out of town," she said. "You mean we have more in common than the fact that I like to break the law and you like to arrest me?"

"I have never arrested you."

"But you wanted to."

He raised an eyebrow. "No comment."

"So the ex. What's she like?"

Sam didn't respond right away. "Emory was a lot."

"Emory," she said. "That's quite a name. She sounds expensive."

Sam glanced over. "You're not wrong. Emory is an influencer. She decorates homes and posts stuff about her projects. Our house in Chicago was how she got her start."

"Your ex-wife is Emory St. James?!" she exclaimed.

Sam gave her a cool look, and she felt instantly contrite.

"Sorry, I promise to unfollow her as soon as I get home," Whippet said. "So what happened?"

Sam shrugged. "I don't know. She wanted . . . more."

"More what?"

He pointed his drink at her. "That is the question. More followers, more travel, more money. Just more. Evidently, I couldn't give it to her. After a while, I stopped trying. End of story."

"It's a short story."

Sam's smile tipped sideways. "I didn't ask you up here to spend the evening talking about my ex."

"I can appreciate that. What do you want to talk about?"

They fell into easy conversation. Sam told her about his family—a sister and his parents—all still in the Chicago area. He talked a little about what brought him out here, the disaster he'd inherited from his uncle, and what a cheap old goat his uncle had been. "He kept everything. Boxes of old magazines. Newspapers. Drawers and drawers of socks. He had a box labeled 'correspondence.' I almost chucked it. At the last second, I decided to look through it. Good thing I did. He had envelopes stuffed full of fifties stashed in there."

She told him about her life in Texas, her many jobs, and the unexpected inheritance from her grandmother. She looked out over the valley. "Everly and I have moved a lot," she said. "A couple of times in the last year. Sometimes I worry it's been too much for her."

"She's a great kid," Sam said. "Proof enough that you're doing a good job, don't you think?"

Whippet blushed. "Thank you."

Sam cleared his throat. "So are you staying in Normal?"

"I don't know. I'd like to." Sam's dog put his head on her knee, and she scratched him behind the ears. "My family has this crazy idea that I should open a bakery," she confided.

"That's a great idea," Sam said.

"Really?"

"Absolutely. I'm there every Thursday morning when Luna puts out the triple chocolate cake. Last week, Lester Barton was in line ahead of me and got the last piece."

Whippet flushed at the compliment.

Stars started to appear as little pinpricks of light in the indigo sky. Whippet relaxed into her chair, enjoying the company and the quiet. She was so comfortable she would have liked to stay here forever.

Just then her phone buzzed with a text. "Oh, it's Luna," she said, looking at Sam. "She's bringing Everly back in about ten minutes. I need to get home."

Sam gave her a ride down the hill. When they turned onto the gravel drive that led to the B&B, she put a hand on his arm. "Drop me off here," she said unclicking her seat belt.

"I can walk you to the door."

"No! I . . . here's fine," Whippet said.

It was the wrong thing to say. Storm clouds gathered in Officer Beaufort's blue eyes. "You trying to hide the fact that you were out with me tonight?"

"No. It's not that."

"What is it then?"

Whippet bit her lip. "Look, you're Normal's most eligible bachelor, and I'm the screwy waitress who yelled at the chief of police her first week at work." She shrugged. "People talk."

He looked at her a long minute. "You don't see yourself very clearly, do you?"

She smiled. "You sound like my brother."

Sam nodded, "Smart man. You should listen to him, or me. I wouldn't be here if you weren't worth my time, Daphne."

A glowing warmth spread through her, and a smile crept across her face. Not trusting herself to speak, she impulsively planted a kiss on Sam's cheek. Before she could think too much about what she'd done, she hurried out of the truck and up the drive to the B&B.

# CHAPTER TWENTY-FOUR

Sam liked Whippet Moran and all her sharp edges. He'd thought about that little kiss she'd given him all week. How he'd fought the urge to grab her and turn it into something more.

Not many women of his acquaintance would say, "I had a good time," after having their date interrupted for a ride-along that involved wrangling the town drunk into the back of a police car. But then, she was the one who'd finally gotten him into handcuffs. The thought had him grinning. And they had another date tonight.

"You just got back from a meeting with the planning commission," Didi said. "Those things usually make you cranky. What are you smiling about?"

Sam walked past her on his way to his office. "I wasn't smiling," he said.

"Uh-huh. Your sister called while you were out," she said.

Sam went into his office and called his sister back. Lanie issued a belated warning that Emory was nosing around again. Sam gave Lanie a hard time for talking to his ex in the first place and explained that hurricane Emory had already landed.

"Advance notice would have been nice, Sis," he said.

"I know," Lanie said. Sam heard a crash, and everything went muffled for a minute. There was a shriek and then his sister was back. "Sorry about that. Ian is going through an oral stage. Everything goes into that kid's mouth." She went quiet and there were more muffled noise. "Okay," Lanie said breathlessly. "Stay away from the harpy, Sam. Maybe you should go into witness protection or something."

"I might have to if I'm going to avoid her," he said. Sam hung up after Didi slipped him a note informing him that Erica had called in sick for her shift. That left him with traffic duty for the rest of the afternoon.

Blessedly, the day passed without too much drama. A couple of parking tickets and one traffic violation when Early Jackson drove the wrong way down a one-way street.

"I do it all the time," she confessed. "Gets me to the courthouse about three minutes faster."

While he was out on patrol, he got a text from Sharon O'Neil asking him to call her. He knew he'd have to talk to her sooner or later, but he was going out with Whippet tonight and decided it would have to be later.

Sam drove home after work to change for his date. Whippet had hinted that she'd like to keep things on the down-low and suggested they give the restaurant in Branson another shot. He understood she didn't want to give the local gossips new material, but he had no interest in hiding out. He'd already fallen for one woman who didn't want him. He wasn't interested in repeating the experience.

Not that he was in love with Whippet Moran.

Sam drove down the hill and pulled up in front of her house. She must have been watching for him because before he could even open his door, she was running down the front steps and letting herself into his truck.

"All set," she said as she dropped into the seat next to him and put on her seat belt.

"Fine." He gave her a hard look and pulled away from the house. They drove through town and pulled off Main Street to park behind the police station.

"Are you kidding me?" Whippet said. "You haven't even read me my Miranda rights."

Sam grinned at her. "Summer Movies in the Park starts tonight. They usually show classics no one born in this century has heard of, but I thought we'd give it a try."

Whippet was quiet for a minute. "Then we're not going to Branson?"

"No," he said and watched that eyebrow of hers make the trip north. "What?" he asked.

"You didn't tell me we were coming here. I'm not comfortable parading around in front of the whole town with the chief of police on my arm," she said.

"I wasn't planning on parading," he said, then turned to face her. "Look, you're right. I should have told you what my plans were. But I'm not going to hide the fact that we're out on a date. I don't like it. I won't do it. So, if you have a problem with being seen with me, you better let me know right now."

Whippet's eyes narrowed on him. "Okay, fine!" she said and got out of the truck.

Sam retrieved a couple of camp chairs, and Whippet held out her arms, offering to carry her own. They walked behind the courthouse and stopped at the edge of the park to buy a bucket of popcorn from a stand sponsored by the Elks Club.

Bernie Chastain eyed the two of them. "You here together?" he asked, scratching his head. "Hey, Chief, isn't she the gal that yelled at you that one time?"

"I told you," Whippet muttered under her breath.

"Nice to see you, Bernie," he said as he nudged Whippet out onto the green.

They walked through an alley of tall maple trees, string lights hung between the branches lighting their way. The park looked great in the evening light. A couple of years ago, the mayor had cracked open the civic budget and allocated some money for city beautification. Common areas were landscaped, benches installed between trees, and the parks were well maintained in hopes of attracting the tourists who shuttled between Springfield and Branson.

Sam and Whippet wound their way through the maze of people sprawled across the grass on blankets and lawn chairs. He nodded at Myrna Hudson. Her clutch of cronies whispered behind raised hands as they walked by.

Whippet waved enthusiastically at Myrna. "Your evil plan is becoming clearer," she told him. "You're hoping if the senior set sees you out with me tonight, they'll think you're off the market. Am I right?'

"Side benefit," he said.

"I'm so glad to be the object of speculation."

"You can handle it," he said grinning. But the farther they walked into the park, the more Sam thought maybe Whippet wasn't wrong. It seemed like someone waved or slapped him on the back every few steps they took. Ronnie Stephens walked up to him and pumped his hand.

"Mighty proud to have you as chief of police, son," the man said affably. "What you did for the O'Neil family, well, no one will ever forget it. I tell ya, we all rest a little easier at night knowing we have a bona fide hero watching over us."

Sam felt a rush of discomfort. He responded with something appropriate, he hoped, then pointed at Whippet and used her as an excuse to keep moving. They finally found a spot by a copse of trees. It was nice and secluded so Whippet could hide the fact that they were on a date. He jerked the cover off his chair and put it next to hers. He sat down, trying to shake off the exchange with Ron.

"Why are you being so quiet?" Whippet asked. "And your face is all grumpy. What's wrong?"

Had he said he liked her? These unusual powers of observation almost made him change his mind. "I don't know what you're talking about."

"Sure, you do. You were fine until that guy stopped you. Your face went all funny when he called you a hero." She wriggled around in her chair to face him.

"Can we not talk about this?"

"Okay, Captain Avoidance," Whippet said, taking a handful of popcorn. "But I don't see what the big deal is."

He turned to her. "The big deal is," he said a little too loudly, then looked around. "The big deal is," he repeated, lowering his voice. "I'm not a hero."

He watched as she tossed a handful of popcorn into her mouth. She was looking at him. A steady stare that had him thinking maybe she could see right inside his head. Which was a disturbing thought considering right now he was thinking about how much he'd like to kiss her.

"I think you're a hero. From what I've heard—"

"You haven't heard everything," Sam interrupted. He glanced at her and then looked around again, not wanting anyone to overhear them. "The night of the fire, I panicked. Not something I'm proud of, especially as a public safety employee. That night"—Sam closed his eyes—"I went in without thinking."

"Which I believe qualifies you as being a hero."

"No. No, I went in, and the adrenaline took over. I slammed through rooms and pulled out whoever I found first." Sam sat back. "I got the boys out first, then Sharon O'Neil. I waited to get Isaac last. I-I shouldn't have done it that way. I should have assessed the situation and noticed where the fire was coming from. I should have gotten Isaac out first. Because I waited, he's still being treated at a burn center in St. Louis." Sam looked down. "Every time someone calls me a hero, all I can think about is Isaac."

Whippet was quiet for a moment. The mayor, Dolly Bricknell, stood and tapped the microphone. She welcomed the crowd and the lights in the park dimmed.

Whippet took another handful of popcorn, then asked, "Have you been to see him?"

"No."

"Do you think it might help if you did?"

"I don't know."

"I think you should. That way you'd be able to see for yourself how he's doing." She paused. Sam remained quiet and she said, "Should I stop talking about it?"

"That might be better," he said.

Whippet was blessedly quiet. He didn't know why he was burdening her with this. This was not the impression he wanted to make tonight. He turned to her and said, "Look, I'm sorry. Maybe we should call it a night."

Whippet looked steadily back at him and then covered his hand with hers. "Nah," she said. "Let's watch the movie."

She smiled at him. Man, she was pretty.

The opening credits started to roll, and Whippet turned toward the screen.

"Oh! *The Quiet Man*. My dad loved this movie!" she exclaimed, her hand still covering Sam's.

He began to unwind. And while Whippet watched the movie, he watched her, fascinated by the way her face changed in the reflected light of the screen, every emotion playing out on her face. This woman was full of contradictions. She was fierce and reckless one moment, compassionate and kind the next. She started to laugh and turned to him with a smile so bright it went straight to his heart.

In that moment, Sam decided he wanted to take a chance on her, to see where this could go. Because it seemed like Whippet Moran was worth the risk.

# CHAPTER TWENTY-FIVE

"Everly, sit down and eat," Whippet told her daughter.

Everly was a blur of constant motion. "I can't, Mom. I'm so excited to see my room!"

"Hon, I don't even have the key yet. Your uncle is picking them up from Cam, and we're meeting him at the apartment in about an hour. You have plenty of time to eat." Whippet pushed out the chair next to hers. Everly sat down with a huff.

Cam had called Whippet the night before and given her the all-clear. The drywall was done. She and Everly would spend the weekend painting to save money. Next week, the finish trim and floors would be done. They were getting close to moving in.

"When can we leave?" Everly asked in between bites.

"After I do the dishes," Whippet said, hoping to slow her down.

Everly finished in record time, put her own plate in the dishwasher, and ran upstairs to grab her sketch pad. Whippet's mother had given it to Everly last week along with a set of colored pencils and suggested she draw a plan for her room.

"She's excited." Mom came in through the back door carrying a basket of peonies.

"Yes, she is." Whippet glanced at the flowers. "Those are pretty," she said as she piled dishes in the sink.

"Aren't they? Miss Lily planted these a couple of years ago. This is their first bloom." She joined Whippet at the sink, filling a vase with water. "How's the business plan coming? Are you and Emma making any progress?"

"Sure is hot today," Whippet mumbled.

Her mother set down the vase. "You know the bank won't even consider the loan without a business plan."

She did know. "We're working on it. Emma thinks it'll be done in a couple of days."

To be honest, when Emma started talking to her about time frames, stakeholders, and financial projections, Whippet got a little nauseous. She was way out of her depth, and she knew it.

"It's a good thing you aren't dating anyone," her mother said, and Whippet looked at her.

"Huh?"

"Well, you're so busy working at the diner and keeping an eye on the apartment. Then there's the business proposal and all the recipes you've been testing for the bakery. A relationship would just be a distraction."

"Right," Whippet said with an uneasy laugh then turned to focus on the dishes while her mother arranged flowers.

She hadn't told her family she was dating Sam. It was a secret for now.

He'd been busy lately too. "Staffing issues," he'd told her a couple of nights ago at the dock, because, yes, she'd started to sneak out to see him. It was always late at night, after everyone was asleep. Which meant Whippet was both busy and sleep deprived.

She was slowly opening up to him. She figured she owed it to him after what he'd revealed about the fire and Isaac O'Neil. Last night she'd slowly unspooled the tale of her broken marriage and her divorce. It wasn't her favorite topic, especially since it meant admitting to a host of character flaws, but she'd rather be honest and scare him off now. It turned out Officer Beaufort wasn't easily spooked.

She'd told him how she ended up with Cal in the first place, and Sam had won another piece of her heart when he'd put his arm around her and said, "You've been through a lot, but you must be doing something right. Everly is a great kid."

Sam had bristled when she mentioned the issues at her last job, a subject she cut short when he'd threatened to drive to Texas and "chat" with Anthony Bannon himself.

"File a report!" he'd said, as he stalked through the woods behind her.

"Fine," she'd said over her shoulder. "I'll file the report as soon as you go visit Isaac!"

They were slowly learning about each other, and the more Whippet discovered, the more she liked him.

"It's probably a good thing that you and Cam broke up," her mother said, interrupting her thoughts.

Whippet gave her mother a tight smile. "Oh! I forgot to tell you," she said, changing the subject. "Remember the card Luna gave me? The lady who wanted the cakes? I called her. She wants to place an order for her restaurant. I told her we were opening a bakery, and she said she'd like to see a menu."

"Honey, that's fantastic! See, I told you you'd be a success," Sophie cheered.

"Mom, she wants three cakes next week. I'm not gonna get rich off three cakes."

"But it's a start! Have you told Luna about the bakery yet?"

Whippet swallowed. "Not yet," she said hesitantly. "I thought I'd wait until we got approval from the bank, and I've officially hired a contractor to do the work. No sense in rocking the boat prematurely."

"Very wise," her mother said.

Whippet finished the dishes just as Everly came crashing down the stairs, calling, "Let's go! Let's go! Let's go!" she called.

The three of them piled into the car.

"This is so exciting!!" Everly gushed. She couldn't sit still as they drove into town, fidgeting until they pulled into the alley behind the empty building. Sam had told Whippet he wasn't thrilled that the only way to access her apartment was through the alley. "Bad things happen in alleys," he'd said gruffly, and for a moment Whippet had relished the fact that he was concerned.

Everly paused before getting out of the car. "Barely Blush, right, Mom? When can we pick up the paint?"

"Tomorrow." Whippet had been secretly stashing items she'd ordered for Everly's room. White dragonfly lights, a giant bean bag, a soft chenille comforter. Emma had offered up an old dresser. She and Whippet had painted it a soft sage green, and Whippet could hardly wait for Everly to see it.

They went up the stairs. Whippet pushed through the front door—her own front door!—and saw Tucker duck into one of the bedrooms carrying a ladder.

"Hey," she called and followed him into what would soon be Everly's room.

"You're early," he said. "Em will be here in a bit. She stopped at the hardware store."

"What are you doing?" Her brother had traded his business casual attire for a pair of ripped jeans and a stained T-shirt.

"We're painting. Barely Blush, right Ev?" He held up a hand and Everly jumped to give him a high five.

"Tucker, you guys have done enough. Everly and I were going to paint this weekend."

"Too late," he said as he climbed the ladder to start taping off the ceiling.

With a tingling sense of anticipation, Whippet wandered into the space where the kitchen would be. She'd put most of her budget here. The cabinets wouldn't be installed for a couple of weeks, but she could see that the galley kitchen would have plenty of room. It seemed surreal, a kitchen of her own. Surreal, but wonderful.

Her apartment shared the north wall with Myer's Hobby Shop. The Myer's building was a few feet shorter than hers, which meant Cam had been able to get a bank of narrow windows up high. They cast golden blades of sunlight on the floors.

There were no neighbors on the south wall. She walked over and looked out the window at the vacant lot next door. According to Gran's will, Whippet owned that too. Next to the lot was the library. Convenient, since her daughter was becoming quite the reader.

Whippet drifted over to their future living room and opened the French doors. Cars passed by on the road below. If she leaned over the balcony, she could see all the shops along Main Street with their pretty awnings and colorful pots of cascading flowers. This would be a great spot to watch the Fourth of July parade. Eventually. There was still so much work to do. So much money going out of the account and into. . .

Whippet closed her eyes and took a deep breath. *You can do anything you set your mind to, Pumpkin,* her father's voice reminded her.

Tucker walked up behind her and flung an arm over her shoulders. "Nice view," he said.

"Yep."

"You excited?" he asked.

She nodded. "Nervous too."

"About?"

"Everything," she confessed. She turned to look at him. "Tucker, what if I fail?"

The front door opened, and the happy chatter of Everly, Emma, and Mom washed over them. Still, she heard her brother whisper, "What if you don't?"

\* \* \*

Nine twenty-two on a Friday night. Whit Coleman was on call, which meant Sam actually had a shot at getting the dining room painted before the weekend was over. Not that he needed a dining room. His kitchen was plenty big if he ever did decide to entertain, which frankly, he couldn't picture. That brought him to the question he always raised as he continued to work on this old monstrosity: what single man needed a house this big? Certainly not him. Sam bent to open the paint when the dog started barking and ran to the front door. A moment later he heard a knock.

"You're a pretty good alarm system," he told the pup.

He opened the door and felt a surge of adrenaline. Whippet Moran was standing there dressed in cutoff shorts, a T-shirt, and tennis shoes. Painting clothes, he thought. "You're just in time," he said, pulling her inside.

She raised her eyebrows. "I am? For what?"

"Painting the dining room."

Whippet groaned. "Really? I just came from painting Everly's room at the apartment."

"Then you're already a pro. C'mon. Everything's set up. I'll go high, you go low."

For the next hour and a half, Whippet cut in while Sam painted. Whippet talked about her new place: the kitchen, the bathroom, the privacy that having her own bedroom would give her. He listened. He knew he should be supportive. She was excited. But he wasn't thrilled about her impending move.

When they finished, Whippet took a step back to survey the walls. "We do good work," she announced.

Sam grinned at her. "That we do."

Whippet put the lid back on the paint can, and Sam pulled away the tape. He shoved the drop cloth into a garbage bag and took it out back. When he returned, Whippet had wandered into the family room. "That is a disgrace," she said, eyeing the threadbare futon. "You need actual, adult furniture. I need to take you shopping."

He hated furniture shopping, but the idea of Whippet putting her stamp on the place held enormous appeal. "Sounds like a plan to me," he said. He wandered into the kitchen, and she followed. "I just realized something," he said as he pulled open the fridge.

"What's that?" Whippet came to stand beside him. He handed her a bottle of water.

"You're the first person I've invited up here."

Her blush was back. It was adorable. "Well, tonight I just sort of barged in," she pointed out.

He looked at her. "I'm glad you did."

Whippet bit her lip and wandered over to the doors leading out to the deck. "Your view is spectacular. This is probably my favorite part about the house."

"You haven't seen the upstairs yet."

"Is it better than this?"

Sam ran a hand through his hair. "No. It's a bit of disaster. Peeling wallpaper, toilet in the bathtub, chipped tile. That kind of thing. I focused on the downstairs first."

"And the downstairs looks fabulous." They were quiet for a minute. "I'll be moving into my new place in a few weeks," she told him.

"Hmm."

She turned toward him. "What does 'hmm' mean?"

"I don't know. I kind of like looking down the hill and seeing your lights on."

Whippet bit down on a smile. *Man, there was something about that mouth*, Sam thought.

"Very stalkerish of you," she said.

"Just keeping an eye on the good citizens of Normal. Or in your case—"

"Hush, you." She put a hand over his mouth and the air between them changed. Whippet must have felt it too because she started to pull her hand away. He grabbed it and linked his fingers with hers. "I like having you close," he murmured.

"My apartment is ten minutes from here."

"Not the same," he said, stepping closer.

"You're sweet." She looked down to where their hands were joined and pulled hers free. "I should probably get back," she murmured. "I just snuck out to say 'hi,' so . . . hi! I've been working all day, first at the diner and then at the apartment you're so grouchy about, and now painting here with you, which you know, obviously because—"

He kissed her, his hands coming to rest on her waist. He noticed right away how their mouths fit together, how her body lined up with his. It was kind of perfect. A moment later, he pulled back, not wanting to press his luck. They looked at each other, and for a second, Sam was nervous that maybe he'd pushed things tonight. But then she smiled and kissed him again, wrapping herself around him like a vine of creeping jenny. Not that he was complaining. Nothing felt better than finally having Whippet Moran in his arms.

Sam rested his forehead against hers. "I gotta say, I wasn't sure if you even liked me."

She grinned up at him. "I know. Me neither."

He chuckled.

"I do need to go though," she whispered.

He nodded and walked her to the door. He looked outside. No car. "Did you walk up here?" he asked in his sternest cop voice.

"Nope," she said, pointing to the beach cruiser resting on the brick sidewalk.

"I guess that's okay." He brushed his mouth over hers. Once. Twice. "Be safe," he muttered. "Text me when you get home."

She rolled her eyes and headed toward her bike.

"Hey, Daphne." She looked back at him. "We're a thing now. That okay with you?"

She gave a short nod and smiled.

That smile. It did something to him.

No doubt about it, he was in trouble.

# CHAPTER TWENTY-SIX

Sam cut across the green and walked up the north end of Main Street on Monday morning, out on patrol. He really just wanted to walk past Whippet's building to check on the progress.

There was none. Which was not great for Whippet, but excellent for his plans for their date later that night.

Her loan had come through, and in short order, permits for the new bakery had been filed. She'd hired Joe Prentiss, a local contractor, for the project. Through it all, Whippet had been an anxious mess. She'd told him that when she saw the amount she had to borrow, she'd just about thrown up. "How am I supposed to pay that off?" she'd asked him. "I'm going to have to sell a million cupcakes!"

He had every confidence that she would.

He walked back to the station, thankful for the blast of cold air that hit him as he opened the door. Normal's weather had turned oppressive over the last couple of days, and Didi had used her pregnancy as an excuse to keep the temperature at just this side of arctic.

He switched on the lights in his office and started as he saw Everly Moran spinning around in his chair. He paused, a little wary at seeing Whippet's daughter. "I see you used your ninja skills to get past Didi again."

Everly giggled. "Do police departments ever hire ninjas?"

"I don't know, but maybe this one should. Does your mom know where you are?"

"Yes. I'm hanging out with Max today. He had to return some books to the library. He's gonna meet me out front soon. Katie Harris is watching us at his house until his mom gets off work. Then we're gonna watch *Harry Potter and the Prisoner of Azkaban.*" Everly gave another spin in his chair. "Hey, have you named your dog yet?"

"I have not." He leaned down to switch on his computer.

"You should do that soon. What if he gets lost? He won't know what to listen for when you call him."

"Good point. Any suggestions?" he asked.

"Um, what color is he?"

"Black."

"All black?"

"Mostly. His paws are white."

"You could call him Blackie, or Socks because his paws are white like socks."

"'Socks' sounds like a cat's name to me."

Everly gave another spin. "I'd like to meet your dog someday."

"I'd like that too." Because for that to happen, Whippet would have to tell Everly they were dating.

"Hey, Chief," Didi said from the doorway. "And hello to you too, Miss Moran. There's a boy outside with his face pressed against the glass. Is he looking for you?"

"Yep," Everly hopped up. "Good talk, Chief." She gave him a thumbs up.

Sam suppressed a grin. "Glad you think so." He looked behind him. Didi had disappeared. "Everything going okay with you, Ev?" he asked in a low voice.

"Yeah, I guess so. Why?" she asked.

"I don't know. Just checking in. If you need anything, you know you can ask me, right?"

"Well, yeah. You were my first friend in Normal," she said. And with that, she was off.

\* \* \*

It was after nine. The hour designated by Whippet as ideal for their date. Everly was asleep, and things were slowing down around town so, in theory, no one would see them.

Chicken.

"C'mon," Sam said. Whippet sat in his truck, door open, looking up at her building.

"Why are we here?" she asked. They had a deal tonight. He would provide the entertainment, and she'd bring dessert. He was curious about what was in the brown bag she had on her lap.

"You'll see." He grabbed her hand and pulled her out of the truck.

"You have the key?" she asked, looking surprised.

"Joe made me swear I'd return it to him first thing in the morning," he reassured her as he slid the key into the deadbolt.

"Are you trustworthy?" Whippet asked, head tilting to one side.

"I don't know," he said, leaning over and kissing her. "Am I?"

She smiled up at him. "Yes, I believe you are."

He held the door for her then followed her inside.

"It's kind of disappointing," Whippet said, looking around. "Mr. Prentiss said they'd get started last weekend. Now they're saying it'll be next week."

At least the awful wood paneling and acoustic ceiling tiles were gone. And the pony wall had been demoed. Sam thought it looked better already. "Once they get going, it shouldn't take too long," he said.

Whippet shrugged. "From your lips to the Big Guy's ears. I'd love to be open by fall so I can start paying back the enormous—"

Sam raised a hand. "None of that. Not tonight."

"You're right. In the meantime, I've been working on my menu, which brings me to . . ." She pulled a stack of takeout containers from her bag. She hesitated. "Do you like pumpkin? 'Cause I've got a lot of pumpkin here. Not exactly summer fare, but this is what I've been perfecting all week. Pumpkin cookies, a mini pumpkin Bundt cake with a chai cream cheese frosting—my favorite, by the way—and pumpkin chocolate chip muffins. Oh, and a brown butter apple crumble."

Sam looked at her. "Any pumpkin in that?"

"You can't have everything."

"These look amazing." Sam took the containers from her and put them on the blanket he'd set up earlier. "Care to join me?" he asked, lighting the candles he'd bought for the occasion.

"Why, Chief," she said. "This is downright romantic."

"Yeah, yeah, yeah. Sit down, Moran."

She complied, sitting beside him. "What are we doing after this?"

"I brought a paste compound that's supposed to remove paint from brick," he said, nodding to the painted brick wall behind them which, until last week, had been hidden behind paneling.

She sat back on her heels. "What is it with you and hard labor on date night? I feel like I'm in a work release program."

"I can arrange that if you like."

"No, thanks," she said, offering him a cookie.

Sam tried everything and Whippet listened to his feedback, taking notes on her phone. He liked it all, especially the muffins and the apple crumble. She asked his opinion about serving sizes and price points, even though he was sure she had that stuff buttoned down.

When they were done, they gathered up their trash and put it in the bag she'd brought. He blew out the candles and switched on the utility lights. "Ready to get to work?"

She looked pretty cute, standing there in her shorts and T-shirt, feet bare. She wasn't afraid to get her hands dirty. She picked up the can of compound and read the directions aloud. They pulled on rubber gloves and painted the paste onto the brick. "This is kind of like waxing," she informed him as she pulled back fabric strips to reveal the original red brick. "Oh, I like that," she said. "The brick showing through the paint looks really good. Why don't we just do that? That way we don't have to strip the whole wall."

"Great idea. I'll go high, you go low." Just like when they had painted at his place.

They worked for over an hour until Whippet begged for a time out. Sam climbed down from the ladder and slid an arm around her shoulders. "What do you think?"

"I think my arms are tired." She wrapped her arms around his waist. "This was fun. Thank you for showing me what it could be."

He pushed a strand of hair behind her ear. Kissed her nose. Now or never. "You and Everly want to go out to dinner tomorrow night?"

Whippet dropped her arm and went quiet.

"Daphne. I asked you a question."

"I know. I heard." She walked over to the blanket, suddenly very interested in folding it.

Sam sighed. "You haven't told Everly about us."

Whippet's hands stilled. She didn't look at him. "Is it really such a big deal?" she asked.

"Yes. It feels like you're holding back when I'm trying to move forward. Are you?"

"I don't know," she said. "Maybe."

Sam frowned. "Sneaking around feels juvenile," he said.

"Doesn't it feel adventurous or challenging or something?" Her voice faded.

"I'd like to drive up to your place and actually make it to the front door before you come sprinting out of the house like you're being chased by a colony of vampire bats." He paused. "And I'd like to be able to hold your hand in public once in a while."

"You would?" A blush flared. "That's sweet."

"I'm not interested in sweet. I don't see why people can't know we're together, Whippet."

"Daphne."

"What?"

"You always call me Daphne," she mumbled. "I like it."

That made him smile. "Well, then, Daphne. When are you going to tell your daughter about me?"

She paused, twisting the ring around her little finger so hard he was pretty sure another turn would sever the digit. He grabbed her hand.

"Soon," she finally answered.

"Soon," he repeated. "This week soon? Or sometime before Christmas soon?"

"Before Christmas." She winced. "But probably not this week."

"Whippet—"

"I know, Sam. But I'm busy with work and starting a new business. It's a lot. And do you really want to go public with this? We went to the movies that one time and I fielded questions—very personal questions by the way—for the next week and a half."

"What kind of questions?"

A blush crept up her neck. "Uh, Eden Turner wanted to know if you were a good kisser." The blush went deeper. "Alice Treemonton asked if we were serious because she has a niece she'd like to introduce you to if we're not, and Jenny Barrows—you know what? Never mind." Whippet retrieved her bag from the floor.

"Uh-uh," he said spinning her around to face him. He brought her chin up. "Jenny Barrows—"

"Fine," she said, not looking at him. "Jenny Barrows wants to know how many kids we want and if we'll be living in your house. Or if she could interest us in the nice little bungalow over on Franklin Avenue that has just come on the market."

"How many?"

"How many what?" Whippet asked.

"How many kids did you say we wanted?"

She raised an eyebrow. "I told her seven. Four boys and three girls since I already have the one," she said, tugging on her purse strap. "And that's not the point. I don't like being talked about. It leads to misunderstandings that could potentially affect my daughter."

"Is that what this is all about?"

She seemed to hesitate. "I think so, yes."

"But Everly likes me," he insisted.

"Yes. She likes you as *her* friend. Not as *my* boyfriend."

He took a step closer. "Am I your boyfriend?" he asked in a low voice.

Whippet rolled her eyes. "Sam—"

"We'll deal with it," he promised.

She was quiet for a minute. Sam didn't like the hesitancy he saw in her eyes. "Well, what if . . ." She paused for a moment. "What if I told Everly by July third?" she suggested.

His brows came together. "Why the third?" he asked.

"It's the day of the Patriot Festival. I have a booth in the park. After I close up, we could hang out. Hit some rides. Everly loves that kind of stuff." She twisted her purse strap. "Maybe after, we could do dinner at your place."

Sam grinned down at her. "That sounds like an excellent plan."

"It does?"

He nodded. "Everly's been wanting to meet my dog. Even if she's not happy that we're together, at least she'll like my dog."

"Clever. Using the dog as leverage. Maybe we should—"

His lips caught on hers and she stopped talking.

"Wait!" she said, pushing away from him. "Turn out those lights."

"Daphne—"

"I don't care what our relationship status is, but I am not kissing the chief of police for all to see." She waved her hand at the front windows.

Sam happily obliged.

# CHAPTER TWENTY-SEVEN

"Are you dating Sam Beaufort?" Luna asked her the next morning at work.

*And here we go,* she thought. Whippet unloaded the tray of dirty dishes into the washbasin before she turned to face her boss. "Why do you ask?" she asked, all innocence.

"Because Myrna Hudson was in here for breakfast, complaining very loudly that my waitress had stolen the police chief right out from under her poor granddaughter's nose. And I'm pretty sure she wasn't talking about Jan." Luna nodded toward the other waitress. "Is it true?"

"Yes. No. I mean, maybe?" Whippet's cheeks felt warm.

"That covers all the bases," Chuck said, wiping his hands on a towel.

Sam would be annoyed if he could hear her now. But she had a very good reason for keeping their relationship just between them. If fewer people knew about them, there would be less pressure on Whippet when it ended. Which—in all probability—it would. Because when had Whippet Moran ever been able to keep hold of a good thing?

Luna went to the fridge and pulled out a gallon of milk. "Well," Luna said. "You might want to proceed with caution."

"Why?" she asked. But did she really want to know? What if Sam wasn't divorced at all? What if he had three kids, a wife, and a labradoodle all crying into their pillows at night because Sam Beaufort was a lying, cheating . . .

"Because your daughter has a crush on him."

Whippet's head came up. She must have heard that wrong. "What did you say?"

Chuck gave a low whistle. "That's awkward."

"How do you know that?" she asked, following Luna out into the dining room.

"She told Max, and Max told me." Luna poured the milk into a carafe.

"When? When did Max tell you this?" Whippet demanded.

Luna thought for a minute. "A few weeks ago."

"A few weeks ago," she repeated.

"But Max made it sound like she's liked him for a long time. She goes to see him at the station sometimes, I guess," Luna said.

"What?" This was news to her.

"I'm sure it's no big deal. A little crush. Just, you know, be sensitive." Luna patted her arm and went over to the cash register to ring up the next customer.

\* \* \*

"She likes Sam?" Emma asked, later that night. She tossed another throw pillow onto Everly's new bed. "That's rough."

Whippet's mom had taken Everly shopping, a ploy to keep her busy while Emma and Whippet put the finishing touches on Everly's room at the apartment.

"I know," Whippet said. She wound the dragonfly lights around her daughter's headboard. Whippet tilted her head. "What do you think?"

"About what? The lights or you dating your daughter's first crush?"

"Emma!"

"I'm sorry," her sister-in-law said, barely suppressing a grin. "But seriously. What are you going to do?"

Whippet flopped down on the bed. "I have no idea."

Emma looked thoughtful. "Okay, Everly aside, how do *you* feel?"

"Sad. I think I really like him, Em. I put off telling Everly because she never did warm up to Cam."

Emma sat next to her. "Yeah, but Cam wasn't the one for you. That boy is sloppy in love with Luna."

"Great to hear," she said dryly.

"That's not a reflection on you. Luna is just his person. Are you using Everly as an excuse because you're scared Sam might be yours?"

Whippet's arms broke out in goosebumps.

"How do you feel when you're with him?" Emma asked.

Buoyant. The ridiculous word came almost unbidden, but she sure wasn't going to say that out loud. "I don't know. Good."

Emma frowned. "Good? I think you can do better than *good*."

Whippet propped herself up against the headboard. "Okay, I guess I feel light. Being around him is easy. I feel like I can be myself. He's fun too. He makes me laugh."

"I like it. Do you think about him when you're not with him?" Whippet felt her face heat. "Oh, my. You've gone all blotchy," Emma said. "I'll take that as a yes."

"Don't tease me. He . . . I don't know. It wasn't like this with Cam. Cam was like an old pair of sweatpants, you know? Comfortable."

"Sheesh. No wonder you broke up. What's it like with Sam then?"

Whippet thought for a minute. "When I'm with Sam—and please don't repeat this to Tucker or, heaven forbid, my mother—but sometimes it feels like my heart's going to beat right out of my chest. It happens every time I see him at the diner or just walking down the street. I mean, it eventually calms down, but being with him is chemical."

"Oh, Whippet." Emma's face went soft. "You deserve it."

"Yeah, but now I find out Everly likes him. This move wasn't easy for her. What if this makes everything worse? I don't want to hurt her."

Emma nodded. "I can see that. When is your next date with Sam?"

"Tomorrow night. He's helping me set up for the Patriot Festival. Time is running out. I told him I'd tell Everly about us before July third."

"It will work out. You'll see." Emma looked at her for a minute and then nudged her. "Can we talk about me for a second?" she asked reluctantly.

"Yes, please. I'm kind of sick of thinking about this."

Emma twisted her fingers in the blanket. "So I have something to tell you." She looked down. "I'm late."

"For what?" Whippet asked.

Emma raised an eyebrow, and Whippet jerked upright. "Oh. Oh! Oh, my gosh! You're late!" Whippet clapped a hand over her mouth. "How late are you?"

"Just three weeks, but I'm pretty regular so . . ."

"Three weeks! Emma this is fantastic! This is amazing!" Whippet lunged for her sister-in-law.

"Don't hug me!" Emma shrieked, and Whippet froze.

"Why not?"

"I don't want to jinx it."

After a year of disappointing news, Whippet could see her point. "Fine. How 'late' do you have to be before I get to hug you?"

Emma pretended to think about it. "Two more weeks. I need to take a test. And I should probably tell Tucker first if I'm, you know, pregnant." She whispered the last word.

"Yes, the husband should definitely know. Emma I'm so excited!"

But her sister-in-law's expression turned uncertain. "What if I'm not? All the other times I—"

Whippet shook her head. "Nope. No bad thoughts." She took Emma's hands in her own. "You've been my cheerleader since I moved here. Now let me be yours."

Emma nodded. "Thank you." She took a deep breath and let it all out in a whoosh. "I'm so glad you're here," Emma said.

Whippet squeezed her hand and smiled. "Me too."

# CHAPTER TWENTY-EIGHT

The Patriot Festival was a logistical nightmare. Sam glanced at the packed street and leaned over to slap another ticket on a windshield. Double parked. He had half a mind to call the tow truck, but he'd already sent the Buckmans to help with a stalled vehicle on Warren Street. He shook his head at the line of cars that stretched down the road, all jockeying for vacant parking spots. There weren't any.

He knew the town relied on revenue brought in by events like this, but the whole thing tested his patience. The festival meant traffic increased by seventy percent, and tourists got very inventive when competing for parking spots. Which was not great when there were only three police officers in town.

The sidewalks were jammed with people. Shop fronts were decked out in patriotic bunting. Some businesses had gone a step further and had planted red and white flowers that dripped over terra cotta pots. Anything to get busy tourists to stop and come inside. Sam had to dodge a bunch of star shaped balloons outside Myer's Hobby Shop. Which was right next door to Whippet's building.

Whippet and Everly had moved into their new apartment a couple of days ago. He'd offered his truck and his services to help her move. His hackles had risen when she'd declined, making all kinds of excuses. Sam guessed that probably meant she hadn't told her family about him yet.

But when he'd helped her set up her booth in the park last night, her brother had walked right up to him, clapped him on the back, and said, "I hear you're dating my sister. You have my condolences." Sam had glanced over at Whippet, but she'd refused to look at him. He'd walked over to her and asked in a low voice, "Did you tell Everly too?" Her eyes went wide, but she gave a short nod.

"Hey, Chief," Whit's voice came over the radio. "We've got a situation over on Christopher Street. Some joker's moved the traffic cones. Everything's backed up."

"I'm on it," he said into his shoulder unit, heading back to his cruiser. He could hear music coming from the festival grounds in the park. The air carried the scent of sugar and hot oil. A child cried, and a blue balloon floated into the sky. He'd be on duty until this evening when he'd promised Whippet he'd stop by her booth, help break it down, and clean up. Then they'd head back to his place for dinner. He, Whippet, and Everly. Something to look forward to.

He glanced at his watch and started down the street. Time to get back to work.

\* \* \*

Thousands of people were crowded onto the green. Or at least it seemed that way. Enough people to make the already hot day just that much more stifling. All of humanity appeared to be jostling in line outside her booth.

Whippet didn't mind. In fact, just the opposite. She felt a hum of excitement every time she glanced down that line. These people wouldn't be here if they weren't interested in what she was selling.

Sadly, the line was currently stalled. Little Theo Barton was in meltdown mode because she'd just sold the last of the chocolate chip cookies to a woman whose T-shirt proclaimed, "I Stop for all Buffets."

"Would he like a snickerdoodle?" Whippet asked the boy's mother, hoping to avoid a full-on tantrum.

"That would be great," the frazzled woman said, and Whippet slipped the boy a cookie, crossing her fingers he wouldn't notice it wasn't chocolate chip. "Have a good day," she said to his mother.

She was only here today by the grace of Luna. Whippet had asked for the day off. Not something to be taken lightly as the Patriot Festival also made it a busy day for the diner. When Luna asked her why, Whippet had swallowed hard and told her the truth. Luna was silent for a long minute. Looking at the ceiling, Luna said, "I knew it. You'll be competing with me."

Whippet reassured her that it wasn't true. The bakery's selections would be vastly different from the diner. Luna, gratefully, seemed to buy her reasoning.

"Is it really this hot or am I having a hot flash?" Whippet's mother asked as she stood there fanning herself with a stack of napkins.

"It's hot, Mom. Do you want to take a break?"

"Honey, look at that line. There's no time for a break."

After the parade this morning, Whippet and her mom had hauled wagons and coolers full of baked goods over to the festival grounds. Emma was supposed to help, but morning sickness had hit, and she went home before they even made it to the park. With the record heat today, Whippet was glad she and Sam had set up the booth the night before.

She hadn't seen him all day.

She knew Sam assumed she had told Tucker about them, but she hadn't said a word to her brother. She'd confided in Emma and relied on her to spread the news, although her mother still seemed oblivious.

She still hadn't said anything to Everly. She'd lied to Sam when he asked about it last night and had been feeling sick about it all day. But how was she supposed to explain this to her daughter?

"Mom, could you run up to the apartment and grab some more cupcakes?" Whippet asked.

Her mother surveyed the shelves. "I think I'll grab some shortbread too. We're running low. Back in a bit."

She shot her mother a smile and muttered, "Hurry," as she greeted her next customer. "Hi, Mrs. Madris. How are you today?"

She felt like she was running a glorified bake sale. Initially, she'd hoped to sell enough to make back what it cost to be in the festival. But if things kept going the way they were, she'd be sold out before sundown. But better than that, this meant exposure and eventually—fingers crossed—customers.

"Here you go, Mrs. Madris," Whippet said, handing her a bag of sugar cookies. "I put a coupon for the bakery in there too. We open in September. Thanks for stopping by!"

"Mom!" Everly bounced up beside her. A couple of seconds later, Tucker dashed over.

"Ev, next time tell me when you're taking off," Tucker said, looking a bit harried. "I couldn't find you." Tucker and Emma were supposed to be watching Everly together while Whippet ran the booth, which would have been great if Emma weren't at home throwing up. No official pregnancy news yet, but Tucker had volunteered to watch Everly solo, mentioning something about "practice."

As if on cue, Tucker's phone rang. "Hey, babe. You need something?" He walked away a couple of paces.

Everly scooted into the booth behind her. "Mom, when are you going to be done? I'm bored." Everly fiddled with a stack of bags.

Whippet rang up her next customer. "Wasn't Uncle Tucker going to take you on some of the rides?"

"No. He said it's too loud over there, and he wouldn't be able to hear the phone if Aunt Emma called." Everly looked up at her with those wide blue eyes. "Can you take me home? There's nothing to eat here."

"Sweetheart, there's a lot to eat here." Whippet handed a customer a stack of napkins.

"Not cookies. Real food. Like a hamburger or something."

"Ask Uncle Tucker—"

"Puppy!" Everly exclaimed and wandered over to pet a dog standing in line next to its owner.

Tucker strolled back, still talking on his phone. "Are you sure? She's got some cookies left," he said, perusing Whippet's inventory. "And brownies. You like brownies—okay, okay! Sorry I mentioned it. No. I won't. I know. Uh, call if you need anything." Tucker hit the end button like it was on fire. He glanced at Whippet. "Her stomach is bothering her," Tucker said, looking a little sweaty.

"Uh-huh." She grinned at him.

His face fell. "You know, don't you? Of course, she told you first." He threw his hands in the air.

Whippet laughed. "She didn't tell me anything. Last I heard, she only suspected. So is it official?" she asked, making change for a twenty.

Tucker rubbed his neck. "Yeah. We drove to Springfield on Friday to see the OB-GYN," he said sheepishly. "We're excited. A little freaked out too. She's throwing up a lot. Aside from that, we're really happy." His phone rang, and he looked at the screen. "Gotta take this," he said and stepped away from the booth again.

"Okay." Her mother hustled toward her. "We're out of the celebration sugar cookies," she said, hefting a bin out of the wagon. "Too bad too. They were so cute with the red, white, and blue frosting. We're really low on brownies, and this is the last of the red velvet cupcakes." Her mother paused. "Whippet, look at that." Both women glanced up at the line stretching past the old oak tree and twisting around the gazebo into the middle of the park.

"Oh, my," Whippet said.

"Hello, ladies." Whippet jumped as Sam materialized beside them. "Looks like you're a hit," he said.

"Hey, uh, Sam. I thought you'd be working," she said, eyes darting to where Everly was holding the puppy.

"Nah. Everything was pretty much contained once the parade was over."

"This is contained?" she asked, looking at the crush of people mobbing the park.

"Better than it was this morning. The volunteer fire department is helping out too." He gave her a pointed look. Ah. He was letting her know he was off duty.

"Cut me a decent-sized slice of that cake, will ya please?" Ronnie Stephens asked Whippet's mother.

"Hi, Sam." Her mother beamed at him while handing Mr. Stephens a slice of triple chocolate cake.

Sam smiled at her mother, then for her ears only said, "I thought we had plans."

What to do, what to do? "Mmm-hmm." She boxed up a half dozen cupcakes.

"Hey, Sam!" Everly rushed up to him, her face lighting up at the sight of him. Whippet's stomach gave an uneasy flip-flop.

"Hey, Squirt. How's it going?" He held up a hand for Everly's high five.

"Okay, except I'm hungry. But the parade was fun! Did you see it? Hey, see that puppy over there? Does your dog look like that? We should go get your dog and walk it around the festival. It'd be good exercise." Everly was talking a mile a minute.

"I don't know," Sam said. "My dog is kind of lazy."

Tucker picked that moment to rejoin their little party. He was holding his phone against his chest. "Whippet, I've got to run. One of the Turley kids put a sparkler out with his mouth. I've got to go into work."

"What? You were supposed to watch Everly until I'm done here."

"I know, but this is an emergency. Ev will be okay. Won't you sprout? Unless she wanders off again." He gave Everly his best stern-uncle look, and she laughed.

"Fine," Whippet said. "Go."

"Yeah, I'm on my way," Tucker said into his phone before he was swallowed by the crowd.

"What am I going to do?" Whippet asked, turning to her mother who was handing change to Eden Turner.

"What about Luna? Who's watching Max today?" her mom asked.

"Max is spending the Fourth with his dad in Kansas City," she lamented.

"I can take her," Sam offered, picking up Whippet's hand and stroking it with his thumb. Whippet saw Everly's eyes track every move.

Whippet pulled her hand free. "Oh . . . um." She bit her lip. "I-I don't know."

She looked at her daughter whose glance bounced between the two of them, expression curious. Sam's hand went to the small of Whippet's back. Everly's eyes were still on them.

"Whippet—" Her mother nodded toward the next customer in line.

"Wait, Mom." Everly's voice rose in pitch. "Are you his girlfriend?"

Whippet's stomach bottomed out, and she took a step away from Sam. "Honey, I—" She reached for Everly, but she jerked away.

"Are you?" Her daughter's face held a look of disbelief.

Whippet turned to Sophie. "Mom, can you take over for a minute?" she asked. Her mother nodded and gave her a sympathetic smile. Whippet placed a guiding hand on Everly's shoulder. "Let's go over here."

"I don't want to go anywhere! You are, aren't you?" Everly face crumpled. The crowd stared. Sam had gone eerily quiet. "Why didn't you tell me? I hate you!" Everly exclaimed and broke away. In a flash, she had disappeared into the crowd.

\* \* \*

Sam walked through his front door and stood there a moment, adrenaline still surging through his body. The dog raced toward him and began walking in circles, head occasionally butting against Sam's leg. "Not now," Sam said, but the beast stayed with him.

It had taken them two hours to find Everly. Half the town had joined in the search. They'd split up, canvasing every place she would have likely gone. He'd been checking Luna's house for the second time when he got word. Everly had been found at Miss Lily's House, hiding up in the cupola. She'd fallen asleep and didn't hear her family calling. If he weren't so relieved, he'd be furious.

Scratch that.

He was furious. Whippet had lied to him. She hadn't told Everly about them. He rubbed a hand down his face. What did that say about their relationship?

Throughout the search, Whippet had avoided looking at him, talking to him. When he'd asked for a list of Everly's friends, she'd kept her head down and mumbled her response. When he couldn't handle it anymore, he'd left with Whit to continue the search.

Sam rubbed his eyes. He was tired of thinking about it.

He went into the kitchen, tossed his keys on the counter, and headed to the fridge for something cold to drink. The dog had his sights on something outside, his nose pressed to the glass, giving a low growl.

Sam opened the fridge and saw all the fixings for the nice barbeque they'd planned to have when Whippet and Everly came back here for dinner.

"Terrific," he mumbled, grabbing a water and heading to the French doors where the dog was pawing at the window.

"What's out there, huh? You see a coyote or something?" Sam went to unlock the doors, but found they weren't locked. That was weird. He pushed them open, and the dog was out like a shot, barking fiercely. Sam followed him down to the firepit and stopped short.

An elegant form unfolded from Whippet's Adirondack chair. Strange that he already thought of it as hers.

Just when he thought the night couldn't get any worse. "Emory."

"Your dog doesn't like me," she said, tossing her glossy brown hair over one shoulder for effect. Because Emory did everything for effect.

Sam reached down and scratched the dog's bony head. "Good boy," he muttered.

Emory's smile turned into a smirk. "You blocked my number, didn't you," she said with raised brow.

Sam didn't want to get into a thing with her, so he just stood there.

Emory shook her head. "Sam, I can see those gears turning. I don't have an agenda, I promise. I just wanted to check on you."

"There are no gears turning, and you always have an agenda, Emory."

She trailed her fingers over the back of the chair. "It's been over a year since I've seen you."

"Really? Doesn't seem that long." He didn't want to court crazy, but he had to know, "Why are you here?"

She gave him a faint smile. "I told you. A client is opening a spa resort in Branson. I'll be in the area for a few weeks."

"No. Why are you here. At my house?" Then it dawned on him. "You found the hide-a-key, didn't you?"

Emory smiled. "Inside the front left screen, same as it was at our place."

"How did you find my house?" he asked.

"I stopped by that cute little diner for lunch. This town is so charming, Sam! A very helpful waitress with pink hair gave me directions."

"Look, Emory. This is a waste of time. Whatever it is that has gone sideways in your life, I can't help you. It's been a long day, and I'd like to go to bed." He gave her a hard look. "You need to leave."

"I can't," she said.

"What do you mean you can't? How'd you get here?"

"An Uber dropped me off."

"Then call another Uber," he said.

"Really? It's after midnight, Sam."

Vintage Emory. Everything planned down to the smallest detail. He grabbed his keys. "Let's go. I'll drive you myself."

# CHAPTER TWENTY-NINE

In the days following Everly's stunt at the Patriot Festival, a cold war ensued. Everly had traded in walking for stomping and grunting for speaking. She was upset because she was grounded. And Whippet was feeling the consequences of parenting on her own.

"It's not fair! All I did was ride my bike!" Everly stomped her foot. Good thing there were no tenants below their apartment.

"Along a busy highway and without telling anyone where you were going." Whippet mentally counted to ten.

It had taken a long time to find Everly. Whippet had been tense and anxious and imagining the worst. Everly could have been taken; she could have been hit by a car. She wasn't at the B&B, and there had been no sign of her at Miss Lily's House. A search party had fanned out through the woods, down to the lake. Whippet still had nightmares about that. What if Everly had drowned? In the end, it had been Whippet who found her. Spying the small door that led to the cupola, she'd followed a hunch and went up the narrow stairs to find Everly curled up on the floor, fast asleep. Whippet had been so relieved that she'd burst into tears. Her daughter woke up confused, sweaty, and very, very sorry. That lasted maybe an hour.

Now Everly wasn't speaking to her. Whippet couldn't tell if it was because Everly was grounded or because—Whippet hated to think it—she was nursing a broken heart. Emotions were so high that Whippet began to wonder if the move to Missouri had been a colossal mistake.

Whippet strode from her bedroom into the family room where Everly was slouched in front of the TV. Whippet picked up the remote and turned it off.

"Mom!" Everly dragged the word out into a three-syllable wail, and Whippet felt the beginnings of a headache. This was the part of parenthood those cute baby-food commercials failed to warn about. "I was watching that," Everly whined.

Wow, actual words coming from her daughter's mouth.

Whippet's hands were clammy, and she wiped them on her sweatpants. "I need to talk to you," Whippet said, coming to stand in front of the TV. "Do you want to go back to Texas?"

Everly said nothing, just looked off into the distance.

"I was wondering if maybe you'd like to go stay with Grandma Fancy for the rest of the summer. Maybe get away from here for a while."

Everly's face crumbled. "You want me to go? Because I ran away?" Everly launched herself into Whippet's arms. "Mom! I'm sorry!"

Whippet's arms closed around her daughter and relief flowed through her. "Why did you do it, Ev? You scared the entire town. You scared me."

"I don't know," she mumbled into Whippet's shirt. She sniffed and looked up. "I thought Sam was *my* friend."

"Oh, honey. Of course he's your friend. He likes you a lot."

"Are you guys together?" Everly sniffed.

Whippet remembered how tight Sam's face had been while they'd searched for Everly, only speaking to her when necessary. Eventually, he'd left the group to search Luna's backyard. He hadn't called or texted since. "We were. I—I don't think we are anymore."

"Because I ran away?"

"It's complicated. Don't worry about that right now, okay," Whippet said.

"I don't want to stay with Gramma Fancy. I want to stay with you. Please don't make me go."

Whippet felt the sting of tears and hugged Everly close. "Oh, baby. I wasn't trying to get rid of you. I just thought maybe you could use a change, that's all. So much has been going on. I thought you'd like to get away for a while. Maybe see your dad."

Everly looked up at her. "Did Daddy call?"

"No, sweetheart." She watched her daughter's face fall. "Look, we've been living on top of each other since we got here. Maybe you need a break." She stroked Everly's long golden hair, almost white where the sun had bleached it.

"I don't need a break. I want to stay with you." Everly held on tighter.

"Okay, sweetie, but you'll need to apologize to Sam."

"I know. I'm sorry," Everly cried, then ran to her room and slammed the door.

"And so will I," Whippet added to the empty room.

\* \* \*

He was surprised to see her. He'd fully expected Whippet to take the easy way out and never talk to him again. He could imagine how it would be between them. They'd slowly become polite acquaintances and eventually forget they'd ever dated.

Sam glanced toward the door. He'd have to choose his words carefully. He'd bet a lot of money that Didi was right outside, eavesdropping.

Sam didn't get up. He just looked at Whippet, so pretty standing there in her sundress, pinching her little finger. She only did that when she was nervous.

"Um, Sam," she started then cleared her throat. "I—uh, came to apologize," she said.

"Okay."

She gave a little laugh. "You're not going to make this easy, are you?"

"Any reason why I should?" Sam asked, his voice tight.

"No. You're right. I made a mess of things," Whippet said in a small voice.

Sam gave a short nod and looked down at his desk. "How's Everly?"

Whippet gave a slight smile. "Grounded. Upset. She'll be by to apologize too. She knows what she did was wrong." She took a deep breath. "She just needs a little time."

Sam nodded, and then stood to face her. "You didn't tell her." He didn't try to keep the accusatory tone from his voice.

Something shifted in her expression, and her eyes went cold. "Well, you were coming on a little strong out there on the festival grounds, Sam. Grabbing my hand. Rubbing my back."

"Normal behavior between two people who are in a relationship. But are we in a relationship, Whippet?" He gave her a hard look.

Whippet said nothing. She just gave her little ring a twist and sighed.

Sam felt a roiling in his chest. He didn't like this. The uncertainty. The emotions. The feeling that at any moment the rug could be jerked out from under him. It had been like this during his marriage. And then Emory had left him.

Sam ran a hand down his face. "Yeah. This isn't working," he said.

Whippet's mouth opened. "Wait. Sam—"

"I think we need to be done."

"You're breaking up with me?!" She actually looked surprised.

He threw up his hands. "How can I break up with you when I'm not even sure we're together?" He shook his head. "Whippet, you lied to me. You hid our relationship from your family, and more importantly, from Everly. You think she would have reacted that way if she had known the truth?"

Whippet wrapped her arms around herself, utterly silent.

It made him angry. He tamped down on the feeling long enough to repeat, "I think we're done here."

And the killer was, Whippet didn't argue. Didn't fuss or put up a fight. She just jerked her purse over her shoulder, turned that frosty gaze on him, and stalked out, skirting around Didi before shutting the door behind her.

Sam went to his desk and sat down. He swung around and looked out the window.

Whippet was his first real try at commitment since his divorce. He'd dated here and there. Gone on the occasional second date, but nothing stuck. No one seemed like the right fit until now. His sister was always telling him he needed to have a rebound relationship. Maybe that's what Whippet had been. A rebound relationship.

The thought made his chest ache.

\* \* \*

When the elevator doors opened to the third floor, Sharon O'Neil was standing right there, refilling a pitcher of water at an ice machine.

Two nights ago, she'd called Sam and he'd actually answered. Their conversation had been short.

"Isaac would like to see you," she'd said.

It was a pretty simple request, but it brought up a lot of complicated feelings. *"You should go see him."* Sam remembered the conversation he'd had with Whippet a while ago. Putting aside his anger with her, he'd decided she was right.

"Sharon," Sam said now, and she turned.

A smile broke over her face. "Oh, Sam. Isaac will be so happy to see you."

They walked in silence and stopped outside of Isaac's room. "I think I'll let you two talk," she said. She gave his shoulder a squeeze and walked back down the hall.

Sam paused. His heart was pounding, his shirt damp with sweat. He took a deep breath and walked in.

Isaac was sitting upright in the hospital bed, but he was asleep.

Sam knew his friend was recovering from a second skin-graft surgery. All things considered, Isaac looked good. There was a slight puckering of the skin at the base of his neck, and his left arm was almost completely bandaged.

"Good-looking, right?" Isaac muttered and opened one eye to look at Sam. "Are you going to sit down? It's kind of intimidating, having a police officer hovering over me."

Sam sat on the hard plastic chair next to the bed. He didn't say anything.

They were silent for a moment before Isaac said, "Sharon thinks you're avoiding her calls."

Sam was nodding before Isaac stopped talking. "She's right."

Isaac gave a short laugh. "Why?"

"You have to ask?"

"Yeah, I think I do."

Sam leaned forward. "You're at a burn center, Isaac. And it's my fault."

"Your fault?" his friend echoed.

"Absolutely," Sam said.

"How is this your fault?"

Sam looked down. This was what he was here for. He took a deep breath and then told Isaac everything—how he'd panicked, how he'd forgotten his emergency training and just started pulling whoever he found out of the house. "I should have assessed the situation and gotten you out first," he said, eyes trained on the floor.

Isaac held up his right hand. "Hang on. Did you think I wanted to see you because I blamed you?"

"It makes sense."

"No, man." Isaac shook his head. "I wanted to thank you."

Sam's head came up. He knew Isaac wanted to reassure him, but praise would make him feel worse. That's why he'd spoken first. "Isaac—"

"Listen to me for a sec, okay?" Isaac's head rested against his pillows. "I'm grateful you showed up at all. We were asleep. From what I understand, the whole house was in flames. If you hadn't come in, if you hadn't pulled the boys out, they would have died. We all would have died. The smoke would have gotten us."

Isaac gestured at his bandaged arm. "This isn't proof that you failed, Sam. If anything, it's proof of how stupid *I* was. I caused the fire. I was the one who set up the space heater. If you hadn't rushed into a burning house, things might have turned out very differently. And if that had happened"— he swallowed hard—"I don't think I'd be able to live with myself. So if you're sitting there thinking your best wasn't good enough, take that into consideration."

Sam gave a short nod, still feeling uncomfortable.

The mood was somber. Isaac seemed to pick up on it as well, because he suddenly said, "Look at this." He held up his injured arm and wriggled his fingers. "You know what this means?"

"Haven't got a clue," Sam said.

"It means I can still hold a 5-iron. This time next year I'll be back to schooling you in golf." He grinned.

"You're on," Sam said. He almost managed a smile.

They talked for the next half hour about everything but the fire. The kids were doing great but driving Isaac's in-laws crazy. They were staying with Sharon's parents until she and Isaac got their housing situation sorted. She had taken a job as a teacher in Town and Country, in west St. Louis County, and would start in the fall.

Sam left, promising he'd visit again soon. It was a promise he would keep.

It was a long drive back to Normal, but it gave him plenty of time to think. Hearing Isaac out had been a good thing. It didn't mean the guilt was gone. No, that would take a while. But Sam was hopeful that maybe, over time, he'd be able to forgive himself.

He grudgingly admitted to himself that Whippet had been right. Seeing Isaac had helped.

He really wanted to call Whippet. She would have applauded what he'd done. He held his phone in his hand, his thumb hovering over the screen. It would be so easy to connect to Bluetooth, hit her number, and spend the rest of the drive talking to her, unpacking everything that had happened that day. Then he remembered her standing there, tight-lipped at the station, essentially throwing in the towel on their relationship.

He looked straight ahead, tossed his phone onto the passenger seat, turned up the radio, and drove home.

# CHAPTER THIRTY

WHIPPET ATTACKED THE GAS RANGE with ferocity. She removed the cast-iron grates and scrubbed around the burners. Nothing like a clean stovetop. Not that she'd had time to get it dirty. They'd only been in the apartment a few weeks. But still, a clean kitchen was something to be proud of.

She had a lot on her mind. Three days ago, Whippet had made a call to Bannon Corporation. She'd almost lost her nerve when an actual person had answered the phone. Gathering every ounce of courage, she'd said, "May I please be connected to your HR department? I'd like to file a complaint."

In less than twenty-four hours, she'd received an email from the company basically summarizing what they'd discussed on the phone. She'd been asked to submit a notarized testimony listing dates and details of each of the perpetrator's offenses. She'd sent it the next day, grateful that she'd kept detailed notes on her phone. When she'd left the post office that day, she'd felt lighter and the bands caused by that ugly memory felt looser. She hoped this would keep Anthony Bannon from harassing other employees.

She hadn't told her family yet, but she was proud of herself. Maybe the girl she'd been, the girl who'd run away from her problems, was growing up.

Whippet looked at the clock on the microwave. Five forty-four in the morning. The construction crew would show up soon, and she and Everly would eat their breakfast to a symphony of skill saws screeching downstairs.

Whippet was doing a good job keeping herself occupied. She worked steadily on recipe development. Emma had helped her set up an Instagram account for the bakery. Whippet also settled on a name: The Bakery on Main. She knew it was kind of prosaic, but she had quickly vetoed Tucker's suggestion of Whip-it Up!

So yeah. She was busy. Very, very busy.

But it didn't stop the sadness that settled over her when everything was quiet. Like now.

She hadn't slept last night. After Everly had gone to bed, Whippet had stayed up, scrolling through Instagram and staring at pictures of people whose lives seemed pretty near perfect. That was when it hit her. She didn't have a single picture of Sam. The thought opened a chamber of misery deep inside and before she knew it, she'd collapsed onto the couch, hot, silent tears sliding down her face, soaking her hair. She told herself to snap out of it, that as relationships went, theirs was barely a blip. A month of sneaking around and making out like teenagers. So what if she had nothing to show for it? No selfies, no ticket stubs to put in an old shoe box. They didn't even have a song. Why was she so sad?

Whippet blinked away new tears and faced the truth. She was sad because what she'd had with Sam had bordered on ideal. It represented a chance at something great, right up until she blew it.

She scrubbed the burner a little harder. Next, she'd tackle that sink full of dishes.

Whippet wasn't used to living in town yet, particularly the sounds that came with it. The sounds of people on the sidewalk. Cars driving by. In a couple of hours, she knew she'd hear Mr. Myers whistling as he opened his shop. She did love looking down on the town as it slowly came alive, feeling the way the air changed when the sun came up. But she felt kind of lonely just now. It was funny how quickly you could get used to the noisy intrusions that came from living with family. In moments like this, she missed Emma popping in unannounced and her mother's chatter. She even missed her bossy big brother.

And she missed Sam. A lot.

It had been a couple of weeks since their breakup debacle. Just thinking about it made her stomach squeeze. She knew she'd let Sam down. He'd fairly assumed he'd been getting into a relationship with a grown-up. If only that were true. She could still see him standing there, waiting for her to put up a fight or explain, anything! But she couldn't. Wouldn't. Because Whippet was terrified she'd fail at another relationship.

Mission accomplished. She had done that.

Whippet walked to the sink. Time to get to those dishes.

"Mom? Why are you up so early?"

A bleary voice came from behind her, and Whippet looked over her shoulder. "Oh hey, sweetheart. What woke you?"

"I had a dream that we had a dog. He jumped on me, and I woke up." She yawned.

"That sounds like a nice dream." Whippet turned the water to hot.

"It was. What are you doing?" Everly asked.

"Cleaning up." She smiled at her daughter. "Are you hungry?"

Everly shrugged. "I dunno. What would you make?"

"What do you want?" Everly appeared to be too tired to answer. "You know what? Get dressed. Let's go see Grandma."

"It's early." Everly yawned again. "She's prob'ly sleeping."

"Nah. Grandma's up. I bet she's getting breakfast ready for the guests. Let's go help her."

Thirty minutes later, Whippet was in her element. She threw together a batch of blueberry streusel muffins and got them in the oven. She sliced a loaf of almond poppyseed bread she'd made the day before and set it out. The chafing dish was full of bacon and sausage. Everly cut strawberries while Sophie whipped some cream. Whippet filled the juice carafes and pulled yogurt from the fridge.

As soon as the guests started coming in, Everly disappeared. Whippet's mom seemed to have breakfast under control by then. Whippet went out back and slid onto the glider swing. She kicked off her sandals and propped her feet up on the table.

The B&B sat in a little valley. She could just make out the road that wound its way up to Miss Lily's House. The morning light fell on the barn Gran had built for the remaining livestock after Emma converted the barn behind Gran's house into an events venue. A couple of goats grazed in the field, and a horse stood next to the fence, its tail flicking at a swarm of flies. A few yards away, the colorful residents of the chicken coop squawked and pecked around, enjoying their breakfast.

"Hey." Her mother's voice came from over Whippet's shoulder.

"Is the breakfast rush over?" Whippet asked as she stretched.

"Pretty much. Everyone is sitting down. I figured I'd take a minute."

Whippet nodded and fell silent.

"What is it, honey?" her mom asked, coming to sit beside her. "You seem sad. Is it Sam?"

Whippet drew back. "You knew about Sam? Did Emma tell you?"

"No, I found out last month when I stopped by the bakery to drop off some paint." Her mother raised a brow. "I saw you through the window, making out like it was the end of days."

Whippet's mouth dropped open. "Oh, my." Embarrassment aside, that night with Sam had been nearly perfect. She smiled thinking about it. Of course, that had also been the night she'd promised him she would tell Everly about them. A promise she'd broken.

"I haven't seen you two together since the Patriot Festival." Her mother's eyes were full of sympathy as she leaned over and wiped something from Whippet's face. Whippet touched her cheek, and her hand came away wet.

"Come here," her mother murmured, gathering her close.

Whippet had done a lot of crying in the past couple of weeks. After the ground-level annihilation Cal's cheating had caused, the only way she'd been able to keep going was to build a protective wall around her heart. She hadn't cried in years. She was kind of proud of it, in fact. Yet, a couple of weeks into a broken heart and here she was drawing sloppy, wet breaths and soaking her mother's shirt.

"You're in love with him, aren't you?" Moms asked quietly.

"I don't know," Whippet moaned. "Can you be in love after only a month?"

"You might have only been dating for a month, but you've known each other longer than that."

"Yeah, but before that he mostly just bugged me," she said, pulling back and giving her mom a weepy smile.

"Maybe the annoyance was a cover for something deeper. Stranger things have happened."

"I feel like he saw me," Whippet confessed, swiping at her cheeks. "When he'd come into the diner, it was like everyone else disappeared and all I could see was him." She looked at her mom. "That sounds corny, doesn't it?"

Her mother smoothed the hair from Whippet's face. "Totally corny."

"He knew the worst, and he still wanted to be with me. Well, until two weeks ago, I guess." She drew a shuddery breath. "I thought he felt it too. But he just let me go." Self-pity took a seat at the table, and the tears started again.

Her mother got quiet, highly unusual during times of distress. "What?" Whippet asked.

Mom sighed. "I don't want to invalidate your feelings."

"But?" Whippet prodded.

"Didn't you let him go too?"

Whippet drew back and looked at her mother.

"I don't blame you," she rushed to say. "You survived your marriage. Honestly, what that man put you through—"

"Mom."

"—but since your divorce, you seem to have one foot out the door when it comes to relationships."

"I wasn't like that with Cam," she pointed out.

"Mmm, I think you saw an out and took it."

"Mom!"

Her mother gave a dismissive wave. "But I wasn't just talking about Cam."

"What—?"

"You're that way with us too. Tucker, Emma, and me. When you first got here, all you talked about was leaving."

"I—" Whippet stopped. Her mother was right.

"I know it's hard for you to trust people. But we just want the chance to prove we *can* be trusted."

Something shifted in Whippet's chest. "Mom, I'm staying."

"And I'm so glad you are." Her mother took her hand. Whippet put her head on her mother's shoulder. "It felt different with Sam, didn't it?" her mother asked.

Whippet looked at their entwined fingers and nodded.

"So can I ask? What happened?"

"He broke up with me because I . . . I lied to him. I promised him I would tell Everly about us, but I didn't. He accused me of hiding our relationship, and he was right."

"Why would you do that? We all like Sam a lot."

"I know," Whippet said. "But I wasn't sure I could make it work. I fail at relationships, Mom. It's what I do."

Her mother made a tsking noise and held her hand tighter.

"But that wasn't all. Everly likes him. That's why she ran off at the festival."

Her mother was quiet for a minute. "That sweet girl," her mother murmured. "Honey, Everly is beautiful and smart, and she's young. Talk to her. She's resilient, and I bet she'd get over whatever qualms she has if she knows Sam makes you happy. But whatever you do, don't use her as an excuse not to try with Sam. You'll regret it."

Whippet pulled her hand away and sat back with a huff.

"Can I give you some advice?" her mother asked quietly.

"Can I stop you?" she asked grumpily.

"Give yourself a chance. I know you blame yourself for the divorce. I know you worry about Everly. You constantly put yourself last, but sometimes I think you do that to avoid taking chances. You don't want to get hurt."

Whippet snorted. "Can you blame me?"

"No, but you're going to miss out on the best parts of life if you're always playing it safe. Love means risk, but isn't it a risk worth taking?"

Whippet looked at her mom. There was a very large part of her that wanted to slap both hands over her ears and start humming "The Battle Hymn of the Republic." Loudly. The rest of her acknowledged that her mother knew what she was talking about.

"You might be right," Whippet whispered, lying down and putting her head on her mother's lap. Whippet closed her eyes, allowing the rhythmic glide of the swing to sooth her worries, if only for a moment.

Her mother ran her fingers through Whippet's hair. "Whippet, I'm sorry if I've been tough on you," she said. "I know I probably held on too tight when you were younger, but you were my baby. I poured everything I had into you." She sighed. "I'm not perfect. I know you sometimes felt like you were alone. I just hoped love would somehow make everything all right."

Whippet let the words sink in. She felt the same way about Everly. So, maybe this was the way of mothers. Trying the best you can but being pretty darn sure you're making a mess of it anyway. Whippet sat up and smiled at her mother. Impulsively, she leaned over and kissed her on the cheek. "Mom, thank you for loving me." Her mother pulled her in for a hug, and Whippet could hear her sniffing.

"You're precious to me. It was hard to let you go and watch you—"

"Screw up?" Whippet supplied.

"Falter. I always believed in you. I just couldn't make you believe in yourself."

Whippet looked at her. "Maybe that's changing."

Her mother nodded. "I think it is," she said, sitting up straighter and dabbing at her eyes. "You should go talk to Sam."

Whippet pulled back. "What?"

"Yes. It's early. Maybe you can catch him before he goes to work," her mother said.

"Now? Mom. . ."

"Come on, sweetheart. Time to be brave." She gave Whippet a nudge. "And tell him the truth this time. I'll watch Everly for you." Her mother stood up. "I need to get back in the house before Mr. Mendoza eats all the bacon." Her mom winked at her. "Good luck," she said, patting Whippet's shoulder before she disappeared into the house.

Whippet watched her mother go then started the glider rocking with her foot. She let the swing propel her onto her feet. Emboldened by her mother's speech, she put one foot in front of the other, hurried down the porch steps, circled around the house, and started up the hill toward Sam's place.

But, oh, she was scared.

Whippet walked slowly, twisting her ring, and practicing a speech full of declarations about mistakes and the beauty of second chances. As speeches went, it stank. Her heart clattered against her ribs so violently that if she did manage to make it to his doorstep, she might just pass out.

She came around the bend, and the house came into view. She walked up the steps to Sam's front door, sorely tempted to turn tail and run. *If you keep doing what you're doing, you keep getting what you've got.* She took a fortifying breath, raised her hand, and knocked.

A moment later the door swung open, but it wasn't Sam standing there. A slender brunette stood on the threshold; glossy hair pulled over one shoulder. Creamy, perfect skin, not a blemish to be found. Her large brown eyes assessing as she asked, "Can I help you?"

Whippet swallowed hard. She recognized Emory St. James from her social media posts. She was even more beautiful in person.

"I, uh, I'm looking for Sam," Whippet said. The woman was dressed very elegantly: a white cotton shirt tied at her waist, loose fitting linen capri pants, and wedge sandals with narrow straps tied around delicate ankles. The woman was a picture. Or a nightmare, depending on your perspective. In contrast, Whippet wore ratty cut offs, a white T-shirt that said, "Nope, not today," and a pair of flip-flops. She felt a bit like Cinderella before the fairy godmother showed up.

Sam's ex-wife leaned casually against the door, looking Whippet up and down. "He's not here right now. May I take a message for him?"

Whippet's curiosity got the better of her. She stuck out her hand. "I'm Whippet Moran. Sam's neighbor down the road."

The woman looked at Whippet's hand before she took it. "Emory Beaufort. Sam's wife," the woman said with a slight smile.

Whippet tilted her head to one side. "You mean ex-wife, don't you?"

"I see he's mentioned me." Emory's smile turned sly. "Actually, the *ex* part is under negotiation."

Whippet's throat constricted. "Really?" she managed.

"Mmm. We reconnected a couple of weeks ago. We're talking about reconciling. That's why I'm here." She raised an eyebrow at Whippet. "So, I guess that would make you my neighbor too."

"Guess so." Whippet looked at her for a beat. "Well, I should get going."

"Okay. I'll be sure to tell Sam you stopped by." No, she wouldn't. Maybe it was just as well. A clean break.

Whippet gave Emory a tight smile, then turned, intensely aware of the slap, slap, slap of her flip-flops hitting her heels as she walked away.

"This is how you answer prayers?" Whippet muttered fiercely, aiming her comment to the sky. But who was she kidding? This wasn't God's fault.

Anger roiled in her stomach as she started down the hill. Two weeks! It kind of seemed like Sam had broken up with her then picked up the phone and called his ex. All that talk about her lies and hiding their relationship. It was just a ruse so he could get back together with *her*.

Whippet felt the hot rush of tears but dashed them away. No more crying! She stalked up the drive to see her mother and Emma sitting on the front porch.

"How did it go?" her mother asked, hands clasped as if in prayer.

"Fine," Whippet said, jaw tight.

"Oh," Emma said in a low voice. "That's code for 'not fine.'"

"Definitely not fine," her mother repeated.

"It also means I don't want to talk about it," she said, as she walked inside and slammed the door behind her.

# CHAPTER THIRTY-ONE

It was only eleven in the morning on a Saturday, and Sam's day was already in the tank.

First, there was Emory. She'd left a text before he was even awake. Her message—*See you soon!*—was both vague and ominous.

Then there was the delivery of the couch. It was the sectional he and Whippet had picked out together on one of their last dates before they broke up. "To replace your frat-boy futon," Whippet had said as she'd sat on the display model in the furniture store, looking up at him with those cornflower-blue eyes.

Just what he needed. Another reminder of Whippet.

The sectional had arrived a couple of hours ago and now sat in his family room. He hadn't even bothered to take the plastic off his new furniture; instead, he decided to avoid it by going to work. There he sat, in his office, hitting the backspace button on his computer, frowning at the budget proposal he was working on. A budget proposal that wasn't due until the end of September.

There was a knock on his door. Sam looked up to find Erica Allen standing there.

"Hey," Sam said. "I thought Whit was working the day shift this weekend."

"He was supposed to, but his kid's birthday party is today. His wife wanted him home, so I traded him."

Sam nodded.

"You got a sec?" she asked.

Sam gestured at the chair in front of his desk. "Sure."

Erica walked into his office but didn't sit down. She stood there, hands behind her back, looking everywhere but at him. "You okay?" he asked.

"Yep. I'm good. Everything is good."

Sam waited.

Erica took a deep breath then blurted, "I'm quitting!" She slapped a hand over her mouth in the next moment like maybe she hadn't meant it. "Sorry. I didn't mean to say it like that," she said.

Sam leaned forward. "Wait. You're serious?"

Erica gave a jerky nod.

Sam threw his hands in the air. "Why? You're doing great now. You've been coming in on time. You don't complain about your assignments. What's going on?"

"I'm going back to school," she explained. "All that stuff with Lyla and her kids—I felt like I made a difference there."

"You did," Sam agreed.

Erica took a seat. "I really like it here. Our team is great. But I'd like to get a degree in social work. Then maybe someday I could come back and work for the department in a different capacity."

As inconvenient as this news was, Sam couldn't fault her for wanting a change. He shook his head and smiled. "Erica, that sounds perfect for you. But you don't have to quit. I might be able to arrange it so you can go part time. We could try to work around your school schedule."

Erica's head came up. "Seriously? You'd do that for me?"

"Are you kidding? I'm doing it for me. The planning commission is talking about letting a developer put up some high-density housing on the east side of town. If it goes in, there will be a bump in our population. The city will have to hire at least one more police officer. Maybe I can talk the mayor into one and a half."

"That would be so great!" Erica's face lit with a smile. "Thanks, Chief. I know I gave you a hard time. Sorry it took so long for me to figure out what I wanted."

"Glad you'll be staying on," Sam said, surprised that he meant it.

Erica looked at the clock on the wall before getting up. "The Elks' meeting gets out in twenty minutes. I think I'll head over there and make sure everyone is okay to drive."

Sam watched her go. He looked at his computer and closed the document. Maybe he'd go home and set up the sectional after all.

\* \* \*

Whippet lay in a hammock under the dappled shade of a great white oak. It was Saturday afternoon, and she was completely content here on the back patio at Miss Lily's House. Every day should be like this, she thought, her eyes falling closed. She and Everly were spending the weekend with her family, a welcome distraction from reality, if only for another—Whippet opened one eye to look at her phone—thirty-six hours.

She had worked a double shift at the diner yesterday. Summer crowds might be good for business, but they weren't great for her already frayed nerves. As soon as she'd clocked out, she'd rushed down the street to conduct her first-ever employee interview in the hollow shell that would soon be the bakery's dining room.

It had been an intimidating ordeal. She'd stuttered her way through the questions, hiding trembling hands underneath the table. Her first applicant had been Emma's friend, Rose Arnell. Rose did catering at The Barn. With her youngest son heading off to college, Rose figured a part-time job might fill the extra time. By the end of her interview, Rose had been asking the questions and Whippet thought she'd have to be crazy not to hire her on the spot. So, she did.

A soft breeze stirred the leaves above, which was unusual for late July. Whippet had more interviews Monday morning, but for now, she pushed her foot against the patio to start the hammock swinging.

Her phone rang.

She was so content that she didn't open her eyes to answer it. "Hello?" she murmured into the phone.

"Whippet?" a familiar voice came over the line.

"Meggie?" Whippet bolted upright, and the hammock swayed precariously.

It had been a week and a half since she'd sent her testimony in to Bannon, Inc. A few days ago, she'd received an email from a lawyer representing the company telling her that Anthony Bannon was on temporary suspension pending an investigation into her allegations. The email also contained an apology and an offer to have her old job back. Through all of it, she'd prayed that none of this would adversely affect her friend.

"Hey, Meggie," she said. "How are things going?" she asked cautiously.

"You did it, didn't you? You filed a complaint?" Meggie asked.

Whippet swung her legs over the side of the hammock. "Uh, yeah, I did," she said.

An unexpected whoop came from the other end of the line. "Girl, you are not going to believe what has been going on around here."

Whippet listened with interest as Meggie continued. "You should have seen the fit Tony threw when a couple of reps from corporate marched in here this week and suspended him. Suspended!" Meggie laughed. "I'm just sad they couldn't fire him."

"Why not?"

"There's some law that says you can't turn a creep like that loose on the general public. Just in case the slimeball keeps doing what he's been doin', you know what I mean?"

"I guess that makes sense," Whippet said.

"And get this," Meggie continued. "The CEO came in to interview all the female employees to make sure no one else was affected." Meggie paused for a moment. "Whip, the CEO is his mother. She was so cool." Meggie went on about the changes being implemented, starting with mandatory harassment training for all employees.

"And one more thing," Meggie said. "Mrs. Bannon did my performance review, right there. Remember how Tony kept putting it off? She said I was a valued employee. She liked that I had goals, you know, with college and stuff. Whip, she gave me a raise!" Meggie crowed.

"Meg, that's awesome," Whippet said.

"Whippet," Meggie's voice got quiet. "You were so brave. Thank you," she said. Whippet flushed with pleasure at her words.

They talked for a couple of minutes about Meggie's course load and her boyfriend. Meggie asked Whippet about Everly and how it was going with her family. By the time Whippet got off the phone, she was jubilant. All that worry had been for nothing. She'd made the right choice. She'd made a difference in someone else's life just by standing up for herself.

Whippet jumped out of the hammock and rushed into the house. She flung open the back door. "Mom!" she called, stalking into the kitchen.

"I'm right here," her mother said, coming through the swinging door. "What's wrong? You sound upset."

"Not upset," Whippet said breathlessly. "I need to tell you something."

Her mother's expression turned inscrutable as she sat down. "The last time you sounded flustered like this, you told me you were moving out," she said.

At that moment, the back door swung open, and Tucker and Emma walked in, bickering. "Hon, I don't know what it is," Tucker said, throwing his work gloves on the island counter. "I can call the extension service and see if they know."

"That's what you said last week. Can you do it now? Those red tango roses were Miss Lily's favorite." Emma seemed to notice Whippet and her mom. "Oh, hey, guys. What's up?"

"Whippet has something she wants to tell me," Sophie said.

Emma pulled a face. "Oh, gosh. It's not bad news, is it?"

Whippet shook her head. "No, I—"

"Hey, hon. Where's the smoked turkey?" Tucker asked as he rummaged through the fridge.

"You didn't ask me to buy smoked turkey. You told me you wanted smoked ham."

"Are you sure?"

"Where's Everly?" Whippet's mother asked.

"She's in the side yard climbing the sycamore tree," Emma answered.

"Whippet, I wish you'd tell her not to do that. It's dangerous."

Tucker snorted. "That's what you used to say to us when we were kids."

Their mother frowned. "Yes, and as I recall you broke your arm falling out—"

"I lied to you when I moved here," Whippet said loudly. Everyone stopped talking and stared at her.

She started over. "Mom, when I showed up here, you asked me if I'd been fired again. I lied to you. I did get fired. But it wasn't my fault." Whippet swallowed. "My manager wasn't a good guy. He was always making inappropriate comments to the female staff. When I asked him for time off to come out here, he made a pass at me." Whippet knotted her hands together. "And when I wouldn't cooperate, he fired me."

Emma took a seat next to Sophie, and Tucker moved behind her. "When I got here, I didn't want to tell you the truth. I was ashamed. I thought what happened was my fault. But it wasn't." She looked at Tucker. "A couple of weeks ago, I filed a harassment complaint with the company.

"I wasn't sure it would do any good. The Maxi Mart where I worked is owned by my manager's family. I also thought that it would make things harder for the other girls that work there if I complained." A slow grin spread across Whippet's face. "Turned out I was wrong. I just got off the phone with one of them. My old boss got suspended because I filed that complaint. Harassment training will be mandatory for all employees now, and my friend ended up getting a raise." She drew a long breath. "Which isn't the point."

Whippet turned to her mother again. "I'm sorry I wasn't honest with you. I was pretty desperate when I got here." She glanced at Emma and Tucker. "Thank you for being patient with me. You've all been so supportive. Without your help—and God's I guess—I'm sure I'd still be lost. Now, it feels like I belong here. With you."

Her mother was on her feet and around the table in a second, her arms going around Whippet. "I'm so proud of you," her mother cried.

"For what?" Whippet asked and returned the embrace.

"For all of it. For having the courage to stand up for yourself. For working so hard since you've been here. For being patient with *me*. Thank you for having the faith to keep going." Her mother gave her another squeeze. "I'm so happy you're here," she said.

Over her mother's shoulder, Tucker gave her an oh-so-subtle thumbs up.

Whippet smiled at him. She wrapped her arms even tighter around her mother. And in that moment, she felt like a bright and shiny new dime.

# CHAPTER THIRTY-TWO

THE LUNCH CROWD STARTED TO trickle in at about eleven. Whippet reached under the counter for an order pad, but Luna breezed past her. "I've got it," she said. Whippet looked up to see who was waiting to be seated. The Treemontons and the Begleys were both there with their broods, each of their three kids bent over their phones.

Whippet's stomach dropped. Behind them stood the entire Normal City Police Department. Whippet grabbed a coffeepot and decided now would be an excellent time to refill it. Out of the corner of her eye, she watched as Luna seated the party near the window. Sam held Didi's chair, and at that moment, he looked up and their eyes locked.

There it was. That tug, the undeniable pull of attraction and something more. Whippet leaned against the counter, wondering if the feeling would ever go away. The mayor walked over and put a hand on Sam's shoulder, and he turned away. The two of them talked for a moment. Someone laughed, and he finally sat down with his back to her. Just as well. Luna laid out menus, then glanced at Whippet and gave her a wink.

Whippet hadn't seen Sam in weeks. To her utter humiliation, she'd taken to hiding behind the pillars on her terrace, watching for him, waiting for him to pull someone over or walk down the street and slap a ticket on an illegally parked car. It was pathetic. He probably didn't even think about her.

Blessedly, Whippet hadn't seen his ex-wife since that morning at Sam's house, even though she'd heard Emory was still around. According to Luna, Sam's ex had stopped by the station a couple of weeks ago while he was out on a call. In his absence, Emory had set up camp in his office and managed to earn Didi's ire by asking for a bottle of water and the Wi-Fi password so she could get caught up on emails. Evidently, by the time Sam got back, Didi was spitting nails.

Whippet pretended it didn't matter. Secretly, she was mentally preparing for the day when she'd run into the two of them together, walking down the sidewalk hand in hand, gazing into each other's eyes and...

"Whippet? You all right?" Monica Turley asked.

"Just fine!" Whippet said a little too cheerfully as she rang up Monica's bill.

She managed a smile at Early Jackson who was next in line. Whippet took her order then went into the back, handing it to Chuck with a trembling hand.

"Get a grip," she muttered to herself.

"You okay, kid?" Chuck asked her, his eyes kind.

She must look pretty bad if Chuck was being nice to her. "Just dandy," she replied.

Ex-wife or no, Whippet was still crazy about Sam Beaufort. And she knew she was going to run into him often. The town was too small to avoid him. She took a deep breath.

She'd be okay. She had a good life. A wonderful life. She had Everly and Tucker and Emma. There was a new dynamic with her mother and, soon enough, there would be a niece or nephew to love. The bakery would open, and she'd be busier than ever.

Jan stuck her head through the swinging door, eyes narrowed. "You on a break or omething'?" she asked.

Whippet pasted on a smile. "I'll be right out," she said, and Jan disappeared. Life was full. Life was good. Time would fix the rest.

At least she hoped so.

* * *

Sam could feel her behind him. He'd purposefully chosen this seat, hoping to keep her out of his direct line of vision. Because, frankly, looking at Whippet Moran was about as comfortable as having a fly ball hit him in the chest.

Man, he missed her.

He'd balked when the team suggested the diner for their monthly staff meeting, but short of a potluck at the station, there weren't many options in Normal for lunch.

They didn't accomplish much during these meetings. It was more about team building than anything else. Today wasn't any different. Didi brought up how much time she was taking for maternity leave. Whit Coleman recounted a call out at Minnie Jones's house. Minnie had needed a light bulb changed, but when Whit got there, she'd forgotten which bulb it was that needed changing. It had taken him an hour to find it. Officer Allen announced to the team that she was going back to school to become a social worker, and they all congratulated her. Sam half listened, but his mind was on the pretty waitress behind the counter. He finally came out of his mental fog when Didi leaned over to remind him of a meeting with the planning commission later that afternoon.

The bell over the diner door rang. A moment later someone planted a swift kiss on his cheek. "Do you mind if I sit here?" a familiar voice asked, and Sam froze.

Emory stood behind them holding a chair. She was asking Didi to move so she could sit next to him.

"That won't be necessary," Sam said, jumping to his feet. He looked around the diner, and thankfully, didn't see Whippet. He took Emory by the elbow and escorted her to the exit. He had just opened the door when he looked back and saw Whippet standing behind the counter, face pale.

Sam looked away. He couldn't think about her right now.

He towed Emory outside. When they turned the corner, he faced her. "You can't keep doing this," he said. "We're not together anymore."

"Sam, we need to talk." Emory's voice was insistent.

"Emory, go home. I've got about a million things going on, and I don't have time for this."

His ex-wife's expression turned mulish. "I'll see you later," she said.

Sam walked away.

Later that afternoon, Sam hit the blinker and pulled off the highway onto the gravel road that led to his house.

The planning commission was the usual snooze-fest. Proposals from developers, requests for zoning changes. Boring. The only entertaining moment had come when Bernie Chastain asked for a special exception request. He wanted to build an additional dwelling behind his house. "A miniature medieval castle," he said. "To rent out on Airbnb. Vacationers pay top dollar to stay in weird places." His special exception request had been denied.

Sam pulled into his garage. He sat there for a moment, recalling the haunted look in Whippet Moran's eyes today. He hated the thought of hurting her, even inadvertently. For the last month, he'd done his best to avoid running into her. It had not been ideal for Emory to show up when she had.

Sam got out of his car and went into the house. The kitchen was dark but soft light came from the family room. Sam hung his head. That light could mean only one thing. He walked into the room. "Emory, what are you doing here?" he asked wearily.

She looked at ease on his new sectional. "You told me to go home," she said.

Sam rubbed his eyes. "*Your* home, Emory. Not mine. What do you want?"

"I told you. I want to talk to you."

"So, talk," Sam said, acknowledging defeat.

Emory looked at him for a beat. "I'm getting married," she said.

Sam stared at her, not sure he'd heard her correctly.

"You're getting married," he repeated.

"Yes."

"That is not what I expected you to say." Sam sat down. "Uh, congratulations."

Emory looked annoyed. "That's all you have to say?" she huffed.

"Well, 'I'm relieved,' sounded rude."

"Sam . . ."

"When?" he asked, still processing the news.

"June of next year," Emory replied.

"Is he a good guy?"

"Yes. He's an investment banker. I met him when I redesigned his Gold Coast apartment."

Sam nodded and found he didn't have anything more to say. A pretty good indicator that he was well and truly over her. But he'd already known that. It was time Emory figured it out too.

"Are you . . . okay with it?" Emory asked tentatively.

He leaned forward. "Sure. Why wouldn't I be?"

Emory looked down. "No reason, I guess."

Maybe she wanted reassurance. "Emory, I'm okay. I've moved on."

"Yes, that's obvious," she snapped. "But that's not why I'm here."

"No?"

"No. I came to see if *I* was over *you*," she cried.

Sam's mouth opened. It took him a minute to speak. "Really? And what's the verdict?" he asked.

Emory was quiet for a moment. When she looked up, there were tears in her eyes. "I seem to be having a hard time falling out of love with you."

Sam sat back, stunned. "Emory, you left me," he reminded her. "Three years ago."

"I know. I know! But it doesn't mean I'm over you," she said, sounding a little lost. "Don't get me wrong. Noah is a great guy. I'm crazy about him. But there's this tiny little spot in my heart that's still yours, and I cannot seem to get you out of there. Believe me, I've tried." She looked down at her hands. "When I left you," she started, "my mother said I was making a big mistake. I didn't believe her at the time. I was high on my success, too full of myself." Emory glanced over at him. "But she was right."

Sam shook his head. "No, she wasn't. We wanted different things. I didn't know it when we got married, but thank heaven you figured it out for both of us. You're a bright, ambitious woman. You have so much going for you. You don't need me."

Emory threw her hands in the air. "What do I have going for me, Sam? All my friends are settled and having children. And me? I was divorced before my second anniversary."

"You're a great success. You're good at your job."

She sighed. "I do love my job." Emory leaned toward him. "Sam, can't we—"

"Emory, no."

"I'd do better this time," she promised.

Sam shook his head.

Emory gave him a sad smile. She dashed a hand across her eyes as she unfolded from the couch. She walked over to him and kissed his cheek. "I'm sorry if I made trouble for you," she said.

Sam chuckled. "No, you're not."

She bent to pick up her purse. "I guess you're right. Don't get me wrong, I meant what I said. I'm not taking it back." She was quiet for a moment. "But you should know, I'm not proud of leaving you. It was the stupidest thing I have ever done."

Huh. Emory St. James admitting she'd made a mistake. There must be snow in the devil's backyard. Sam could have given her a hard time, but instead he just said, "Thank you."

Emory called an Uber, and Sam walked her to the door. He heard the crunch of tires on gravel. Emory squeezed his arm. "Goodbye, Sam," she whispered and started to walk away.

"Oh," Emory snapped her fingers and turned around. "I almost forgot. That waitress at the diner today. The blonde one with the strange first name."

Sam's head came up. "Whippet?"

"That's the one. Very odd name. She stopped by a few weeks ago."

Sam's brows came together. "Stopped by where?"

"Here."

"Here? You were here?"

"Mmm, you should really move your hide-a-key," she purred.

"What did she say?" Sam asked, laser focused on the fact that Whippet had been here, and he'd known nothing about it.

"Who?"

"Emory!" Sam barked.

"Fine. Um, she didn't say anything. Not really. She asked to see you, and I told her you were out." Her expression turned thoughtful. "And I might have mentioned we were getting back together. I was still hoping for a reconciliation at that point, and all's fair, you know? Don't get upset," Emory said.

Too late. Sam's irritation shot into the red zone. "You need to leave," he ground out.

Emory smiled. "You must really like her." She reached up and touched his cheek. "Pity," she said and opened the door. Relief mingled with anger as Emory left the house for what he *hoped* would be the last time. Sam looked at his watch. Was it too late to call Whippet?

Emory was almost to the Uber when he looked up. "Hey!" he called. "I need my hide-a-key back!"

Emory gave a low laugh and got in the car.

# CHAPTER THIRTY-THREE

"Why haven't I noticed this before?" Whippet asked Joe Prentiss as they looked out the impressive floor to ceiling windows into an abandoned wasteland. She glanced back at Everly sitting at a wobbly card table, completely engrossed in whatever she was watching on the iPad. Good. Maybe she wouldn't notice when Whippet burst into tears.

"You own the lot, right?" Joe asked.

Whippet swallowed hard. "I sure do," she said. Unfortunately, the lot next to the bakery was little better than a landfill. Trash caught in the straggly remains of dead bushes. Plastic bags stuck along the edges of the lot. An entire newspaper plastered against a rusty wrought-iron fence. That fence, which divided the lot from the alley, was twisted with dried weeds and dead vines. Her customers would sit next to the beautiful picture windows eating pastries and gazing into a junkyard.

Joe pointed out the window with his pen. "The good news is the fence is in decent shape. Paint it, get rid of the trash. Maybe plant some forsythia bushes or lilacs. Something."

"Who, me?" Whippet asked in alarm. "I don't know anything about that stuff."

Joe shrugged. "Maybe you should hire a landscaper."

Whippet's shoulders sagged. She didn't have the budget for a landscaper.

"We need to fix these too," he said. He walked over to the French doors and tried to wrangle them open, but no luck. Whippet bit her lip. Every time Joe uttered the word "fix," it ended up costing her money.

She rubbed her head. "How much do you think—"

"Whippet Moran, do you like me?" A voice came from behind them, and Whippet whirled around.

Sam stood just inside the front door, hands planted loosely on his hips. She just stared for a moment, trying to process the fact that he was *here*.

Then she looked around the room, crowded with workmen. Her eyes landed on Everly, who had perked up at their unexpected visitor.

"Well, do you?" Sam demanded.

"Excuse me?" she asked.

He walked toward her slowly. "Do. You. Like me?"

"S-Sure, Sam," Whippet said hesitantly. Sam was here. Here! She felt her face flush and her heart fluttered in her chest like a trapped hummingbird. She glanced at her daughter. Everly looked back at the iPad. They shouldn't be talking about this.

"Not very convincing if you ask me. What do you think, Joe? Did that sound convincing to you?" he asked her contractor.

"Not really. But then I should probably mind my own business, so I'll just leave you to whatever this is," Joe said before rejoining his crew in the dining room.

Sam was right in front of her now. "Emory thinks you do."

"Your ex-wife?" she snapped, brows slamming together. She walked around him.

"She told me you stopped by," he said quietly.

That was unexpected. "She did?" Whippet said.

Sam nodded. "Of course, she didn't share this information with me until late last night. If I had known . . ."

"It doesn't matter." She didn't want to talk about this in front of Everly.

Sam frowned. "I think it does matter. Why did you stop by that day?" Sam pressed.

There was a rap at the window. Whippet looked over to see Kara and Max making fish faces at Everly through the glass.

Her daughter waved at them and hopped up. "Mom, it's okay," she said. "I heard you talking to Grammy that day." Everly turned to face Sam. "My mom came to see you because she wanted to tell you that she likes you, but she doesn't think she should because she doesn't want me to be sad." Everly plucked at her shirt. "That's because for a while, I kinda liked you too," she mumbled.

Whippet felt her face heat. Neither she nor Sam moved.

"Um, when we moved here," Everly started. "Well, you were the first person that was nice to me," she explained.

Sam cleared his throat. "I'm glad you think so."

"I ran away at the festival because, I dunno, I thought you liked me too, but you were holding my mom's hand and stuff, and it made me mad. Mom thought I'd be sad if she was your girlfriend. She worries a lot. But it's okay now. Promise." Everly looked at Whippet. "Mom, can I go hang out with Max and Kara?" Everly started for the door.

Whippet nodded mutely. "Wait, Everly," Whippet called. "When did you hear me say those things to Grammy?"

Everly lifted her shoulders. "You were on the back porch at her house. On the swing."

Whippet was confused. "But you weren't there."

"Yes, I was." Everly's expression turned impish. "I was sitting in the willow tree above you." Everly waved at her friends. "Gotta go! Sam, it's okay if you date my mom. She still likes you." With that, Everly raced out the front door.

Sam rubbed his neck. "Well, that was enlightening."

Whippet's thoughts were in a jumble. She wanted privacy for this conversation, not saws going off in the background. Every joint in Whippet's body buzzed with adrenaline. "You know what?" she said, "I'm busy. I'm very, very busy." She walked away, but Sam followed her.

"You!" She pointed a finger at him. "You stay over there," she said, putting a table between them.

"Daphne," he said in that low, warm way of his that drove her crazy. She leaned over and began fumbling with the blueprints. Sam's hand covered hers.

"I'm sorry, Daphne," he said in a low voice. "I shouldn't have jumped to conclusions. I should have been more patient with you." She looked up at him. "I should have been paying attention," he said.

"Attention to what?" she whispered.

"Attention to who you really are. Steadfast and loving. Protective." His face was serious. "I shouldn't have let you go, but I was hurt," he confessed.

Whippet frowned. "What about your ex-wife?" she reminded him. "She said—"

"I know what she said. Emory was trying to make trouble. Her favorite pastime. But it's not true."

"Really?" Whippet's voice still held a note of skepticism. "So, you're not getting back together?"

Sam shook his head. "No. She's getting married. To someone else," he clarified. "She wanted to tell me in person. That's all."

She sucked in a shaky breath. "Oh. That's good, I guess," she said looking up at him. Something like hope flared in her chest.

Sam took her hand. "When you walked into my office that day, I should have fought for you. I should have told you we'd go slow and work it out. You, me, and Everly."

She managed a nod. "Well, to be fair, I didn't—"

Suddenly he was around the table, her face was cradled in his hands, and he was kissing her. She didn't mind that there was a dining room filled with workmen watching the show. Sam was kissing her. And it was slow and deep and perfect. His hand went to the back of her head, maybe trying to keep her in place. He needn't have bothered. She wasn't going anywhere.

Her heart was pounding so hard that it took her a moment to realize he had stopped. "I love you," he said, and she drew in a surprised breath. A smile pulled at the corner of his mouth. "Sorry. I probably should have led with that." He rested his forehead against hers, and she let the words wash over her. "What do you say, Daphne? Will you give me another chance?"

Whippet smiled up at him, but instead of answering, she launched herself at Normal, Missouri's chief of police. And she didn't care who saw.

# EPILOGUE

"What about Zeus?" Everly asked, tapping the pen against her chin.

"Zeus? What kind of name is Zeus?" Sam said, raising an eyebrow at Everly.

Seated at a table in the bakery, the two of them had been trying to decide what Sam should name his dog for an hour.

"Okay." Everly looked pensive as she wrote something on the paper in front of her. "How about Boomer?"

"My dog is quiet. I'd expect a dog named Boomer to make a lot of noise."

Whippet slid two slices of warm apple pie onto their table and came to stand next to Sam. "Any progress?" she asked, leaning into him.

"It's not going very well." Everly sighed and looked at Sam. "What about Frank?"

Sam shook his head. "Frank isn't a dog name," he insisted.

"I know. But it's funny."

"No human names for the dog, okay?" he said.

"But I—"

Sam gestured at the notepad. "Write it down. On the 'no' side, Everly."

Sam slid an arm around Whippet's waist. It was nice, these little displays of affection. They were always careful not to kiss in front of Everly, though. She'd caught them a couple of weeks ago and had walked away, stiff as a starched collar, muttering, "So gross."

"All right. You two geniuses keep at it." Whippet looked at her watch. "It's almost time to close up." Sam winked at her as she walked away.

Tomorrow she was taking her first day off since opening the bakery. Rose would manage things while Whippet and Sam drove to St. Louis to visit the O'Neils. They'd just purchased a home, one built in this century. "No more renovations for me," Isaac had said. He had almost a full range of motion in his left arm, thanks to physical therapy. Sam hadn't said anything, but she was pretty sure Isaac's progress was a relief.

The side windows were open, letting the cool October breeze pass through. Whippet loved this time of year. The days were still warm, but evening brought the chill wind of autumn.

Everly and Sam were pals again, and the awkwardness between them had disappeared. Which Whippet was grateful for, because Sam had quickly become a fixture in their lives. He was a regular at dinner, offering wild praise for Whippet's culinary skills. After dinner, he often helped Everly with her math homework, something that qualified him for sainthood in Whippet's eyes.

He'd ingratiated himself with her family too. He and Tucker golfed when the weather was good, and Sam made himself available whenever her mother needed help fixing things around the house. He was a regular prince, her guy.

But maybe best of all, Sam sat next to them at church on Sundays, his arm around Whippet as he and Everly looked up at the stained glass windows and played whispered games of I Spy.

These moments were very nearly perfect, but sometimes Whippet still found herself battling against the panicky feeling that it would all go up in smoke tomorrow. At those times, she reminded herself to breathe deeply and look for the good. So far it was working.

Whippet went behind the counter to help Mrs. Taft, sliding a box of leaf-shaped sugar cookies into a bag before ringing her up.

The bakery had been open for a month. So far, she was holding her own. On Saturdays, her cinnamon rolls and chocolate brioche drew the crowds, and Sam had threatened to implement riot control when the line stretched down the block. Luna still ordered cakes for the diner, and now that fall was coming, she was thinking about switching things up and ordering pie too. Whippet still supplied the woman in Branson with desserts, but she'd declined the woman's offer to spread the word among fellow restaurateurs. Whippet was getting used to being a business owner. There would be time to expand in the future if she wanted to.

She wished her dad were here. He would have been her biggest cheerleader. When she'd mentioned this to her mother on the night the bakery opened, her mom had said, "Oh, don't you worry. He's watching."

"We're closing in fifteen minutes, Mr. Cochran," Whippet announced cheerfully, topping off his coffee anyway.

She glanced out the large-paned windows and watched Rose Arnell fold back the awning and secure it for the night. It was beautiful out there.

Early Jackson had come up with the perfect solution for the vacant lot. Whippet had come out one afternoon while the bakery was still under construction to see Early regarding the wasteland, making a tsking noise. "Sort of a sow's ear next to a silk purse, isn't it?" Early had said, and Whippet couldn't agree with her fast enough. "What if you turned this into a community garden?" she'd asked, gesturing toward the weeds and trash. "I bet I could get the city council to cough up some money, civic beautification and all that. Put in some raised beds for growing vegetables and herbs. String some globe lights across the way. It could be real nice out here."

Nice indeed. There was a new cement patio edged in reclaimed brick. The brick carried on through the garden, winding in paths around planter boxes full of basil and rosemary. It was too late in the year for new planting, but the attractive wood beds held mounds of gold- and rust-colored mums that would be transplanted in the spring to make way for the Normal City Produce Patch. The fence had been cleaned up, repaired, and painted black. Whippet, Tucker, and Sam had spent hours weeding and preparing the soil for the clematis and lilacs she'd planted in front of the wrought iron. There was an apple tree in the corner. It would be spectacular in the spring and, fingers crossed, would bring her plenty of fruit for tarts and pies in the future. Next weekend, she and Emma would line one side of the garden with tulip and daffodil bulbs. There was so much to do, but the work was deeply satisfying.

There had been a lot of changes over the past few months, but if she ever felt too overwhelmed, she reminded herself that the goal was to embrace uncertainty and keep her heart open to possibility. She prayed a lot too.

Her mother was dating again. The online thing seemed to be working for her. The other night when Whippet and Sam had walked past her mother's Camry, parked on the side of Shep's house, the windows had been all fogged up.

"Is that . . . Is she . . . ?" Whippet sputtered, but Sam towed her away. "Keep moving, Daphne."

Her mother had walked into the house five minutes later, cheeks flushed, holding hands with a silver haired gentleman. Her mother had a boyfriend. He was a sixty-year-old ophthalmologist from Rolla. Very respectable and very nice. But like Everly had said, so gross.

Whippet stuck her head into the kitchen. "We all wrapped up back here?" she asked. She'd hired a couple of high school kids as dishwashers. They worked hard and ate the leftovers. The kitchen was beautiful, bright, and gleaming. After they left, Whippet looked everything over before she walked back into the dining area.

She went back out front. Mr. Cochran gave her a wave on his way out the door, and Whippet stowed her apron behind the counter. Sam was the only person in the dining room.

"Where's Everly?" she asked.

"With the dog," he replied, taking her hand, and leading her outside. She locked the front door. Sam's dog was tied up to the bike rack under a maple tree, its red leaves shivering in the breeze. Everly knelt next to him, stroking his bony head, causing the pup's tail to thump against the sidewalk.

"What about Trixie?" Everly suggested, squinting up at Sam.

"You do know my dog's a boy, right?" Sam untied the leash from the bike rack and handed it to Everly. "You can drive this time," he said, and a smile burst like sunrise on her daughter's face. The three of them set off in the direction of the diner for dinner. Whippet watched Everly skip along until the Jackson boys stopped her and asked if they could pet her dog. Her dog. Whippet was pretty sure Everly felt like the luckiest girl alive.

"Hey," Whippet called. "What if you named the dog Lucky? I mean, he's lucky he found you, right?" she asked, looking up at Sam. He grinned and looked at Everly, whose eyes had gone wide.

"Lucky! That's perfect!" Everly tugged on his leash. "C'mon, Lucky, let's go!"

Whippet began to follow, but Sam had hold of her hand and didn't budge.

"You all right?" she asked with a frown that mirrored his own.

"I know you don't like surprises," he started slowly. "So, I'm telling you right now. I'm going to ask you to marry me. Not this minute. I think I can do better than a proposal on the sidewalk in front of the library. But someday. That's where I see us heading. If you don't agree, I need you to tell me."

Something bloomed, warm and sweet, inside her chest, and she gave him a wobbly smile. These days, when she got all weepy, it was because she was happy. Still, Sam made a noise and touched her cheek. He didn't like it when she got emotional. It made him protective. And it was wonderful. Whippet was crazy about the man. Life was good. Even the hard things seemed easier because these days she was surrounded by love.

Still, she couldn't let things get too sentimental. She cleared her throat. "Well, I guess we'll just have to wait and see." She tugged on his hand.

"Whippet—" Sam's voice held the warning note that she knew was mostly bluster.

"I'm a woman of mystery," she said, waggling her eyebrows at him.

He gave her a tolerant look. "Fine, but can you maybe give me a clue?"

Whippet rolled her eyes. "What, and ruin the big moment?"

"Fine," he said, grabbing her and kissing her right there in front of the whole town.

"You know I love you, right?" she asked, thinking that was an answer in itself.

Sam nodded, then grinned. "I'm a lucky, lucky man," he said. He picked up her hand, kissed it, then tugged her toward the diner.

Lucky indeed.

# ABOUT THE AUTHOR

ELLE M. ADAMS LOVES NOTHING more than a sweet and sassy romance, and that is what she endeavors to bring to the pages of her novels. Elle was born in Washington state but raised in a small Missouri town that still owns a hefty chunk of her heart. She holds a degree in English and has a deep and abiding love for literature, travel, and chocolate. Elle lives in the Intermountain West with her family and a dog named Bee.

Learn more about Elle at ellemadams.com and follow her on social media.

Facebook: Elle M. Adams
Instagram: @ellemadams